A COMPANY OF
MONSTERS

SHAMI STOVALL

CAPITAL
• STATION BOOKS •

Published by
CS BOOKS, LLC

A Company of Monsters
Copyright © 2019 Shami Stovall
All rights reserved.
https://sastovallauthor.com/

Cover Design: Darko Paganus
Editor: Jessica Meigs, Tandy Boese

IF YOU WANT TO BE NOTIFIED WHEN SHAMI STOVALL'S NEXT BOOK RELEASES, PLEASE CONTACT HER DIRECTLY AT
s.adelle.s@gmail.com

ISBN: 978-0-9980452-5-2

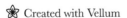 Created with Vellum

A Company of Monsters

by Shami Stovall

To John, for being the first to see.
To Beka, who eagerly awaited this one.
To Tiffany, who wants to know if Capitan UK dies or not.
To Gail and Big John, for all the support.
To Michael Neff, for the support and ideas.
To Ann, for being the best schmoe.
To history, for being so interesting.
And finally, to everyone unnamed, thank you for everything.

ONE

1917

G eist made an art of stealth.

She slipped through the moonlight shadows around the Watson Manor House, keeping to the grass to stifle the sounds of her steps. Cloaked in invisibility, she made her way across the vast front yard. Her sorcery—specter sorcery—gave her all the power and versatility of a ghost.

Geist. German for *ghost*. The magics in her blood had defined her codename.

Once she reached the west wall of the manor, Geist peered in through the nearest window. No lamps. No electric lights. And the crescent moon didn't help with visibility. Despite those limitations, Geist took in a deep breath and calmed herself. Specter sorcery gave her the portfolio of a ghost, but apex sorcery gave her all the super-human abilities of a peerless predator. Like any jungle cat, she saw through the dim lighting, her vision perfect and unobscured by darkness.

The Watson Manor House, built in 1837, had all the posh and luxury of a grand palace. The ceilings were carved into twisting, vine-like designs, the marble tiles were arranged to create smoke patterns, and massive paintings adorned every wall. Most notable were the bronze, iron, and steel statues of people long since dead. A statue for every corner of the room.

Although it was midnight, someone should've been awake and walking the manor—house staff who tended to the fireplaces or groundskeepers going about their duties while the lord slept.

Instead, the chimneys were cold and the estate as quiet as a graveyard.

With enough focus, Geist stepped through the manor wall, her body, Springfield rifle, and uniform incorporeal until she reached the other side. A shiver ran down her spine as she released the magic. A twisted scar on her wrist burned afterward—a souvenir she had acquired in the German trenches. Unlike a knife or bullet scar, the waxy sheen on her wrist represented damage on a magical level. She pulled her sleeve down to hide it and suppressed the terrible memories associated with the event.

Only fools trip on what's behind them, Geist thought as she examined the dusty dining table and china cabinets. No one had used either in some time.

Geist snuck across the room and into the nearby hallway.

The Watsons were sorcerers with an unusual sorcery—they could shape metal as if it were malleable clay, and while most Watsons used it for artistry, as evidenced by their many ornate statues, some used the magic for crafting weapons. They had provided specialty equipment for the Allies, outfitting soldier sorcerers in the Ethereal Squadron.

But no one had heard from them in weeks. No letters. No shipments. Not even the nearby town of St. Peter Port had any information. The Watsons allowed their servants to live on their property, and the deliverymen couldn't get past the gate. Their sudden seclusion baffled everyone.

Which was why Geist had been sent. She needed to investigate their disappearance and report back to the Ethereal Squadron in Verdun.

Please let me find someone here, Geist thought. *Anyone.*

The wood floor threatened to creak if Geist became careless. She took her time and tiptoed through the dark atmosphere of the

Watson Manor House. The shadows of the copper statues created human silhouettes on walls, and while a civilian might feel terror for the unknown, Geist had been through hell and back.

She chuckled to herself. *I'm the thing lurking in the darkness that men fear.*

After slinking through the foyer and making her way upstairs, Geist slowed and crouched close to the ground, hoping to find signs of a struggle. Sure enough, when she came to the bedrooms, she found the hallway carpets disturbed and upturned at the edges. Instead of opening the doors and potentially alerting someone to her presence, Geist ghosted through the wood, maintaining her invisibility and becoming incorporeal.

A child's bedroom.

It took Geist a few moments to take in all the details. Stuffed animals. Dolls. Blocks stacked into a house-like shape. She caught her breath when she examined the bed.

Pink sheets and a white comforter were twisted around the pale corpse of an eight year old. Geist walked over, her teeth gritted. Apex sorcery heightened all her senses. When she strained her ears, she couldn't hear shallow breaths, or even a heartbeat.

Geist touched the skin of the corpse and recoiled. The icy chill of death unnerved her more than the thought of battlefields and combat. The child had died long ago.

She unrolled the body from the sheets. Her hands shook as she pulled back the collar of the child's dress. Deep puncture wounds over the jugulars told a terrible story of a slow death, and the bruises on the arms screamed struggle and terror. But there wasn't any blood. None on the dress. None on the sheets.

None left to coagulate in the body.

Geist didn't look at the corpse's face. Instead, she covered the body once she had concluded her examination, determined to give the little girl dignity, even if she wasn't alive to appreciate it.

After a brief moment to steady her breathing, Geist made her way to the next bedroom. A little boy, two years younger than the girl, sat atop his bed in a similar fashion. Cold to the touch and drained of all blood. Nothing but a husk of his former self and shriveled from decay.

The next room was the same. A small child, barely able to walk. The master bedroom, on the other hand, had two corpses, but the room itself had been twisted with bits of metal—even the iron bars over the windows and copper bedframe were warped. Had a fight broken out? Geist took note of the destruction, especially the shattered vase and bullet holes in the wall. One of the corpses held a gun.

With her heart pounding in her chest, Geist made her way back downstairs. War took its toll on everyone, but nothing stung more than seeing defenseless children wrapped up in the violence. She entered the servants' quarters and gagged on the strong copper scent that wafted out.

Ten men and women lay in the corner of the room, their necks slashed, their clothes and beds black with dried blood. The whole room screamed *massacre.* If there had been a struggle, Geist couldn't detect it, which meant fiends had slipped into the sleeping quarters, cut their throats without any of the other servants waking, and then stacked them in the corner.

Sorcerers were far stronger than the average man, and the trained soldiers who fought in the war were far scarier than anything else. The servants never stood a chance, even if they had been awake.

Geist exited the room and searched the rest of the house, her frustration turning to poison in her system without an outlet. *Someone should pay for this. A man of honor would never have participated in such a slaughter.*

Her findings were what she had feared—every Watson sorcerer had been drained of blood while every civilian in their employ had been murdered.

Geist exited the house, her concentration wavering. With each disturbing thought, her invisibility slipped. She walked down the main road of the house, confident the murderers had left the manor days prior.

Two members of the Ethereal Squadron awaited her at the

gates. Even without her apex sorcery to see through the shroud of darkness, Geist knew them by mannerisms alone. One fidgeted with his belt and backpack while the other stood perfectly still, coiled to strike like only trained killers could.

"Geist?" the fidgety one called out. "Thank goodness you came back."

"What did I tell you?" the other growled. "Of course she would return."

"She was gone for over ten minutes. That's longer than her average whenever she goes to investigate."

"I'm fine," Geist said with a single chuckle. "You fuss too much, Battery."

Battery stepped out into the moonlight, his khaki British uniform a sight for sore eyes. He stood the same height as Geist, shorter than most in the Allied forces, but not by much. His youthful facial features and lack of definition hinted at his age. Despite his lack of stature, he stood straight and offered her a smile.

"I'm sorry I doubted," he said. "But I couldn't imagine this war without you. Who would lead our team?"

The second soldier scoffed. "She can handle herself. And if anything had gone wrong, *I* would've stepped in to kill it."

He stepped out to stand next to Battery, a cold glare set on his face as though it were tattoo—permanent and stark. Even if he had an unwelcoming demeanor, Geist still smiled upon seeing him.

Vergess. A German defector to the United States, and one of her most trusted teammates. He wore the drab olive uniform of the American soldiers, complete with a 48-star American flag. While the United States hadn't officially joined the war efforts, sorcerers weren't bound by the same restrictions as the average man. Many volunteered for the Ethereal Squadron and were accepted into the ranks after agreeing to follow the instructions of British and French commanders.

"*Wie geht es dir?*" Vergess asked, his German smooth and natural.

"I'm fine," Geist replied and with an exhale. "But the Watsons aren't as lucky."

Battery shot Vergess a sidelong glance. "I knew it. You *were* worried about her." Then he turned back to Geist. "Well, I came prepared. If the Watsons are dead, we should use the camera to record the evidence. It'll take me a few minutes to set up, but I understand how to use it."

"Didn't you set a camera on fire back at the base?" Vergess asked with a chuckle.

"Th-that's not accurate! Tinker played a trick on me!" Battery straightened the straps of his backpack. "Besides, I read the instruction manual and trained with the cameramen of the 87th regiment. I'm a professional now."

Battery's huge backpack carried a giant box made of mahogany wood and steel hinges. He kept the tripod strapped to the outside. The entire getup appeared cumbersome, and the straps of the backpack dug deep into Battery's shoulders.

Geist didn't understand cameras. All the reporters said *this would be the first war truly captured in detail*, yet they never explained *how*. Their boxes of lights and pictures confused everyone. It wasn't magic—Geist could understand magic—yet their photographs took still images of reality and made them permanent.

"There are corpses in all the bedrooms," Geist whispered. "And the servants are dead in their quarters. If you want photographs, make it quick. All the sorcerers were drained of their blood."

Both Vergess and Battery tensed, their eyes going wide.

"You think Abomination Soldiers targeted them?" Vergess asked.

"Yes."

They all knew why.

Before the Great War, sorcerers could only develop magic that was in their bloodline. But after the war started—once the Germans and the Austro-Hungarians began fiddling with technologies never thought of—they developed Grave-Maker Gas. It melted flesh together at a baser level, creating deformed monsters of multiple people or animals. They used the gas to melt blood into their bodies in order to steal the magics from other sorcerers.

And now they were collecting rare samples.

Geist's mouth tasted of cotton.

"Major Reese needs to know about this," Battery said. He hustled past Geist and headed toward the Watson Manor House. "I'll be done soon."

Vergess shook his head. "I can't believe they're acting this fast. Especially after we destroyed their stores of gas during the assault on Paris. Do they really have more?"

"Maybe they're just collecting blood for once they have it," Geist muttered. "Either way, we need to stay on guard. If they catch any of us, they'll drain us dry."

Even muttering the phrase *they'll drain us dry* sent a shiver down her spine. She knew the enemy wouldn't hesitate, considering her father and ex-fiancé were top military officers. They had both tried to kill her in the past, and she didn't see why they would stop now that they had a way to steal her specter and apex sorcery.

Geist glanced back at Battery. He came from a long line of sorcerers with rare magic. And not just one magic, but untold numbers. Would he be a target? The thought lingered in her mind for a prolonged moment.

"Stay with him," Geist commanded, "while he takes his photos. I'll go to the port and make sure our ship is ready to take us back to Le Havre."

Vergess replied with a curt nod.

TWO

The Ethereal Squadron of Verdun

Geist tossed the photos down on Major Reese's desk. He stood from his chair and snatched up the documentation, his eyes narrowing as he progressed through the stack.

The poor ventilation of Fort Belleville made everything hot. Cigarette smoke hung in the air, and the copper tang of blood wafted down the halls from the medical rooms. Geist didn't mind the atmosphere. She had come to associate it with safety—all three years of her service had taken place at Fort Belleville, under the command of Major Reese. At a certain level, it was hard to imagine her home being anywhere else.

"You didn't find anyone alive?" he asked.

Geist shook her head. "No, sir."

When he frowned, the age lines on his face deepened. His haggard appearance didn't boost Geist's confidence in the situation. The war sometimes felt like it would go on forever. Day after day, month after month. The enemy wouldn't quit, and they had turned to dastardly tactics. Unrestricted submarine warfare sinking passenger ships like the Lusitania, secret military pacts, dangerous magical-technology hybrid weapons, and now their schemes had turned to espionage. Dealing with such villains would add twenty years' worth of stress to anyone's appearance.

"No blood," Major Reese muttered. "They're trying to steal sorceries."

Geist nodded.

She had given her reports the first time she found the Grave-Maker Gas—the *Grab-Hersteller Gas* in German—known as the GH Gas in their reports. The allies had feared the enemy would capture members of the Ethereal Squadron, but Geist had destroyed most of the gas stores. Obviously, it wasn't a permanent solution, yet she had hoped the gas would never resurface. How did they make it? She didn't know.

"We have counter gas," Geist said. "We could send teams to search for an enemy gas factory. If we can stop their production, we'll interrupt their plans."

Major Reese nodded along with her words. After a moment of silence, he exhaled. "This isn't the first instance of a sorcerer family going dark."

"What do you mean, sir?"

"House Markle. House Livingstone. House Farah. They were all sending aid to the Ethereal Squadron, but one by one, we lost contact."

Geist mulled over the facts. There were thousands of sorcerer houses, and most kept their bloodline secure to keep their magics to themselves. Although Geist didn't know the magics of House Farah or Livingstone, she did recognize House Markle and remembered they had a strange magic over insects. Were the Germans and Austro-Hungarians after bizarre and rare sorceries?

Then again, House Markle was small, just like House Watson. Was the goal to target minor allied houses? Or perhaps it was to start small and work their way up to something larger.

"No matter what we decide to do about this," Major Reese intoned, "we'll need to warn our allied sorcerer houses of the danger."

Geist remained silent. If the minor houses thought they were in danger, they could withdraw from the war altogether. *Was that our enemy's goal? To scare the sorcerers sending us aid, so they would back away?* It was a clever plan, Geist concluded, but what could they do to prevent their allies from abandoning them?

Major Reese exhaled. His pale features matched the haze of smoke above them—an unnatural color. Geist stepped closer to his desk.

"Sir? Are you all right?"

"Geist, my boy, troubling times are ahead of us."

The way he said it, without looking up or adding a hint of emotion, put Geist on edge. "Has something happened?"

"Although Austria-Hungary has functioned with a dual monarchy since 1867, the Austrian Emperor has recently claimed full control of the nation. A true autocrat, that man. And to make matters worse, I've received information that Austria-Hungary has been in contact with the President of the United States. If they form an alliance—"

"They would never," Geist interjected.

"Everyone knows the United States' wartime motto: *war is good for business.* The Americas were on the brink of devastation until the war broke out in Europe. Now they make massive profits on steel and sell to every nation here." Major Reese slammed his hand on the desk. "If helping Austria-Hungary would keep the war running, you better bet the United States has an interest in seeing that happen."

Geist gritted her teeth. She didn't know the politics of the non-sorcerers in the United States, but she did know plenty of sorcerer families who had ties to powerful congressmen. They had never expressed interest in war for war's sake. Then again, she hadn't returned home in three years. Had the United States changed so much? Would they side with Austria-Hungary simply to continue supplying war machines to the European nations cannibalizing each other?

"We need to act carefully," Major Reese said as he paced the room. "We can't afford to lose any more sorcerers, especially if we're about to have a new nation of enemies."

"I agree," she said. "But no matter what the United States

decides, the sorcerers of the Americas will stay with the Ethereal Squadron."

"We don't know that. For now, you'll stay in the fort for the night. Tomorrow, after I speak with the generals, I'll have an assignment for you and your team. Be prepared, understand?"

"I understand, sir."

"You're dismissed."

Geist turned on her heel and headed for the door.

"Wait, Charles."

She stopped.

"You did good work."

"Thank you, sir."

With no other words between them, she exited the room. The drafty halls of Fort Belleville reflected the chill in Geist's thoughts. In her mind, the war in Europe stayed limited to Europe. The United States would stay out of the conflict, and the heart of victory would come from the Russian Empire. But if the United States joined with the sorcerers using monstrous gas and magical-technology, the Allies would surely lose.

Without glancing up, Geist made her way down the southern hall. She knew the fort intimately, from the mail rooms to the recovery ward to the barracks for the French soldiers. When she nearly collided with a fellow soldier, Geist jumped back, her heart beating fast.

Then she got a good look at the man standing in her way.

"Victory," Geist said. "I was just about to look for you."

"I know," he said with a smile. "And I knew you'd be walking down this hall."

"You and your damn future vision." She punched him on the arm and then motioned for him to follow her through the hall. "Do you always use your magic for such mundane purposes?"

"I would win every game of chance with my brothers when we were younger. I was simultaneously the least popular and the most dependable of all my mother's children."

"Is that right? If you all had the same bloodline, why couldn't they learn destiny sorcery?"

Victory shrugged. "It's difficult to understand and use. I just had a knack for it, and my brothers tended toward other abilities."

Victory and Battery both belonged to House Hamilton—one of the most powerful magic families living in Great Britain. Everyone knew they married to diversify their sorceries, and over the centuries, they had amassed hundreds of magics into their bloodline. Geist knew her family had three: specter, apex, and corpus sorcery. Specter to become invisible and incorporeal. Apex to increase strength and agility beyond human limits. And corpus sorcery, to manipulate flesh, either for healing or destructive purposes.

Her house—House Cavell—was a family of assassins known for regicide. That was why those magics had been bred into them.

But House Hamilton acted more like a museum for sorcery. They married sorcerers without houses—individuals who had lost everything or who had nowhere left to go. Their endangered sorceries were added into the Hamilton family with each child, until they had amassed a collection unlike any other sorcerer house.

"Do you know about the missing sorcerer houses?" Geist whispered as they walked. While the occasional nurse and soldier walked by, each had an exhausted expression and were likely far too worn to worry about the random mutterings of fellow soldiers.

"I've heard of them," Victory said.

"We have reason to believe the Abomination Soldiers are targeting sorcerers for their blood." She glanced up to gauge his reaction, but he had none. A perfect poker face. "If we're sent to deal with this problem, I would… worry about you and your brothers. I mean, Blick can be reckless, and Battery only studied the one sorcery. They'd make for perfect targets."

"I doubt the enemy would know who we are," Victory said, nodding along to her words. "That's why we use codenames, after all."

"Still." Geist turned away. "If the enemy ever found out…"

"I'll keep my third eye open to any attacks."

"Thank you."

Having a safeguard against the worst possible outcome gave

Geist a tiny bit of relief. Although she had traveled for days, at no point had she truly rested. Content she had done everything in her power, she patted Victory on the arm and allowed her shoulders to droop.

"You need some rest," he said.

"You're right."

"If you sleep in the second examination room, no one will disturb you."

"More of your destiny sorcery?" Geist asked with a laugh.

Victory flashed a perfect smile. "I love using extraordinary abilities for mundane tasks."

"What would happen if I slept in the first examination room? Or the barracks?"

"Tinker would barge in and disturb you. Twice. Then two nurses would rush in and demand the bed for a wounded soldier. The barracks won't be much better."

The part about Tinker amused her, but the harsh reality of war never stayed hidden long. Of course there would be emergencies, especially since the enemy trenches weren't far from Fort Belleville.

"Joking aside," Victory said, his smile gone. "If you stayed in the first examination room, Tinker would discover more about you than he previously knew before."

He drew out each word but said nothing else.

Geist mulled over the comment, fully aware he was referring to her status as a woman. While everyone in her team knew—Battery, Vergess, Blick, Dreamer, Victory, as well as Cross and Heinrich—the rest of the Ethereal Squadron still hadn't discovered her secret. While female sorcerers often aided the squadron, they weren't given positions in the fighting ranks.

Major Reese would remove me from the front lines in a heartbeat.

"I'll stay clear of the room," Geist said.

Victory nodded. "Then I'll see you tomorrow for the briefing."

THREE

Urgent Operation

G eist awoke in a pool of sweat.

She sat up on her cot, her mind spinning. The darkness offered a comforting atmosphere—she was alone, far from the monsters that plagued her dreams. But she knew that wouldn't last long. Soon she would be out on the battlefield once again, facing down twisted creatures created by the GH Gas.

Geist took a deep breath and then exhaled, allowing her breath to take her anxiety with it.

Now isn't the time to fret.

After another round of breathing, she hopped off the cot and dressed. Although the thin coat of sweat demanded she take a shower, Geist only had an hour or so before she would need to meet with Major Reese.

She buckled her belt, unlocked the door, and stepped out into the hall of Fort Belleville. Vergess stood by the door, his arms crossed, his expression set in a glower. When he turned to Geist, however, he softened.

"You're finally awake."

She glanced around. "You were waiting for me?"

"Tinker was walking around, and I feared he might bother you."

Geist smiled. "Don't worry. Victory told me how to best avoid him."

As if speaking his name summoned the man, Tinker rounded the corner with a bloated satchel held in his arms. He smiled wide as he walked with long strides. "Well, well, well. Two out of three of my favorite people. Where's the other tiny one? Battery is always with you."

He spoke with a lively energy, his voice echoing down the stone hallway.

"What're you up to, Tinker?" Geist asked as she eyed his satchel.

Tinker came to a stop and held the bag close. "Exciting news."

He stood even taller than Vergess, and he had a gaunt frame ill-suited for the British uniform. That didn't stop him from showing off, however. He set the satchel down at his feet and ran a hand through his styled blond hair.

While some sorcerers were suited for combat, Tinker stayed within the confines of the fort, far from conflict. It allowed him the luxury of slicking his hair back with pomade for the perfect wavy hairdo.

Tinker held his head high. "I'm being transferred to London."

"Why?" Vergess asked.

"All sorcerers with an affinity for magic crafting are being summoned to work on magi-tech prototypes. I was near the top of the bloody list thanks to all my work here. I'll be working on top secret projects from here on out. I may even be promoted into the officer ranks."

Geist nodded along with his words. He had helped create a vast store of anti-gas. "You better help with the war efforts. No messing around. You're a real dingbat sometimes."

Tinker dramatically grabbed at his tunic. "I'm wounded, Geist. How many times have I made you custom explosives? And here you're implying I won't be of any use. That's a blow to my honor, I'll have you know." He withdrew a black glove from his trouser pocket and waved it through the air. "You're lucky this isn't twenty years ago. I'd have to duel you to the death."

"This is what I'm talking about," Geist said with a roll of her eyes.

Tinker used his glove to slap her on the shoulder and then offered a smile. "I know you're just jealous. I'm going home to see my girl and you're stuck here on the front lines without the warm comfort of another. Who wouldn't be envious?"

Geist gave Vergess a quick sidelong glance before shaking her head. "That's not it."

"I'll send you parcels from London," Tinker said as he pocketed his glove and snatched up his satchel. "I'll even forget your little insult and get a local girl to write you from time to time." He elbowed Geist as he walked by. "You can thank me once this is all over."

How generous, she thought as Tinker continued on his way.

Vergess rubbed at his chin, half concealing a smirk. "Sometimes I wonder what the man would say if he knew the truth about you."

"I suppose he would get a handsome young man to write me," Geist said.

All mirth disappeared from Vergess's expression. "Feh. Not if he wants to live to see the end of the war."

They both chuckled, but it didn't last long. Geist dwelled on the information, her gaze becoming unfocused. The enemy had started their magi-tech arsenal years ahead of Britain, France, and the Russian Empire. They had the advantage, and with the situation looking so dire, the Ethereal Squadron was finally pooling their resources. What would they create to fight Germany and Austria-Hungary?

Vergess placed a heavy hand on her shoulder. "Let's go see the commander."

"Vergess."

"Hm?"

"You think we'll win this war." She turned to face him. "Don't you?"

He met her gaze with a cold expression. In the long moment between them, Geist understood—he wasn't certain.

"We'll win," he finally said. "We won't allow Germany and Austria-Hungary to rule over all of Europe. Not after everything their royal families have done."

Geist stared at her feet. "Yeah. You're right."

ONLY GEIST'S team had been summoned to speak with Major Reese.

Each of them offered a unique role to the group. Victory could see snippets of the future, perfect for risk-free reconnaissance. Dreamer had his illusions for infiltration purposes. On the other hand, Blick could see through the enemy's illusions, as well as pierce through invisibility. Vergess—his full codename *Vergessenheit*, German for *oblivion*—acted as the team's destructive force. Battery could empower other sorceries, giving them a temporary boost to any power they would need to overcome the enemy.

And Geist considered herself a jack-of-all-trades. She functioned as the leader and participated in almost every aspect of the plan, whenever she was needed most. She'd never had any squad as cohesive as the one she ran, and she suspected whatever Major Reese asked of them, they would be able to succeed.

I hate it when he gets this look on his face, though, she thought, her teeth gritted.

"We have trouble," Major Reese said as he paced behind his desk.

The others said nothing.

He continued, "After analyzing Geist's report, and taking into account intel given to me this morning, I've come to conclusion that our allies are in danger. Small sorcerer houses are being targeted for their sorceries. It's clear the enemy has dispatched small teams of operatives to collect blood for their GH Gas experiments."

Dreamer lifted both eyebrows. "I take it our enemies have forsaken the ways of God."

"So far they've limited their targets to sorcerer houses who aid the military, but given Germany's attack on civilian vessels, I suspect they'll target any sorcerer they feel will add to their strength."

"I know the tactics of cowards well. Civilians make for easy targets."

Dreamer spoke with a proper English accent, his words regal and fully articulated. Even the way he held himself—he never did anything in haste. It was one of the traits Geist admired about him.

"What's the Ethereal Squadron doing about this?" Blick asked. He rotated his shoulders and leaned against the fort's stone wall. "If we know what our enemies are plotting, we should stop them. Beat them to the punch. *Something*."

Major Reese stopped and shook his head. "Communication has been difficult with some of our smaller allies, especially those located on islands or within the Russian Empire."

"What about radio communication?" Battery asked.

"Ha! Those newfangled radios aren't reliable. Their range is too short, and there's always interference. Telephones and telegraphs have been the military's go-to solution, but even that isn't foolproof. The few sorcerers we have who can speak long distances are currently in key operations in the Middle Eastern theatre."

Blick pushed off the wall and wheeled to face his older brother, Victory. "What's the solution, then? What're we gonna do about it? What *can* we do?"

"Calm down," Victory stated. "Major Reese was about to send us to check in on our allies and bring them back to Verdun."

Everyone turned to face the commander. Major Reese offered a slow nod and then returned to his pacing. Geist didn't like the idea of collecting everyone in a single spot—wouldn't it invite the enemy to strike them all at once?—but they had already defended Paris from the worst attack in history. The enemy had been pushed back, and there would be no safer place in Europe than the Ethereal Squadron base of operations.

In theory.

"Geist," Major Reese said, his tone filled with a heavy gravity. "I need you and your team to bring back the sorcerers of four Russian houses."

"Sir?" she asked. "Wouldn't they be safe in the capital city of Petrograd? Surely the Royal House Romanov would send soldiers to protect their sorcerers. And moving four entire houses to France seems like a difficult undertaking."

Battery crossed his arms and then uncrossed them. "I thought the Russian Empire had the largest standing army in the world. I agree with Geist. Why would we bring them to France?"

"Tsar Nicholas Romanov has taken personal command of the military," Major Reese said with a single laugh. "Since then, the Russian Empire has been on a failing offensive. They've lost millions of soldiers yet haven't advanced far into Austria-Hungary, and large segments of the nation have fallen into disarray."

"It would make it easy for specialized enemy sorcerers to sneak into the empire and target non-military sorcerer families," Dreamer concluded. "Dastardly tactics of the highest order."

Vergess shook his head. "There's something else to this mission you're not telling us, isn't there? Let me guess. The Royal House Romanov hasn't approved the relocation of the families we're supposed to rescue?"

"No," Major Reese said. "As a matter of fact, all Russian sorcerers have been instructed to remain within the empire unless otherwise given direct military order."

"So, you want us to run this operation in secret."

"Correct."

"Are these sorcerer houses really that important that we would need to risk a diplomatic incident over them? None of the Royal Houses are known for their reasonableness." Vergess huffed and shook his head. "Why don't we focus on catching the sorcerers who are killing people?"

Major Reese glared at his feet. "The four families I need you to rescue have extremely rare and valuable sorceries. We cannot allow the enemy to have them, especially not because a buffoon wearing the costume of a general thinks he knows what he's doing."

Geist caught her breath. The Royal House Romanov had ruled

the Russian Empire for over 300 years. They were powerful sorcerers in their own right, with their own brand of unique sorcery. Although Geist had never met any of the royal family, she knew the Royal House Habsburg-Lorraine well. They were a royal house of competent and powerful sorcerers. Surely the Royal House Romanov would be similar, or at least far from the *buffoon* Major Reese had painted the current Tsar.

"What if we're caught taking Russian sorcerers?" Geist asked. "Do you think this would anger the Tsar?"

Major Reese nodded.

Victory and Dreamer exchanged quick sidelong glances.

Vergess huffed again. "I still think we'd be better suited to hunting down the perpetrators."

"Germany and Austria-Hungary have thousands of sorcerers they could task this mission with," Geist intoned. "Killing one squad would result in another taking their place. We need a permanent solution if we want to protect our allies."

"Hiding them in Paris is our permanent solution?"

"The war won't last forever."

It can't.

Geist clenched her fists, digging her nails into her palms. Could the Ethereal Squadron afford to anger the Russian Empire? They currently fought on the side of Britain and France—they were one of the three pillars that made up the Triple Entente—and if they exited the war, Germany and Austria-Hungary wouldn't be caught between two fronts. They could shift all their soldiers to fight in France.

And what if the United States joined the enemy forces? Geist thought, her heart rate increasing with each dire scenario she painted in her mind. *We would never win in that circumstance. The Ethereal Squadron would be taken before the sorcerers of Germany and Austria-Hungary and hacked apart for their magic... maybe even melted together to form monsters of war.*

The weight of the operation hit Geist hard. They had to travel into the war-plagued Russian Empire to save sorcerer families from their own Tsar. If they were caught, it could cause an incident, perhaps even worthy of the Russian Empire withdrawing from the war entirely.

"Can we at least attempt to reason with the Tsar?" Geist asked, her voice distant.

Major Reese let out a long sigh. "I've sent word to the Tsar many times. He has not been a reasonable fellow. However, you will need to travel through Petrograd to reach one of the houses. If you think you can get the Tsar to listen, then you have my blessing to attempt it, but no matter his reply, you must continue with the operation."

"Tipping him off to our intentions doesn't sound like a good idea to me," Blick said.

"I would have to agree," Major Reese said.

Before anyone could add anything further, Major Reese pushed a small folder across his desk. Geist walked over and took their instructions. Each page had information on a separate sorcerer family, right down to the living members and their estimated wealth.

"These are your targets," Major Reese said. "House Solovyev, House Lungin, House Menshov, and House Kott. I had been in contact with them until communication over the border basically disappeared. When last I heard, they wanted out of the Russian Empire. I suspect they'll be receptive to your appearance."

Battery glanced over Geist's shoulder to look over the paperwork. "Is there a chance they're already dead?"

"Yes."

Another strike straight to the heart of the issue. They needed to protect civilian sorcerers from the horrors of the Great War.

"Can we at least destroy this team of killers if we find them?" Vergess asked.

"Don't allow a manhunt to jeopardize your goal. None of the houses should be put in danger, but if you can deal with the enemy squad, do it."

Although Geist had agreed with Major Reese about rescuing the houses rather than hunting down the killers, she didn't mind the thought of somehow accomplishing both. The team who destroyed

House Watson had taken the lives of children, after all. They didn't deserve mercy. They didn't deserve anything.

Geist closed the file. "We'll handle this, sir."

The rest of her team nodded along with her words.

"Good," Major Reese replied. "Then you leave this afternoon. Take your equipment and send word right before you cross the border."

FOUR

The Port City of Riga

"We might not see each other for a long while," Cross said. She opened her locker and withdrew her spare gloves and clothing. Then she neatly folded them and placed them into her bag. "I'll be joining the Romanian campaign."

Geist remained quiet.

Cross touched her silver necklace—a holy cross from the St. Augustine's Roman Catholic Church in London. She twisted the ornament between her fingers.

"I'm worried about your safety," she said.

"It'll be easier to remain hidden in the barracks with Victory around."

"I wasn't referring to your gender. I'm worried about whether you'll make it back from your operation."

Before Geist's team discovered her identity as a woman, Cross had been her sole confidant. As the Matron-in-Chief at Fort Belleville, Cross had even helped in disguising Geist as a man. Cross performed all physical examinations and checkups and provided Geist cellucotton for her monthly moments of blood.

I never would've joined the Ethereal Squadron if it hadn't been for Cross. The least I can do is dispel her doubts.

"The Russian Empire is ally territory," Geist said. "I'm more concerned about your assignment in the Kingdom of Romania."

"They need expert healers. I asked to be assigned once I heard the death tolls."

The Kingdom of Romania remained neutral the first two years of the war. They sold oil—their fields rich with it, more so than any other European nation—and allowed Germany to pass through to Turkey without hindrance. Although they had joined the allied powers, everyone knew Romania had strong ties to the enemy. Romania only joined the war on the allied side so they could take back Transylvania under the guise of "fighting the Central Powers," though Turkey wasn't even the biggest threat. The moment Romania had their land, the whole nation could change sides. The Central Powers would probably allow them to keep Turkey in exchange for the troops and tactical advantages.

And then Cross would be in the heart of enemy territory.

Geist folded her arms and gave Cross a long stare.

"What about you?" Cross asked. "Didn't the Austro-Hungarian prince want you for your blood? What if they specifically target you for their blood collection? Specter sorcery isn't common."

Geist shook her head. "I doubt it. The prince wanted me before they created their GH Gas. They no longer need dynastic legacy to pass sorceries from one person to another. Besides, my father and brothers work for the crown prince. If he wanted blood, he could have it."

The locker room grew quiet. Cross finished packing her bag, her eyebrows knitted together. The expression didn't suit her. Her regal posture and perfect golden hair came straight from fairy tales. Anything that marred her stately appearance looked out of place. Geist regretted upsetting her, especially when they would be parting ways soon.

"Have you said goodbye to Victory?" Geist asked, hoping to change the subject.

Cross didn't answer. She hefted her bag over her shoulder and straightened her dress.

"You don't have to hide anything from me," Geist said.

"I've spoken to Victory. He shared the same concerns you did, but I've made up my mind. My family won't be able to deny me anything once I return a war hero." Cross brushed a strand of her hair to the side. She relaxed a bit, her expression neutral. "Once this ordeal is over, Victory and I can be together without fear of protest from my father. I just need to be strong. The light is at the end of the tunnel—I can feel it."

Geist nodded.

Then Cross smiled. "You know, you never did tell me about you and Vergess."

"W-well, that's different."

Heat flooded Geist's face the more she stumbled through excuses in her head. No one was supposed to know about her relationship with Vergess, even if it were obvious to those who knew them.

Cross walked toward the door. She placed her hand on the handle. "Be safe, Florence. I want us all to meet back in Paris once the Central Powers have fallen."

The weight of the request dug into Geist's thoughts. She found it hard to find the words to respond—to promise they would all be together—and decided instead on silence. There were no guarantees in war, even if Geist was determined to make sure her team made it through the Russian Empire without trouble.

"Until we meet again."

––––––––––––

THE SHIP ROCKED with the waves of the Baltic Sea.

Geist read over her operation notes, her focus drifting after the long travel. For some reason, no matter how many times she rode on a ship, the rocking took its toll. Her stomach twisted, and her chest tightened, but she pushed through the nausea.

The top of each briefing page read: OPERATION ORPHEUS. The rest of the page consisted of tiny Corona 3 typewriter print. The paragraphs detailed each sorcerer house, their estate, and any known information on associations and ties to the Royal House Romanov.

The three brothers of her squad—Battery, Victory, and Blick—sat in the far corner of the passenger lounge. The rocking of the ship didn't seem to bother them. Battery and Victory flipped through the operation notes with ease. Blick took his time. His half-lidded eyes and slacked posture betrayed his boredom.

Dreamer and Vergess sat near the windows overlooking the deck. The waves glistened in the light of the setting sun, a glorious sight that Dreamer couldn't keep his eyes off. His operation paperwork sat in his lap while he soaked in the golden rays of a dying day. Vergess didn't glance up. He read through his brief and then read through it a second time afterward.

The last member of the Ethereal Squadron assigned to Operation Orpheus was none other than Heinrich von Veltheim. Heinrich wasn't normally a field operative like the others. Like Tinker, he sat behind fort walls and engaged in a war of information, research, and development. He sat next to Geist and read his notes without a sound, his black-framed glasses occasionally sliding down his slender nose when he reached the bottom of every page.

"I'm surprised you weren't assigned to London," Geist said, keeping her voice low.

No one else sat in the ship's lounge, but she didn't want to disturb the quiet.

Heinrich huffed. "I will be traveling to London after this operation concludes. Major Reese has asked I train several Russian sorcerers on the basics of our magi-tech operations. I *would* have submitted my notes through a coded telegraph, but the major doesn't trust traditional forms of communication."

"Several telegrams have been intercepted by German spies."

"Still. I find his archaic way of spreading information to be troublesome."

"I have instructions to protect you," Geist said. She glanced down to the front sheet of her notes and pointed to the objectives. His name wasn't listed, for security reasons, and instead Heinrich was referred to as *the researcher*. "I also have instructions to pick a codename for you."

Heinrich lifted an eyebrow but didn't glance up from his notes. "I've always found the Ethereal Squadron's use of codenames to be questionable. Germany doesn't require their Abomination Soldiers to choose aliases."

"It prevented enemies from targeting specific sorcerers, especially during the Napoleonic Wars."

"We can choose anything?"

Geist chuckled. "Not quite."

Normally, with field operatives, the codename came from their powers on the battlefield. Researchers, engineers, and medics had other rites of passage. *How did Tinker get his codename?* she wondered. She thought back to Battery and how he earned his name by empowering others.

"I'll think about it," Geist stated. "You have an unusual circumstance. What did Tinker call you when you two worked together on the anti-gas grenades?"

"He called me all manner of derogatory terms, but I suppose his favorite was *traitor*." Heinrich glanced up from his reading and huffed. "If Vergess can have a codename that doesn't directly reflect his turncoat actions, I demand the same treatment."

"*Turncoat* would be an amusing name," Geist said with a chortle.

Heinrich responded with a sharp sneer. "You Americans have an odd sense of humor."

Do Germans even have a sense of humor? Geist glanced over to Vergess. He had a slight smile on his face, and although he sat at least three tables away, she knew he heard the entire conversation. His apex sorcery heightened all his senses, and he tended to use it to his advantage whenever possible, especially when team matters were discussed.

Victory stood, walked over, and took a seat next to Geist, a slight frown on his face.

"We're heading to the port city of Riga," he said as he tapped the papers.

Geist nodded. "That's right."

"We could stay on the ship and land in Petrograd instead. It'll add a day to our travels, but I think landing in the capital of the Russian Empire would be safer."

"We're meeting a member of the Ethereal Squadron in Riga. Plus, one of the houses we need to speak to is located just outside of Riga."

"Two of our target houses are just outside of Petrograd," Victory said.

Geist flipped through her notes until she came to House Kott. "Out of all the sorcerer houses on the list, this one is closest to the Eastern front. They would be the easiest to target for our enemy operatives, and if Germany has plans to invade—and I suspect they do—they might want all sorcerers in the area dead regardless."

Victory stroked his chin as he stared down at the notes. He had a charisma about him, and his neat haircut and smooth face added to his clean-cut mien. Geist understood why Cross swooned in his presence.

"We'll be taking the train to Petrograd afterward," Geist said.

Victory nodded. "I see. Depending on how long we need to speak with House Kott, this may even be faster."

Geist hoped her decisions wouldn't cost them any lives. Would the enemies target Petrograd first, since they could get two houses with one stone? Or perhaps she was worrying for nothing. The variables made everything seem uncertain.

But with magic…

"Can't you use your sorcery?" Geist asked. "If you see something terrible with this plan, you need to tell me."

Victory inhaled, closed his eyes, and then exhaled. Heinrich stopped reading and paid close attention as Victory sat motionless in his chair. Although powerful and beyond useful, Victory's powers were the least flashy in the group. A slight chill filled the ship lounge, but otherwise there was no indication his sorcery had been used.

Geist held her breath. Victory always reported multiple possibilities, since the future wasn't totally determined. Many things *could* happen depending on the actions of a million individuals. What would he see in Riga?

"In all my visions…" Victory scrunched his eyes and rubbed at the bridge of his nose. "We arrive at House Kott. And then we encounter… eyes."

Heinrich straightened his glasses. "Pardon me? *Eyes*?"

"Yes. We will face *eyes* in Riga. That's what I hear Vergess screaming whenever I picture their house and estate. Something about eyes. And then… we're running." Victory rubbed harder at his face, his voice strained.

"Anything else?" Geist asked.

"Death," Victory added. "Geist, I think you might've made a wise choice. So many of my visions involve us not arriving in time because we chose to go elsewhere." He opened his eyes and shook his head. "We must head straight for House Kott once we reach port. But we should be careful. I saw blood everywhere. Like stumbling upon the scene of a gruesome murder."

"Are we walking into a trap?"

"No. The enemy is always surprised in my vision. But they're not helpless, either."

"Who are they?"

Everyone else in the lounge stopped and turned to face them. Geist gripped her uniform pants with a tight fist, her heart beating hard against her ribs. They would engage the enemy the moment they arrived? She could barely believe it.

"*Abomination Soldiers*," Victory muttered. "I would stake my life on it. They're hidden in the shadows, and my visions become too blurry after that. The closer we get to House Kott, the clearer my sight will become."

Abomination Soldiers. The German equivalent to the Ethereal Squadron. They operated with a brutal efficiency, and Geist had fought enough of their sorcerers to know they would be walking into a carnage if they weren't careful.

"You need to keep me appraised," Geist commanded. "Even the slightest detail could make the difference, you understand me?"

Victory nodded. "Yes, sir."

He sat back in his seat and stared at his lap. On several occasions he spoke about how his magic was both a blessing and a curse.

Witnessing death and pain on a near-daily basis, especially during a war, could wear a man down, and sometimes Victory had a melancholy expression unlike anyone else Geist had ever seen.

Had he seen something terrible just then? More than what he reported?

Heinrich picked up his operation notes and glared at the pages. "Eyes?" he muttered. "What an odd thing to worry about."

THE SHIP DOCKED at Riga just as the sun was rising into the sky. The grand city, the third largest in the Russian Empire, rivaled Paris and London. Three-story buildings, painted an ivory white, shone in the new daylight. Wide streets allowed for hundreds of people, horses, and Russo-Balt automobiles. The hustle and bustle of a wartime nation meant everything was crowded. They had to ship materials, men, and medical supplies 24/7.

Geist and her team walked down the gangplank and headed across the port through the massive crowds. Horns sounded as ships finished packing supplies and leaving harbor. A thick smell of fish wafted through the air. In every way, Geist's heightened senses were assaulted.

"This is my first time in the Russian Empire," Battery muttered as he shifted closer to Geist. "Our family technically has a branch here, but my father and his Russian cousins had a major disagreement over a decade ago. They haven't spoken since."

Geist had never been to the Russian Empire. Her father hated slavs and insisted they were lesser peoples. With no evidence one way or another, Geist could never protest, but after one glance around Riga, she knew he had to be wrong.

"I wonder what it'll be like in Petrograd," Geist said.

Battery pointed to a tall building in the distance, one with pillars and a massive statue holding a fountain. "That must be the opera house. I heard it was built for the Germans some fifty years ago. Ironic, isn't it? That the Germans are marching toward Riga as we speak."

Although Geist would've enjoyed seeing the culture of a foreign city, she shook the thought from her head. They had to find their contact and head straight to House Kott. *Victory has never been wrong in the past. We'll have to hurry.*

"There you are," a large man said as he pushed himself through the crowds of Riga. "I vas beginning to think you vouldn't make it." He patted his bulging shoulder and approached with a wide smile.

Blick and Vergess stepped forward, both smaller than the Russian, though neither could be described as a *small man*.

"Do you have business with us?" Vergess asked.

The Russian nodded. "I do. I'm your correspondent. I need to speak vith someone named Geist."

He wore a guard's officer uniform, complete with a long brown trench coat and ridged cap. Like most Russian soldiers Geist had seen, he kept facial hair—a bushy mustache and goatee.

"You may call me *Varnish*," the Russian said. "I'm your guide through the empire. Anyvhere you need to go, just say so."

Heinrich stepped forward and sneered. "Varnish is your code-name? Out of anything you could've possibly chosen?"

Varnish smiled wide. "Alcohol is prohibited in the empire, my friend. It has been enforced for several years now. That doesn't mean ve've stopped drinking, though. This is Russia, after all."

Battery paled. "Wait. Are you saying you… drink varnish? Does varnish even have alcohol in it?"

"Of course! A buddy of mine bet fifteen rubles I vouldn't drink it. So I did. Then another buddy didn't believe the first guy, so I had to do it again for forty rubles. Easy fifty-five rubles, if you ask me." He waved a hand into the air. "And now I have nickname. Excellent for Ethereal Squadron."

Geist exchanged a questioning glance with Vergess before following the lumbering Russian. As far as she was concerned, actual varnish was toxic, but Varnish, the man, didn't seem the least bit fazed. *Or perhaps he started as a genius and this is all that's left*, Geist joked to herself, a slight smile creeping at the corner of her lips.

Dreamer chortled. "Fascinating. You must have an iron stomach. Or perhaps you have a unique sorcery that allows for perfect digestion?"

"You're close, my British friend."

Dreamer's posh accent clashed with Varnish's unrefined English.

"Ve have a long trek to House Kott," Varnish said. "But first you all need rooms."

"No," Geist stated. "We need to visit House Kott right away. No delays."

Varnish pointed to the far road. "I have a vehicle. I can take you."

FIVE

House Kott

G eist hung her legs out the back of the supply truck as it sped south down the earthen road. The slightest divot shook the automobile, and Geist found herself wishing for a horse-drawn carriage. Unfortunately, horses weren't the fastest option, and since Varnish offered a military vehicle, they had to accept.

Vergess sat next to her, his gaze on the dust cloud kicked up by the tires. He hadn't spoken since they began their trek.

"You okay?" Geist said.

The others sat nearby, but the rumble of the engine and muttered conversations made everything difficult to hear.

Vergess nodded, though he didn't look up from the dirt. "Victory said I was yelling in his visions. Something about eyes. I'm trying to figure out what could be waiting for us. I must know if I'm the one trying to warn everyone."

"You have no ideas based on Victory's description?"

"It's... difficult to concentrate at the moment."

He offered nothing else.

His troubled expression ate Geist's confidence. As a commander, she needed all her soldiers at their best, especially on the eve of a fight. As someone who cared for Vergess more than a typical brother-in-arms, she wanted to ease his doubts and assure him that everything would be fine. But she could think of no way to improve his focus, and she refused to allow her affection to dictate her actions. They were a military unit first and a couple second.

It had been so long since they shared any intimacy that Geist almost found it possible to forget they once had experienced loving moments. War tarnished the beauties of the world, stripping humanity of its best parts.

She wanted nothing more than to end it.

Varnish, driving the supply truck with one hand on the wheel, turned to Heinrich in the passenger seat. He smiled wide. "So, you're German, yeah?"

Heinrich pushed up his glasses. "Don't speak to me."

"Why don't you enlighten me about the Russian Empire's logistics?" Dreamer interjected with a smile, so smooth with his delivery Heinrich's insult almost went undetected. "I would love to hear about supply routes, especially those connecting to the ports. My information may be out of date."

Dreamer opened a book titled *Howards End* and readied his pencil. Once upon a time, Geist thought Dreamer kept a book or two for entertainment, but she knew better now. He took notes on everything and hid them in plain sight. His spy tricks came in handy. Geist had given serious thought to imitating his practices.

"Railways," Varnish said. "They are the heart of our operation."

"And you know all the major routes?"

"I do." Varnish hardened his expression and turned away. "But the trains never deliver enough food."

Major Reese had already commented on the Tsar's incompetence. Geist took note of Varnish's harsh tone and shift to a dour attitude. Was the Russian Empire even capable of holding on in the war? Twelve years earlier, they had lost to the tiny island nation of Japan, and now they had lost battle after battle—to the point morale was obviously low.

Geist scooted back in the truck until she reached Victory. "Have you heard much about the Russian Empire?" she asked.

He shook his head.

"What about you?" Geist asked Blick.

He scoffed. "I haven't heard word from the Russians since my father got angry at our uncle."

She turned to Battery, but he replied with a shake of his head.

"I'm sorry," he muttered.

Much to Geist's surprise, Heinrich turned in his seat and glared. "The Russian Empire has been steady on decline for some time. And the Austro-Hungarians and Germans know it."

Varnish lifted both his bushy eyebrows, but said nothing.

"What do you know?" Geist asked.

"I was there when the Kaiser paid to have anarchists and Bolshevik agitators delivered into the heartland of Russia. He shipped them nothing but radicals—anyone the Russian Empire had exiled, the Kaiser had them smuggled back into the country— including Vladimir Lenin, the Bolshevik leader himself. He hoped they would stir up anti-war protests."

"And they've been causing problems?"

Varnish laughed out loud, his deep voice rumbling louder than the engine. Blick joined him with a look of amusement and shock.

"Stop the vehicle!" Victory shouted.

The sudden application of brakes sent everyone tumbling forward. Battery and Dreamer slammed into the divider between the truck bed and the cab. Blick held onto the wood panel sides, his hands bleeding afterward. Geist and Vergess, both with apex sorcery, managed to brace themselves in time.

The supply truck skidded across the dirt road for a foot before stopping. Varnish tapped on the steering wheel and then chuckled to himself.

"Nothing is ever slow with your group, is it? Hurry here. Stop there. Make up your minds."

Heinrich snatched his glasses off the floor before turning back to the truck bed with a glare. He motioned to their surroundings. The empty Russian countryside had a yellow-green glow from the midafternoon sun. The grass swayed with the winds, the trees rustled, and the cloud of dirt kicked up by the tires wafted over them.

Not a soul in sight.

"Is there a reason you turned banshee?" Heinrich asked with a straight face.

"I saw something," Victory muttered. He wiped sweat from his forehead, his hand shaky. "We can't drive up. We... we have to approach the house on foot. They have someone watching the main road."

Leaving the truck would add time to their travel, but maintaining the element of surprise was an advantage they couldn't forsake. Geist exhaled and leapt out the back of the truck.

"Heinrich, you wait here with Varnish," she said. "The rest of us will approach House Kott."

Heinrich gave his Russian companion a sidelong glance.

"Don't vorry," Varnish said. "I'll protect you like a knight protects a princess in a castle."

That didn't seem to help Heinrich's mood. He sneered as he turned away. "Life has a cruel sense of humor," he muttered in German. "Perhaps this is punishment for all my past works."

No one else argued. Although Heinrich had access to anti-magic powers thanks to his nullis sorcery, Geist had seen his feeble attempts at combat. He struggled to use his own luger, for Pete's sake. And he was much too valuable to lose in a skirmish over a small sorcerer house.

Hopefully Varnish will take his duty of protection seriously.

Geist's team exited the vehicle and brushed themselves off, each with a hardened, almost worried, expression. Even if they had stealth on their side, they didn't understand their opponents. What sorcerers would be waiting for them? Was anyone from House Kott still alive? Geist rubbed her sweaty palms along the bottom of her khaki tunic.

They had to act fast.

Varnish leaned back in his seat, withdrew a pack of cigarettes, and lit one up. After exhaling a line of smoke, he said, "Hurry back. I don't think me and the prissy German vill play nice for long."

THE LONG ROAD to House Kott had large trees planted on either side, creating a natural canopy of shade. There wasn't much else. The open fields of grass didn't offer any places for hiding, and the modest mansion kept statues and ponds rather than flourishing gardens. Geist and her team made their way around the edge of the property until they came across a training field for horses. A hay barn, several jumping posts, and a stable, dotted the estate.

And a small path led from the servants' homes to the mansion from the back.

As the sun set, casting harsher shadows across the grass, Geist turned to the others.

"I'll scout first," she said. Then she turned to Victory. "Unless you see something?"

He shook his head. "I'm sorry. Normally I can sense more, but... I don't feel right."

Geist hesitated a moment. None of her team seemed ill, yet Victory was the second one to report he didn't feel well. Perhaps the stress was too much? Or perhaps sorcery was involved. She didn't have enough facts to determine anything one way or the other.

Vergess motioned to the main Kott mansion. "I'll go with you."

"No," Blick interjected. "Let me go." His eyes glowed with an inner golden light, showcasing his ability to pierce through any illusion or shroud of invisibly. "I'm better for a scouting run."

His all-seeing sight would come in handy.

"I'm the better fighter," Vergess said.

"I can hold my own."

"You heard Victory. There's death inside."

Geist held up a hand. "Enough. It's a scouting mission first, then we attack. Blick, you're with me. The rest of you take defensive positions around this field. If I give the signal from the window, you're to move in. Otherwise, you stay put until we get back."

Vergess and the others nodded.

Battery held out his hand. "Wait. Don't go without me empowering you."

"Empower Blick," she said. "If he can spot something crucial, that's more important right now."

The brothers exchanged a quick glance. Battery held out his hand, and Blick took it. After a short second, Blick let go and shifted closer to Geist's side.

Satisfied with their arrangement, Geist allowed her specter sorcery to permeate her being. The process of becoming a ghost always gave her a rush of raw power. Incorporeal and invisible, she could move around, free from the concerns of solid objects and spying eyes. Sometimes, whenever she pushed her magic too far, she would slip a foot into the ground, still drawn by gravity, but free from the earth. Those moments had startled her enough to break her concentration and end her sorcery.

The others in her team—all but Blick—stared at her last location, their eyes searching. The moment Geist made her way for the mansion, Blick hefted his SMLE rifle and followed, staying a short distance behind her, all the way until they reached the stable. The snorting and neighing of horses echoed from within.

Geist slid along the backside of the building.

"It's odd," Blick murmured.

"What?"

"We haven't seen any people. Not one."

The agitation of the horses became more apparent.

It's just like House Watson, Geist realized. *They don't care if they leave corpses. They just don't want any witnesses.*

"We need to know how many there are," Geist whispered.

Blick leaned around the corner, his gold eyes shining in the low light. He pulled back and shook his head. "The curtains are drawn on all the windows. I can't see anything inside."

"Are there any signs of a struggle outside?"

Blick took another second to chance a glance. "No. Nothing looks out of place. Just deserted. But…"

"But what?"

"After Battery empowered me, I can see a lot of magic in the air. Like a dust. It's everywhere. I hadn't noticed it before. I hadn't even felt it."

Geist lifted her tunic to cover her mouth, but she knew without a gas mask it wouldn't make much difference if she were breathing something toxic. They had already been through the thick of it.

"Do you know what it does?" she asked.

"My sorcery doesn't give me hard data." He offered half a smile. "It's just hanging in the air as far as I can see. All around the estate and a little beyond. We must have been in it for a few hours now."

We shouldn't stay here longer than necessary then. A quick scouting mission. In and out.

After a moment of shallow breathing, Geist crept around the corner and ran to the mansion. She kept low, just in case the enemy had someone with Blick's style of all-seeing sorcery. Once against the wall, she crept to the back door, plunged her hand through the handle, and unfastened the lock.

She motioned for Blick to join her.

The darkness of night settled over the estate as Blick ran across the yard, his rifle held close. He stopped once he reached her side and then waited.

He exhaled and closed his eyes. "I, uh…"

Geist placed the back of her hand on his chest. "It can wait."

"You don't understand," he whispered. "I've been practicing a new sorcery."

"*You?*"

Blick stifled a laugh. "Don't sound *too* shocked."

"Sorry. I suppose we could use a little more of what Battery and Victory have."

"Yeah, well, I can't… learn sorceries like those. I've tried. They're too complicated."

She lifted an eyebrow. "And you wondered why I was shocked."

"Don't give me that look. Those aren't easy sorceries."

He was right. Some sorcery required more of the sorcerer than others. Geist couldn't even imagine learning Victory's destiny magic. How did someone go about looking into the future?

Not only that, but mastering a second sorcery required a lot of time and concentration. Hell, mastering *one* sorcery usually took a fair amount of effort—some never managed it. The process was like mastering an instrument. People could become a professional violinist, but most people couldn't stack professional trumpeter on top of it. Some could. But they were the exception.

Although Geist had started learning apex sorcery, she knew it would take a considerable amount of time and effort to fully take advantage of it. Still, having more than one sorcery had its usefulness, especially in a time of war. And Blick was a member of the Hamilton House—they had all sorts of useful sorceries.

"Then what're you learning?" she whispered. "How can it help us now?"

"I've been learning *communis* sorcery. It allows me to speak to others telepathically."

Every soldier knew of the importance of communication. Without the proper orders, battles could turn into a real problem, real fast. Speaking to someone over long distances, free of spy intervention, would prove beyond useful.

"How far?" she asked.

Blick glanced down at his feet, a sheepish smile at the corner of his lips. "A few feet."

Silence descended upon them.

Geist sighed. "Look, I appreciate you letting me know, but now isn't the time. If you can't use the ability properly, then we'll have to—"

"That's the thing. With Battery, I feel like I can reach farther. Like… I can reach out and talk to someone." Blick turned to face her, his gold eyes almost transfixing. "I can sense the others like a switchboard operator staring at the empty connectors, ready to make a connection. There are people in the house. At least eleven."

"Enemies?"

"I don't know. But if I speak to them, they'll know we're here."

"Don't. I'll search inside first."

A loud crash of porcelain sounded inside the mansion, followed closely by the scraps and slams of a struggle. Geist and Blick tensed, each listening to the conflict with rapt attention. It lasted thirty seconds. No screams or cries for help. Then nothing.

Blick gave Geist a questioning glance.

Their mission was to recover the Russian families and prevent their blood from falling into the hands of the enemy. However, they still didn't know what they were up against. Geist gritted her teeth, hesitating between getting the rest of her team and gathering valuable information. Someone had been attacked.

"Do you want me to call the others?" Blick whispered.

Geist shook her head. "Stay here."

She ghosted through the wall, an odd tingle sweeping through her body when she entered and exited solid matter. After a moment to shake off the sensation, she found herself in the middle of a kitchen. The hexagon tiling, alternating between black and white, shone with the luster of a mirror. Every inch of walls were covered in windowed cabinets, all of which were stuffed to the brim with spices, dried food, and containers of water. Nothing looked out of place.

"*Geist.*"

The voice, not spoken, but clear in her ears, startled Geist. In her brief moment of confusion, her sorcery flickered. Once she regained her invisibility, she turned to face the wall. Had Blick spoken to her? Was it possible for her to speak back?

"*Lights came on in a room above you.*"

Again, Geist didn't know if there was a way to respond. She had no blood relation to any sorcerer with *communis* sorcery, so she could never learn it, and no one in the Ethereal Squadron had ever used it with her.

With her new knowledge, Geist shifted through another wall and found herself in an eighty-foot long hallway. The potted plants and paintings on the wall were undisturbed, but several vases had been shattered across the rugs. Blood speckled the blue and white porcelain, still wet and glinting in the light of the hallway's electric chandeliers.

Geist stepped around the shards of vases and made her way for the staircase. A corpse waited on the first step, its body curled in on itself, as though half rotted from decades of decay.

It wasn't old, though. Geist had seen *ruina* sorcery at work in the past. It aged and rotted everything, including flesh.

By the looks of the clothes, the corpse had once been a nobleman, most likely someone who lived in the house, but perhaps a visitor. Geist knelt and examined the body. Slashes across the neck. Bashed in eye sockets. The man had been fully incapacitated.

Geist stepped around the body and made her way upstairs, each step quieter than the last until she was on the second story landing. She turned and made her way down the hall, her attention drawn by the bright light shining from under one of the doors. The beating of her heart rang so loud in her ears she suspected someone standing a few feet next to her could hear it. There still hadn't been any sight of her enemies.

Were they invisible, too?

The thought almost got her laughing. Geist didn't have a way to find others with *specter* sorcery. They might as well be blind submarines, waiting to strike.

Once she reached the door, she stopped.

"*Wir haben drei vermisst*," a man said, his German distinct, even when muttered.

We missed three.

"*Härter aussehen*," another man replied.

Look harder.

Geist had her Austrian father to thank for her knowledge of German. Her father had specifically kept them with German language tutors, even when they lived in the United States.

Floorboards creaked as someone walked toward the door. Geist readied her Colt M1911. Whoever it was, they weren't an ally. And once she disposed of the two men in the room, she could signal the others.

"Wait," a third man said in German, his speech muffled not just by the walls, but by something on his face. A mask. A gas mask.

The man heading for the door stopped. "Is there not enough blood?"

"That's not the problem."

The voice behind the gas mask sounded familiar. Geist took a step back, her mouth dry. Although she couldn't place the tone, her stomach twisted into knots, as though her body already knew the answer—it just wouldn't share it with her.

"We have a visitor," the gas mask man said. "In the hallway, just outside the door."

SIX

The Eyes of the Kaiser

G eist jumped through the wall of the next room over. A second later, the three enemy soldiers opened their door. It took them a few moments before they entered the hallway, precision in their movements befitting elite soldiers. Geist moved away from the wall at a slow pace, holding her handgun close. She had entered a study with no exits other than a lone window.

"There's nothing here," one of the men muttered from the hall.

"No," the man with the gas mask said. "He's moved. You two get downstairs. I can sense another outside the kitchen door." He snapped his fingers. "Dispose of that one."

The other two took off down the stairs just as Geist registered the command. They were heading for Blick. She didn't have much time, and she still needed to contact the rest of her team.

Then the door to her room opened, and Geist caught her breath. The voice, his appearance, the way he walked—everything came together. She knew exactly who he was.

Amalgam.

He was a German soldier twisted by the terrible GH Gas, his body melted together and fused with the blood of Geist's first sorcerer team. It had been her fault he fell into the gas-filled trench in the first place. And after the "accident," she had seen Amalgam without his gas mask only once—a sight straight from her nightmares. No eyes. A waxy sheen to his deformed skin. How he could still talk with gnarled lips was still a mystery.

"Geist," Amalgam said. "I know it's you. No one else... has an aura like yours."

Somehow his new monstrous form had changed him. Amalgam *saw* things, unlike a normal man with eyes, especially when it came to magic. He turned his gas mask in her direction, the glass of the goggles reflecting the room like a mirror.

She took a hesitant step back. "Amalgam. Hunting civilians? Children? You really have become a monster."

He chuckled, every sound made sinister by the filter of his mask. "None of that matters."

"How can you say that?"

"I only joined this team in the hopes I would find *you*."

Amalgam lifted his hand—a hand repaired through braces and wire, all held together with a gauntlet made of leather, hooks, and black opals. A sickly green flame sprouted from his fingertips and washed across the room, burning paperwork and books in an instant.

As the fire rushed toward her, Geist allowed herself to ghost through the floor. She fell, unaccustomed to the sudden feeling, and lost her concentration a split second before colliding with a table. Her *specter* sorcery failed her, and she smashed through the furniture and rolled to her side.

For a moment, she didn't move. Seeing Amalgam stirred a deep-seated dread. He had tried to capture her before—and almost succeeded in turning her into a twisted monster, just like himself. Was that what he still wanted? Had he come searching just to drag her back to the horror-show they called a research lab? She wouldn't allow it.

With a long groan, Geist forced herself to stand. The throbbing in her side momentarily dominated her thoughts, making it hard to concentrate.

There was running in the house. Shouting in German. It took her a couple minutes to even register what room she was in.

A piano room. Two corpses of children littered the instrument.

"*They're coming*," Blick said, his voice directed straight to her mind. "*Geist, they know we're here!*"

Geist reached for her handgun, only to realize to she lost it when she fell.

I don't have time!

She turned to the window.

The others need to know.

Without giving her actions more than a half second of thought, she grabbed a metal stand for sheet music and threw it at the window. The stand shattered the glass and tumbled into the yard with amazing speed. Geist half smiled to herself, unaware she had tapped into her *apex* sorcery to help with her strength.

She pulled a spark grenade and tossed it into the yard. The grenade wasn't designed to do damage, but to be seen from long distances. The intense flare of light, followed by a sparkling effect after the explosion, was thanks to Tinker's showmanship. He always wanted his gadgets flashy.

A scream from upstairs echoed throughout the mansion.

Geist locked up, painfully aware there were still three Kott sorcerers the enemies hadn't found. Would Blick need her help? Or would the others make it in time? Her heart beat up into her throat as she turned and headed inside. Once again clothed in invisibility, she ran from the piano room, into the hall, and headed for the stairs.

To her horror, Amalgam jumped down the last couple steps and landed hard. He turned in her direction, a greenish flare of fire sprouting around him, catching the rugs and tapestries with stray embers.

He reached into a pocket and tossed shirt buttons around on the floor.

"Hiding from me?" he called out. "Why bother? I'll always know where you are."

If hiding wasn't an option…

Geist ran straight for him. When she reached out with her ghosted hand, she intended to dive into his body, return to her physical form, and then rip flesh right out of his gut.

Unfortunately, her hand slammed against his uniform as a solid object—his entire outfit was some sort of tight suit made of leather bindings and crushed opals. A magi-tech suit of armor. It canceled her magic, preventing her from ghosting through.

When Amalgam swung with his fist, Geist dodged backward, aware it would've connected with her, even if a normal punch couldn't. Then he held his hand up and unleashed a torrent of puke-green flame.

Geist dove through the wall and stumbled into a library. Although she could pass through most sorcery effects, she wasn't willing to test her theory with Amalgam's strange fire. Something told her it would be a great mistake and probably her last.

A smaller spiral staircase sat in the corner of the room. She ran straight for it, painfully aware of the door being slammed open as she climbed the steps, taking two at a time.

More screaming. Something in Russian. Geist couldn't understand the words, but some things were universal. She sprinted down the hall and then leapt through a locked door.

Geist found herself in the middle of a tragedy. An Austro-Hungarian soldier, marked by his country's flag on his shoulder, stood over two small children, no older than five, their blood draining from slashes on their necks, spilling into buckets like they were animals in the slaughter. A single Russian boy, around the same age, cowered in the corner of the room, his leg mangled, his eyes wide, his breathing shaky.

The enemy soldier wore the same damn magi-tech armor.

Geist pulled out her trench knife and charged. The man must have heard her, because he glanced up just as she approached. With one powerful swing, she caught him across the face, her blade breaking bone. The man collapsed to the floor with her weapon embedded in his skull.

The heavy footfalls of Amalgam kept her blood pressure high.

Geist dropped her invisibility, turned to the boy, and hoped her concerned expression crossed their language barrier. He stared at her, his legs trembling so hard he couldn't stand.

"We need to go," she whispered.

Using her *apex* sorcery, Geist scooped the boy into her arms and held him close. Although her *specter* magic allowed her to become incorporeal, she still couldn't use it on others—at least, not without Battery's help.

The door slammed open.

Geist sprinted for the window. She leapt at the glass, shattered through, and sailed through the air until she collided with the ground. Attempting to protect the young boy, she rolled across the grass, her left arm and hand wrapped around his head. The impact, small cuts, and tumbling motion rattled her mind. Again, she lost focus and her sorcery left her.

I need to regroup with the others...

Shirt buttons flew out the window and landed on the lawn.

Geist stood, the world spinning all around her. Amalgam appeared where one of the buttons had landed. He just *appeared*—teleporting to the button's location—and then headed straight for her.

Smoke wafted out of the broken windows, and flames flickered within. Soon the whole estate would be ablaze.

She ran to get around the mansion, but before she could round the corner, Amalgam popped into existence in front of her, his hands coated in a bright green flame, the embers licking at his magic-immune clothing.

"Nowhere to run," he whispered. "You might as well surrender."

Just when he lifted his hand, Victory stepped around the corner and fired his rifle, the crack echoing over the yard. Amalgam stumbled forward and collapsed to one knee, but Geist knew that wouldn't kill him. Hell, it wouldn't even subdue him. She had seen him take much worse.

As though flood gates had been opened, a torrent of gunshots rang out across the estate. A small war had erupted, but the chaos focused Geist's thoughts. In combat, she knew exactly what she needed to do—a skill developed over years of trench warfare and painful battles.

"Victory!" she said as she ran forward. "Where are the others?"

He pulled back the bolt on his rifle. "I knew you might need a hand, so I left them near the stables to come get you."

"You and your damn amazing future vision," she said with a chuckle.

"We need to hurry. Something is about to happen."

They ran together along the side of the mansion, Geist never releasing the Russian boy from her grasp. As they passed a garden door, it opened, revealing two men dressed in bright red tunics with gold switch-back lace—a common Russian nobleman outfit.

"Help us!" one man said, his English clear enough.

The boy in Geist's arms said something in Russian. She stopped, her heart racing.

There were three unaccounted for. Weren't those the children she had seen earlier? Who were these two?

Victory lifted his SMLE rifle. "Look out!"

Both Russian men pulled out pistols, but Victory shot one square in the chest before either could open fire. The second Russian aimed for Geist and pulled the trigger. She ghosted on instinct, dropping the boy to the ground and allowing the bullet to pass through her forehead without harm.

Victory bolt-loaded another round and fired again. The second Russian collapsed onto the stone walkway, his blood pooling out into the dirt and bushes.

Why did they attack us? Geist wondered as she scooped up the crying Russian boy. *The Russian Empire is our ally! We're here to save them. We're even wearing our nation's uniforms.*

Victory closed his eyes and stumbled back a foot. "It's happening." Sweat dappled his skin and hands shook.

"What's wrong?"

"They're here. The *eyes.*"

Another man exited the mansion, clothed in a grey and black version of the German uniform—the kind with a second coat over the tunic, reserved for decorated officials or special operatives. The man tilted up his cap and revealed purple glowing eyes, similar to Blick's. Geist and the man locked gazes, and he smirked. The chill that followed caused her shiver.

"Kill your allies," he commanded in English.

In that instant, something clicked. Geist dropped the Russian child a second time, her vision burning with the details of operative's eyes, even as she turned to face Victory, like the sinister gaze would forever be an afterimage on her sight. Although she wanted to stop, her body moved on its own, her thoughts a dull white noise. She took a step closer to Victory.

Kill your allies.

Victory lifted his rifle and shot at the enemy operative. The bullet cut through the man's uniform, but not his flesh.

Geist rushed forward and ghosted a hand into Victory's arm. She tore flesh away, exposing muscle and ripping his weapon from his grip.

"Geist!" he shouted as he fell back on the ground, his arm held tight against his body. "What're you—"

But she couldn't stop. Even when she wanted to yell at him to run. She couldn't seem to get the words out. All she could think of—all she could do—was follow through with the order.

Kill your allies.

Drowning in her single-minded need to kill Victory, she reached for him a second time. She hadn't noticed Vergess arrive, however. She only just noticed his fist collide with her face, blacking out her vision with a single moment of intense, near jaw-shattering pain. She hit the walkway, her head in so much agony the sensations spread to her neck and shoulder blades.

"Don't look at their eyes," Vergess stated. "They'll dominate you in an instant!"

Geist grimaced as someone lifted her from the ground. The urge to kill still haunted her thoughts, but her dazed body couldn't seem to put the command into action.

"You're lighter than I expected," Dreamer said. "God grants us little gifts."

Vergess jumped for the man with the purple eyes, keeping his own closed. "Don't let her out of your sight! She might not have regained herself!"

"*Her?*" the German operative asked.

Dreamer nodded and turned. He carried Geist away from the garden and straight for the stables. The sounds of gunshots, the bright green blaze of an unnatural fire—Geist couldn't distinguish much else. But by the time Dreamer set her on the floor of the stable, her strength returned. She rolled to her uninjured side and pushed herself to her feet.

"Geist," Battery said as he felt back into the stable, his voice shaky. "Thank the stars you're okay. We counted six enemy operatives. Two of which are—"

Bullets pierced through the walls, agitating the already anxious horses. Some reared up, and others kicked at their stalls.

Battery shouted over the chaos, "—two of which are the Eyes of the Kaiser! Vergess said they were elite members of the Kaiser's Guard. Please, Geist. We haven't found Blick. Where is he?"

Kill your allies.

Geist reached out, but Dreamer yanked Battery away before she made contact. And as Geist prepared herself to launch forward, Dreamer waved his hand. Illusions formed over her vision, obscuring everything and making it appear as though multiple people were around the stable, even if they weren't. Maybe if they weren't in the middle of a war zone, the illusions wouldn't have confounded her as much as they had, but terrible mix of panic and mayhem made everything worse. She flailed around, determined to catch someone with her phantom strike.

"The Eyes of the Kaiser already got to her," Dreamer said. "Focus on holding back the enemy. Vergess and Victory will find your brother."

Although Geist couldn't distinguish Battery from the illusions, she heard him just fine.

"Will she be okay?" he asked. "We have to help her!"

"I… don't know what we can do. Stay out of her reach. She'll tear you apart if she gets ahold of you."

"We can't leave her like this."

"I'll… try something."

Geist closed her eyes and lunged for the people talking. Her mind processed facts she hadn't even considered. She had five allies here on the Kott estate. Two more allies left in the car down the road. Thousands of allies in the docks of Riga. Millions of allies in France and Britain. She had a terrible compulsion to kill them all. For a fleeting second, she had a thought. If she left the Kott estate, she could kill more at the ports. If she made it back to Fort Belleville, she could get away with a slaughter before they caught her.

Shaken with her own gruesome thoughts, she turned away from Dreamer and Battery in favor of returning to Riga.

One of Tinker's flashy grenades went off in the stable, spooking the horses into a full-blown panic and blinding Geist with the after-effects of sparkles and lights. Then someone struck her on the side of the head, rendering her unconscious.

SEVEN

A Company of Monsters

Hot wind rushed over the Kott estate.

Amalgam didn't feel the heat. The bullet hole in his backside stitched itself together, a searing pain dominating his perception until the metal popped out over his flesh and fell onto the grass. He stood and ran a hand over the last of the fading injury.

His *corpus* sorcery had taken care of the life-threatening damage. Once again, Amalgam breathed deep, almost hating the sensation.

He would live. A fact he despised the longer it remained true.

The blaze created by Amalgam's sorcery raged out of control, consuming the house and jumping to the lawn. It would spread to the road and leap into the trees. The whole area would become a twisted landscape, not unlike Amalgam's own body.

He clutched at his magi-tech uniform, his grip so tight it pained his knuckles.

She had been so close! Right in his reach.

Amalgam hadn't expected to see Geist so soon after the start of the operation. He knew their paths would eventually cross, but in the Russian Empire? Fortune had been cruel in the past, but obviously it wanted to make things right now. Amalgam had dreamed of encountering her since their last interaction in the OHL.

"There you are, my friend."

Amalgam turned to face the speaker, though it didn't matter. He "saw" the Right Eye of the Kaiser, even while facing away.

"Did you kill them?" Amalgam asked.

"We shot a few, but they managed to escape on horseback."

Amalgam didn't care whether the Ethereal Squadron lived or died. He only wanted to hear about one of them—about Geist— but his single-minded fanaticism wouldn't be appreciated by his fellow operatives. They thought he was here to serve his homeland, like any good duty-bound soldier, but Amalgam's love for his Germany had died with his real name.

The Right Eye of the Kaiser placed a hand on Amalgam's shoulder and motioned away from the burning mansion. Amalgam gritted his teeth and held back the urge to rip the man's hand off. What was his name again? His *real* name. Hans Lorenz.

"Hans," Amalgam growled.

"I require your insight," Hans said as they walked. "Something interesting happened, and I want to know if you can help me."

"Speak."

"During our skirmish, I dominated one of the Ethereal Squadron and had him attack his allies. A small man. I'm not sure what his sorceries entailed."

Amalgam held his breath and listened to the crackling of the flames. A part of the roof collapsed, filling the crumbling estate with the cries of disintegrating wood and embers.

"I commanded him to attack his allies," Hans continued. "But that's when our traitor, Wilhelm, arrived. He said something inter- esting. He said," and then switching to English, Hans repeated, *"don't let her out of your sight. She might not have regained herself."* After- ward, Hans returned to speaking German and asked, "Fascinating, no?"

Amalgam exhaled and inhaled, his breath trapped in the confines of his gas mask, warming his skin and creating a stale scent of sweat. He didn't want the others to know about Geist. If they knew of her presence, they would target her, no doubt in Amalgam's mind. And he couldn't stand the thought of her captured at the hand of her enemies.

"Are you listening?" Hans asked.

Another hot gust of wind rushed past them.

Amalgam shook his head. "What of it?"

"He called the soldier a *she*. Did you sense anything different about the enemies? Was one a woman?"

"Wilhelm must've gotten his English confused. There were no women among the ranks of the Ethereal Squadron."

"Hm. And here I thought your undead sight could pierce through trickery."

Undead sight. That was what the Eyes referred to his senses. Were they jealous? Sometimes it seemed so, but Amalgam never counted his bizarre vision as a blessing. His "sight" also came with a heightened sense of hearing. No one understood that magic *spoke*. Even as Amalgam walked with Hans, he heard the whispers of Hans's sorcery, revealing secrets of his magic.

… control … order … rescript …

And sometimes, if Amalgam listened hard enough, he could hear the secrets of the man himself.

… brother … Otto … where is he?

"There was no woman," Amalgam stated.

"A shame," Hans muttered. "It would've been interesting to find a female sorcerer in the ranks of our enemy. I never did get to hunt those harpy spies who infiltrated the capital."

Before Amalgam could respond, he sensed the arrival of the rest of their squad. Their whispers, their sorcery, their auras—all were distinct, almost agitating. Whenever they drew near, Amalgam couldn't help but take notice, like a person approaching while wearing bells.

Two sorcerers approached from the fiery mansion. Although they had arrived at the Kott estate with eight operatives, Amalgam could no longer sense two of them. Now they were six.

"Brother," Hans said with a smile.

The Left Eye of the Kaiser, Otto Lorenz, greeted his brother with a tip of his cap. "Brother. Here you are. Did you find the last Kott child?"

"He escaped with the Ethereal Squadron, unfortunately."

"The Kaiser won't be pleased. We had a mission."

Hans and Otto gave each other quick glances, their stares a cryptic language only they knew. The two of them could've been twins. One of them was older by a year, but nobody was sure which. Even their aura and sorcery whispered in the same tone, usually of each other's names.

The second sorcerer to arrive was Dietrich Cavell, an Austro-Hungarian.

Geist's brother.

He carried a bandolier of glass vials and metal canteens and walked with an odd gait, unconcerned with the roaring fire destroying the last of the mansion. Dietrich jogged through the falling embers and ash until he arrived at Amalgam's side.

"The blood," he said, his voice shaky. "I gathered the last of it from Walter's body."

Walter had been a member of their team, but if he was dead, it meant the Ethereal Squadron had gotten to him.

Hans and Otto both gave Dietrich the same sharp look of disappointment.

"You couldn't save him?" Hans asked.

Dietrich shook his head, his gaze distant. "I'm not... skilled enough... with my sorcery."

"Such incompetence would've never been tolerated in the Kaiser's Guard."

Otto smiled. "He wouldn't have lasted a week, brother. Look at him. He's singed."

Amalgam turned away and headed for the road, uninterested in whether they got the blood they were looking for. The last two members of their team waited along the dirt path, among the trees. Lieutenant Markus Cavell—none other than Geist's father—and Pavel Leman, their Russian double-agent and language escort.

The others followed close behind, Hans flanking on the right, Otto on the left, like the positioning was ingrained in their stride. *It probably is,* Amalgam mused. The brothers had been raised in the Kaiser's Guard, the most elite and intense military training course Germany had to offer. They could dismantle and assemble their rifles in their sleep.

The roar of the fire died in the distance, and the smoke blotted out the stars in the sky.

Amalgam stepped onto the main road, and seconds later, he felt the shift of cold magic as Lieutenant Cavell ghosted through the nearby trees. He "showed himself" the moment he reached the group, dropping his invisibility and startling the rest—his *specter* sorcery was unrivaled.

Unlike Dietrich, who held himself like a limp blade of grass, Lieutenant Cavell had an aura that overpowered others. He stood tall, his uniform bloodied, but his pistol clean. The man had a scent of war about him.

He was the type of man Amalgam used to be, before the gas ravaged his body.

"Did you kill them?" Lieutenant Cavell asked.

"They escaped," Amalgam said.

"All of them?"

"And a child of the Kott family."

"Even with the Eyes of the Kaiser?" Lieutenant Cavell barked, his disbelief and anger mingling in equal parts.

Hans and Otto made no reaction nor offered any apology. They stood stiff and cold, only their occasional quick glances between them.

Amalgam found their lack of reaction amusing. They were tools of war. Nothing like the enlisted soldiers. Neither man had lived a life of home and family—they had been offered up as babes and forced to pledge themselves to the Kaiser. While normal German schoolchildren learned their numbers and letters, Hans and Otto had learned discipline and the art of killing.

"*Well?*" Lieutenant Cavell shouted. "What excuse could you possibly have? *No one can escape the Eyes of the Kaiser!*"

"I did dominate one," Hans said, no agitation in his voice, just amusement. That was the word they used. *Dominate.* Like the entire world was subject to their control. Hans continued, "But it turns out Wilhelm is in this group. He knew our tactics. He saved the others from my gaze."

That was the trick with the Eyes of the Kaiser. They were some of the deadliest operatives in the Kaiser's Guard—one glance and the enemy would work for them—but if they couldn't make eye contact, their sorcery couldn't take hold. Amalgam thanked the cruel God in heaven that he no longer had eyes.

"Wilhelm?" Lieutenant Cavell asked. "The one who infiltrated the OHL?"

Hans smiled. "Yes. He attacked, so I had to retreat. With his eyes closed, it was simple, but it'll be different in the future. He'll prepare for us."

"We should just kill him," Otto chimed in with a chuckle. "Then we can drag his head and spine back to the Kaiser."

"He can use it for his collection."

"And his son can animate it with his sorcery."

Lieutenant Cavell exhaled and ran a hand over his smooth chin. The man was older, Amalgam knew, but his *apex* sorcery kept him in his prime. His aura, his magic—they whispered his thoughts and schemes. Amalgam didn't care about Lieutenant Cavell's love for Austria-Hungary or his devotion to the emperor. Amalgam did care, however, about Lieutenant Cavell's hatred for his own daughter. If *he* knew Geist was in the ranks of their enemy, he would seek her out at once.

"We should ignore these Ethereal Squadron agents," Amalgam said. "We have the blood of the Kott family, and we should return it to our base before moving to the next target."

Hans pulled down his cap and buttoned his uniform coat. "They didn't appear here on accident. I suspect they're a team meant to counter our operations."

"I agree," Lieutenant Cavell said. "They even avoided the main road. They knew we were here."

Amalgam rotated his shoulders. "How shall we proceed, lieutenant?"

If he couldn't persuade them to disengage, he would have to get to Geist first. The moment Amalgam had her in his grasp—the moment he could feel and hear her aura—he would finally be able to relax. He would have to subdue her, however. She made it clear she wouldn't go anywhere with him willingly. But that didn't matter. He would do whatever was required. Nothing else concerned him.

And when he had her? He would allow the GH Gas to twist her body as well. Then... Amalgam wouldn't be the only one. If he had that, life would be worth living.

Lieutenant Cavell pushed Hans aside and grabbed his son by the collar. "Come here, boy." He jerked Dietrich close and ripped a blood vial from the bandoleer. "Tell me, were you the reason the team had troubles this evening?"

"No, sir," Dietrich replied, his gaze down.

"Good."

Lieutenant Cavell pulled out a glass container of *Grab-Hersteller Gas*—Grave-Maker Gas—the sinister concoction that had twisted Amalgam's body and left him half the man he once was.

Amalgam took a step back, every muscle in his body tense. While in his anti-magic armor, he wouldn't be affected, but the devilish whispering of the gas always left him rattled. If too close... he would lose his sanity to it.

He didn't know how they made the gas, but he knew he wouldn't want to hear the answer. Something about it wasn't right.

Although sorcerers couldn't learn magics outside their bloodline, the terrible gas fused things together and made them one. Lieutenant Cavell pulled up his uniform sleeve and then opened the vial of blood. He poured the contents across his forearm, coating his skin with a layer of thick crimson.

Then he smashed the container of gas, allowing the noxious cloud to wreck his arm. The gas had its own thoughts, but listening to them could drive a man to madness.

... *dgftheredgfisdgfnodgfescape ... hungerdgfneverdgfdies* ...

Amalgam took another step back, the voices of the gas too much for him to bear. The wind took the sickly green cloud away, carrying it into the trees and dispersing it. Still, the echoes of the dark voice lingered in his thoughts.

One little touch of the gas was all Lieutenant Cavell had needed. His skin warped and twisted, soaking in the foreign blood and adding it to his own. After a few moments, the damage had been done. His arm had a waxy sheen, but otherwise he was whole.

Lieutenant Cavell took in a deep breath, his forehead covered in sweat.

Amalgam remembered the terrible sensation of the gas covering his body. *It burned.* Most men would've screamed. Yet Lieutenant Cavell held back his shouts and remained composed. He had done this before, Amalgam could tell.

"Excellent," Lieutenant Cavell muttered.

Otto lifted an eyebrow. "You wanted Kott House's mastery of insects? I never thought of you as someone who wanted *bestiola* sorcery."

"I want a sizable collection. The rest is to be shipped off to the laboratory."

"Lieutenant," Dietrich said. "Before we return the blood, I… have something to report."

Lieutenant Cavell turned to his son, his eyes narrowed. "Did you manage to see anything while you were hidden?"

"Y-yes, sir."

"Then tell me."

"I counted six of them. One of which was… my sister."

"Florence?" Lieutenant Cavell whispered. "She's here?"

The question silenced the group, each man holding his breath. Amalgam could sense their collective excitement and hear the susurrations of their surprise. And although he wanted to deny Geist's existence, Amalgam knew he couldn't now that Dietrich had seen.

The boy should've been killed ages ago, he thought as he gripped his hands into fists. *Now he's caused me problems.* All plans he had to deal with Geist had shattered. He would have to think of something new. Something that would prevent the others from getting their hands on her first.

Hans chuckled. "I knew it. Wilhelm fights alongside a woman in the Ethereal Squadron. He slipped up when he shouted to help her."

"Is that right?" Otto asked. "Curious. We should question her. Perhaps they're training women sorcerers in the Ethereal Squadron. A new division."

"I will handle my daughter," Lieutenant Cavell growled. "The rest of you will focus on finding the squadron. Dominate and spy on whoever you need—just get me their location as fast as possible."

"We could have our Russian agent inquire about their whereabouts within the empire," Hans said.

"I don't care how you do it. *Just get it done*. We'll assassinate the team and then continue our harvest. Do I make myself clear?"

Hans nodded. "Of course, *lieutenant*."

"By your word, lieutenant," Otto said.

"We'll find them," Amalgam added, his stale breath warming the inside of his gas mask. "And then report to you immediately."

Dietrich tensed, his magic and aura flickering.

… sister … I'm sorry …

"We'll find her, lieutenant," Dietrich muttered. "Rest assured."

Lieutenant Cavell snapped his fingers. "Deliver the blood first."

EIGHT

Dire Mission

G eist woke with the worst headache of her life.

She rolled to her side, her forehead throbbing. But even through the pain, she jerked upward, her chest tight with panic.

What have I done?

"Geist?"

A gentle hand gripped her shoulder. Geist grabbed the arm of her companion, comforted by friendly presence. But was she in control of her facilities? She closed her eyes and replayed the last few moments of wakefulness in her mind. She had wanted to kill— but that urge no longer dominated her thoughts.

"Where am I?" she whispered in a raspy breath.

"Riga. Near the ports."

The timbre of the voice—the way he pulled her close—Geist knew Vergess enough to know she could relax. She exhaled and rested against him. After a few shallow breaths, she opened her eyes.

"Vergess... I, uh, attacked Victory."

"Don't fret," he whispered. "He's being tended to as we speak."

"By a sorcerer?"

"No, unfortunately. All sorcerers with any skill in healing have been shipped to the front lines."

Geist took a moment to let the news sink in.

She had gouged a chunk of flesh straight from Victory's arm. Even remembering it for half a second intensified her headache. She was the leader of their squad—the one in charge of success and failure—yet she had been turned traitor by the mere glance of the enemy and then made to attack her own!

Shaking away her inner dread, Geist glanced around the room. The tiny inn didn't offer much. A bed, a stand, and a lantern. Midafternoon sun shone through the window, illuminating each corner.

She still wore her uniform, as dirty and bloodied as it was at the Kott estate. Only her boots had been removed, likely because no one in her team wanted to be the one who undressed her. Geist glared at her tunic. What if she had internal injuries? *But Victory could use his sorcery to see if some injury was being left untreated,* she reasoned. *Perhaps this is for the best.*

Vergess wrapped his arm around Geist's waist and pulled her close.

"How are you feeling?" he asked in German.

"Better," she replied as she rested her head on his shoulder. "What happened?"

"The Eyes of the Kaiser were among the enemy forces. We were forced to retreat."

"Do you know them?"

Vergess tensed, but he didn't release her. "We were trained together in the Kaiser's Guard. I would say they're the closest thing I had to brothers, though they kept to themselves."

"They dominate people…"

"With their gaze, yes."

Enemy sorcerers always posed a unique problem. Geist had never met anyone who could control another. She recalled Lady Coppins, a sorcerer with the ability to sway those who found her attractive, but her magic had been subtle. No one knew they were being affected until long afterward. The Eyes of the Kaiser would be difficult threats.

"Do you know how we can beat them?" Geist asked.

Vergess took a moment to mull over the question. Then he replied, "Fighting them blind is the best option, but also puts us at a terrible disadvantage."

"What about fighting them in the dark?"

"Their eyes glow. You'd be more likely to stare at them then. It's a tactic I've seen them use in the past."

Damn.

"What about the others?" Geist asked, another spike of panic washing through her veins like ice. "Did they find Blick? What about Battery and Dreamer?"

"Yes. Blick was wounded, but not as badly as Victory. He should be fine."

"What about the little boy I rescued? Have we seen to his safety?"

Vergess nodded. "He's already on a boat heading for Paris."

Knowing that tiny bit of information eased Geist's worries more than anything else. As her muscles unwound, she glanced up, content to stare at Vergess's blue eyes as her thoughts drifted away. He stroked her short hair, his fingers occasionally tangling in the tight curls. He radiated warmth, and although her head still pounded with each beat of her heart, his embrace somehow took the edge off her pain.

"Vergess," she whispered.

"It's just the two of us," he said. "Call me Wilhelm."

Geist gripped her tunic, her fingers twisting into the fabric. He wanted to use real names? The thought bothered her, though she couldn't articulate why. Her name—Florence Cavell—had stopped meaning much to her after boot camp. She wasn't the same little girl afraid of her father as she was years back.

"You prefer your German name?" she asked.

Vergess sighed. "If you want, you may call me by my American name. William." He smiled. "They said *Wilhelm* was too difficult to pronounce, so it needed to change when I became a citizen."

It amused her that both she and Vergess technically had three names. She had her birth name, Florence, her false male name, Charles, and her codename, Geist. It also amused her that she and

Vergess had German words as codenames, though his—*Vergessenheit*, German for *oblivion*—was rarely said in full.

She relaxed a bit. "I prefer Vergess."

He stroked her hair. "I don't actually care what my name is. I just want us to have something intimate between us."

The tension in her body returned in full force. The word *intimate* had never sounded so… well, intimate before.

"The French have interesting phrases for their lovers," Geist murmured. "Would you be irritated if I called you *mio dolce amore?*"

"My sweet love?"

"Y-yes."

Somehow, in English, Geist hated the phrase. At least in French, the language of love, it didn't sound so blunt.

Vergess half smiled, like the entire situation amused him. "What shall I call you?"

"My intended."

Geist knew it was a bit presumptuous. *My intended* was only for couples slated to be wed. Asking Vergess to call her such a nickname, when they hadn't yet solidified their future, meant that—

"Very well," Vergess said. He leaned in close, his lips against the shell of her ear, and whispered, "My intended."

Her face grew red and hot. Unable to find words, Geist turned around and embraced Vergess, her grip tight on his uniform. Despite her troubles and mistakes, Vergess made things right. His steadfast presence—the tender way he spoke those last words—shook her into a realization. She wanted him to stay by her forever.

Vergess leaned down, and Geist sat up to meet her lips with his. She had missed his touch and enjoyed the way he pulled her tight. If she could have, she would have stayed in his embrace for the rest of the day.

The door swung in, and Heinrich walked into the room.

In a rush of movement, Geist and Vergess leapt apart from each other, Geist's face so crimson it screamed the truth of their actions. And in the next second, her headache pulsed back to life, her temples on the verge of rupturing.

Vergess stood from the bed. "What do you think you're doing?"

"What is this?" Heinrich straightened his glasses, a slight blush to his cheeks, and frowned. "You two should keep your fraternization to yourselves."

"You should knock," Vergess growled.

"Funny. I wonder which mishap Major Reese would be more disgruntled hearing." Heinrich held up one hand. "Me not knocking." Then he held up the other. "Or you two locked in a lover's embrace while in the middle of an important operation."

Vergess grabbed Heinrich's shirt collar and jerked him close. "Was that a threat?" he whispered in German.

"Stop," Geist said as she forced herself to stand. "Heinrich is right. We never should have… well, we should never lose sight of our objectives." She rubbed her sweaty palms on the pants of her khaki uniform. If Major Reese discovered anything about their relationship… it could mean more than her military career.

Heinrich knew it, too. Once Vergess released him, he straightened his shirt and gave Vergess a sideways glare. "There are many reasons men and women do not fight on the frontlines together."

"It won't happen again," Geist stated. "It's, I mean, we—" She took a deep breath, her throat tightening. With a shaky exhale, she glanced up at the ceiling. "I know there are—"

"I don't care," Heinrich interjected.

Geist bit back her words and stared.

He dismissively waved his hand. "As long as it doesn't happen again, I'll be happy to move past this. You're anxious and sweaty enough for ten teenage boys. It's uncomfortable. And I didn't come here to discuss the dynamics of your personal relationships and how they relate to your teammates."

Still shaken, but delighted Heinrich wanted to move on to another topic, Geist nodded along with his words. "Good. Yes. This was awkward for everyone. Why don't you just tell me what you needed to say?"

"Our Russian companion, Varnish, spoke with the Kott child. Apparently, an Austro-Hungarian soldier killed his siblings."

Geist waited for Heinrich to continue, but he held his breath and crossed his arms, like he had delivered shocking information.

"I saw the Austro-Hungarian," Geist said with a forced chuckle. "And?"

"What do you mean, *and?*" Heinrich snapped. "I was told the Eyes of the Kaiser were amongst our enemies. Those two killers would never take orders from Austro-Hungarians, no matter how many alliances their countries made. Hans and Otto are loyal to the Kaiser alone."

"What if the Kaiser ordered them to work in a team with Austro-Hungarians?" Geist asked.

Heinrich turned on his heel and huffed. "Clearly you don't know the Kaiser! Something suspicious is going on. This enemy task force is here for more than blood, I guarantee it."

His voice shook for a moment at the end, and Geist lifted an eyebrow.

He's scared.

"I don't think they know you're here," Geist said as she took a step closer to him. "And you'll be protected so long as you follow orders and stay in our safe houses."

"Even if they don't know I'm here now, they will." Heinrich turned back around, stiffer than he usually was. He pushed his thin-framed glasses back up his nose. "I've no doubt the Eyes of the Kaiser will drag me back to Germany in pieces. I'm sure there's a reward on my head for being the one and only magi-tech general to turn traitor."

"Vergess and I were just discussing how we'll deal with those two. You can rest easy."

"I'm not convinced our team can handle the two of them," Heinrich stated in a cold tone. "Especially not when they're with a squad of allies—all of whom I assume are just as deadly."

Vergess stepped between them. "You forget *I* was a member of the Kaiser's Guard. Hans and Otto can be dealt with. I've seen it happen."

"Oh, I remember you, *Wilhelm,*" Heinrich said. "I oversaw the opal research for the Kaiser's sorcerers. I took everything I know into consideration before I made my statements."

His pessimistic attitude didn't help Geist's headache. She rubbed at her forehead and stared at the wood flooring. What was the best course of action? Sending Heinrich home? Focusing her efforts on finding the enemy squad? Rushing to each Russian house and warning them of the dangers?

I could split up my team and do multiple things at once...

Geist shook her head.

But if any one of them were caught by the enemy forces, they would die for sure or potentially get captured and forced to speak about our plans.

The pressure to make a decision ate at her. There wasn't much time. Every second they squabbled was another second the enemy gained over them.

And what if Heinrich was right? What if their enemies were plotting something more than just the blood? Surely the Eyes of Kaiser wouldn't be sent on a simple fetch quest. What were they after?

Amalgam...

Geist took a seat on the edge of her bed.

He said he came looking for me, but he was surprised when I showed up. What else is he doing here?

Heinrich walked back to the door. "I suggest that we don't stay in any one safe house too long."

"We'll head to capital of the Russian Empire," Geist muttered.

"Petrograd?" Vergess asked.

"Yes. I've made up my mind. We'll head to the tsar first and warn the royal family. Everyone should know the Eyes of the Kaiser are within the empire's borders."

"YOU'VE NEVER BEEN TO RUSSIA?" Varnish asked as he drove the truck along the military roads.

Geist shook her head. "Never."

She sat close to him, the stick shift against her leg. Heinrich sat next to her, and the rest stayed in the back. Blick and Battery crowded around Victory, helping him move his arm whenever he needed anything. Dreamer and Vergess spoke in quiet whispers near the back. The whole vehicle rocked with each pothole and ditch Varnish drove through.

"You vill like Saint Petersburg," Varnish said with a smile, a cigarette held with his lips.

"I thought the capital was called Petrograd?"

"Oh, it vas. But after the var broke out, the tsar thought it sounded *too German*, so he changed it."

"That's strange. Does the tsar always make such bizarre decisions?"

Varnish burst into a short round of laughter until his smoke fell onto his lap. He flailed and slapped at his legs in an attempt to snuff it out against his uniform pants. Once the crisis had been averted, he pulled out another cigarette and lit it up.

"Vant one, princess?" Varnish asked.

Geist locked up, her mind immediately grounding to a halt.

Does Varnish know I'm a woman?

Heinrich rolled his eyes and held out his hand. "He's talking about me," Heinrich said in German. "Don't worry. This Russian lout doesn't know your secret."

"Why princess?" Geist mouthed back in German, utterly confused.

"He thinks I'm—to quote him—*stuck up and elitist.*"

"Is that your language for *yes?*" Varnish asked as he passed over a smoke. "It sounds like you're choking." Then he glanced at Geist. "Vhat about you, short one? I get plenty from the messengers."

Geist shook her head. She had smokes, but mostly to trade with other soldiers. Whenever she needed a stiff drink, she knew she could make a deal.

Varnish lit his up and tucked it back between his lips. With one hand on the steering wheel—a decision that keep Geist tense, especially since they were near the Eastern Front—Varnish motioned to a fork in the road.

"Ve'll be taking the southern route," he said.

"Petrograd is north," Geist said. "Shouldn't we head east and then along the main routes?"

"Those roads are for supply trains. If ve head south and then east, ve'll avoid contingents of soldiers. Plus, if one of the majors or staff-captains asks me for assistance, I have to stop my mission and help. It applies to all sorcerers."

"I see," Geist muttered. "Can you make this truck go faster?"

"Ve're already traveling forty-eight kilometers an hour. Any faster and ve could strain the engine."

"It's imperative we reach the capital as soon as possible."

Geist stared out along the road, her eyes searching for anything out of the ordinary. There was a chance the enemy would ignore the attack and continue with their mission, but she suspected at least some of them would come for her and her team. Although Major Reese didn't want the tsar involved with Operation Orpheus, Geist didn't have a choice. The tsar could send out warnings faster and likely had a safe haven for Geist's team.

She glanced back into the truck. Victory forced a smile and chatted with his brothers. He hadn't spoken to her outside of answering a few questions—not about the attack or his recovery. Had she broken his trust? The attack still swirled through her thoughts.

"Are those cavalrymen?" Heinrich asked in English. He pointed up the road.

Varnish stroked his mustache for a moment as he squinted into the distance. "Those *are* horses."

"Blick," Geist called out. "Can you give us details?"

While he shined his golden eyes on the road, Geist turned her attention to Dreamer.

"Make us Russian soldiers," she ordered.

Dreamer replied with a curt nod. One by one, he touched the shoulder of everyone's uniform. His illusions coated the fabric, transforming the colors into the greenish brown of the Russian Empire. If someone was looking for them—searching for a group of Englishmen traveling with a Russian—this would keep their identities hidden, at least in passing. Without the ability to speak Russian, however, the disguise would never work beyond any level of scrutiny.

Blick dropped his all-seeing sorcery. "They appear to be Russian cavalry. Ten of them. None of them radiate magic, though. I doubt they're sorcerers. And they seem in a rush."

Everyone remained silent and tense as the horses drew closer and closer. Geist straightened her posture.

"Let me do all the talking, princess," Varnish said with a chuckle.

Heinrich snorted. "Will you torment me with your infantile nickname the entire time we travel together?"

"Just until it sticks as a codename."

Geist elbowed Varnish in the ribs. "We're on urgent business. We cannot be stopped for any reason. Do you understand?"

"Of course, commander," Varnish replied. "Just let me do all the talking."

NINE

General Volkov

Ten men rode toward the truck. Nine of the horses were a shade of wet mud, but the last one—an Arabian—had a coat of clean snow. The soldier atop, more decorated than the rest, urged his mount to slow as the distance between him and the truck became smaller.

Varnish applied the brakes. The Russian soldiers circled around the vehicle while the command trotted up to the driver-side door.

He said something in Russian. Varnish replied with a chuckle.

Geist waited patiently, her mind on the beautiful horse rather than the situation. The white Arabian stood fifteen hands tall, its dark eyes a harsh contrast with its lustrous coat. Geist enjoyed riding horses, and she liked seeing them from time to time among the soldiers, but she hated how many of them died pointless deaths. Perhaps cavalry had been effective during the times of Napoleon, but that wasn't the case with the Great War. The trenches and heavy artillery made short work of cavalry.

"Beautiful," she heard Dreamer whisper from behind her. He, too, stared at the white Arabian, his eyes wide.

Sometimes she forgot Dreamer was originally from the Middle

Eastern Theater. Although he had a slight Arab accent to his words, he never really spoke about his past life in Saudi Arabia.

Varnish slapped the side of the truck and said something heated. The cavalry officer pointed down the road and barked a few words before jerking the reins of his horse and motioning his soldiers to continue.

The ten cavalrymen took off toward Riga. Geist watched them go for a long moment before turning her attention to Varnish. "What happened?"

"He vants us to speak with Sorcerer General Alexei Volkov." Varnish leaned back and exhaled. "Apparently he *sensed us* coming this vay."

"Those mortal men know General Volkov is a sorcerer?" Geist asked.

"Yes and no," Varnish replied.

Everyone in the truck glanced over at Varnish. Battery even jumped up and moved closer to the front, his eyebrows knit together.

"Didn't the general take an oath of secrecy?" he asked.

It was a long-standing tradition that went all the way back to the first crusade. Before then, sorcerers used their magic for a great many things—history often confusing the use of magic for "miracles" or "mysteries"—but during the holy wars, mortal knights targeted sorcerers to turn the tides of combat. There were more non-magic users than sorcerers, after all. An army could do away with a talented sorcerer house, if they had enough knights. And even a servant could slit the throat of a sleeping individual, no matter how many sorceries they had mastered.

Back then, it was a time of great confusion and death, but the remaining sorcerer houses, from Europe to Eastern Asia, agreed that the mortal population had grown too vast and too bloodthirsty for sorcerers to remain out in the open. Sorcerer houses swore oaths to remain hidden, as magicless men would surely target them as "witches" should they figure out the truth.

And to enforce this rule, sorcerers vowed to kill any who broke it.

She had even reaffirmed that oath when she joined the Ethereal Squadron. If General Volkov *had* told his soldiers of magic, Geist and her team would have to put an end to him. But if the reveal was an accident, counter measures could be employed.

"The Russian Empire is different than Europe," Varnish said as he applied his foot to the pedal. "Ve've alvays had rogue sorcerers, ever since Baba-Yaga. They vere too difficult to kill. Hell, even the tsar's vife, Alexandra, consorted with Grigori Rasputin, the famous swindler sorcerer."

Dreamer immediately opened his book and took notes. "Such actions would have been met with a swift death in my homeland. I almost cannot believe this."

"There was a rogue sorcerer working with the royalty of the Russian Empire?" Vergess balked. "And this is *known throughout the land?*"

Varnish shrugged. "I told you. He vas hard man to kill. Proper sorcerers hated his influence over Alexandra and the tsar, but vhat can you do vith a man of ancient sorcery? He's so long-lived, people thought he vas immortal."

Geist couldn't help but chuckle. The longer she heard the story, the more it sounded like a fairy tale. Immortality? Such sorcery was fantasy. But…

"Wait," she said. "Did Baba-Yaga claim to have ancient sorceries in her blood?"

"That's vhat they say." Varnish laughed aloud, his belly shaking until he calmed himself down. "I remember reading the papers a few veeks back! The bastard Rasputin took a gunshot straight to the forehead and two to the chest. That vas after he ate cyanide-laced cakes. And then he was tossed into the river. I have fifteen rubles that says he's still alive."

The story hit Geist hard. There were sorcerers open about their magic in the Russian Empire. But that wasn't as significant as the thought that followed afterward. She turned her gaze to her team-mates, afraid to voice her hypothesis.

But the others returned her stare with looks of realization and fear. They had all come to the same conclusion.

The enemy squadron—and the Eyes of the Kaiser—weren't just after obscure sorcerer houses. They were looking for sorcerers with long-thought-fantasy sorcery. They wanted ancient magics. Descendants of Baba-Yaga. Immortality. Maybe something more powerful, Geist couldn't even imagine.

"How have we not heard about this?" Victory demanded. "The other allied powers would not stand for a blatant disregard to tradition."

Varnish sped down the road, the smoke of his cigarette trailing out the window. "The enemy nations are betveen us. Communications are limited. Besides, no one tells the tsar vhat he and his family can do. Do you honestly think Britain and France vant Nicolas Romanov dead? Then they vould lose the Russian Empire. The enemy could then focus all their efforts on one front."

As they drove toward General Volkov's camp, Geist's thoughts circled the newest bits of information over and over again. Could she get word to Major Reese? She didn't have a reliable route or courier, and Blick's telepathy couldn't span continents.

We'll have to handle this ourselves, she reasoned. *Under no circumstance can the enemy be allowed to steal the blood of any more sorcerers.*

THE EASTERN FRONT wasn't far from Riga.

Tattered tents, ragged horses, and wary men crowded the side of the road. Trench warfare took its toll on morale. The front lines never moved, and when they did, it had been the Russian Empire who had lost ground. Geist had heard that much through the newspapers. While the Russians had numbers, their wartime strategies were dated. Austria-Hungary and Germany innovated.

Soldiers shuffled toward the truck with bowls and cups. Through their cracked lips they muttered things in Russian, but Geist didn't need a translator to understand they were starving. When the soldiers realized there was no food, they spat and cursed, their eyes hard with resentment.

Varnish didn't speak much. He didn't laugh or joke. He kept his grip tight on the wheel, glaring at the road as he slowly made his way through the squads of soldiers.

"Are we going to run into trouble?" Vergess asked as he turned to Victory. "The air smells of mutiny."

Geist couldn't smell mutiny, but she did detect rotting flesh and human waste.

Victory shook his head. "No. The men might be miserable now, but they'll soon cheer up." He closed his eyes and smiled. A small chill filled the truck as his sorcery took hold. "They'll start chanting any second now… at the arrival of their general."

Sure enough, right on cue, the mood of the encampment shifted. Soldiers got to their feet, each whispering and pointing to a hill not far down the road. Geist followed their motioning and caught a glimpse of a man on horseback. It was easy to see why everyone recognized him.

"Volkov!" the men cheered. "Volkov! Volkov!"

General Volkov wore his hair like he was part lion. It puffed out in all directions, including his thick sideburns and well-kept beard. The red hue shone in the light of the setting sun as he rode for the officer's tent. Each man he passed greeted him with a salute and a smile, completely changed in attitude from moments before.

"Is this sorcery?" Geist asked. "Does he have some sort of power over them?"

Varnish cracked a small smile. "No. General Volkov is just loved among his men. He fights vith them in a battle. Ten men in one, they say."

"So, he's a fierce warrior?"

"And a cunning strategist. If not for him, all of the Russian Empire vould've fallen."

The cheering made sense. Geist always appreciated the leadership of Major Reese. Before she had worked under him, she had a field commander who only cared about his own comfort. The depression of being seen as a tool and nothing more had eaten at her resolve. If Geist hadn't been reassigned, she might've regretted her decision to join the war.

Varnish pulled his truck up to the officer's tent and parked a fair distance behind the horses. He, Geist, and Heinrich exited the vehicle.

"Wait here," she said to the others.

Battery held out his hand. Without a word between them, Geist reached out and took it. His empowerment surged through her palm and straight up her arm until it permeated her whole being.

"Thank you, Battery," she said.

He replied with a smile.

Geist, Varnish, and Heinrich walked together to the front of the tent. Heinrich's tailored coat, button-up shirt, and clean slacks clashed with the dirty uniforms of the Russian soldiers—so much so that the few they walked past stopped their *Volkov* chant to give them dirty glances.

Heinrich straightened his glasses and ignored their glowers.

"General Volkov is one of the men you need to speak to?" Geist whispered.

"A sorcerer general should know where the western research lab is located," he replied. "Or would you rather me wait in the truck?"

"I would prefer you with me, actually. Your nullis sorcery will be useful. If the general and I have a falling out, you're to return to the truck."

Geist wished she had Heinrich's ability to ignore magic. Then she wouldn't have been possessed by the Eyes of the Kaiser—or even affected by the terrible GH Gas.

Then again, becoming incorporeal isn't so bad. Geist smirked. *Perhaps I should take a suit of magi-tech armor from the enemy squad. It might be just enough to save me from hostile magics.*

Varnish approached first. Two Russian soldiers stood at attention in front of the massive tent, each with rifles held at the ready. Varnish said a few things, tapped at his rank insignia, and then motioned to Heinrich. He laughed, said something else, and then the tent guards were laughing as well, both giving Heinrich quick glances.

"Have I mentioned I dislike Varnish?" Heinrich said in casual German. "I didn't decide we wouldn't get along. He did."

Geist gave him a sideways glare and replied in her own hushed

German, "You're taking it too seriously. This is the first time he's acted like his normal self since we've arrived. If anything, I think he likes you."

"Heh. I've never been a fan of *push me down, pull my hair* flirting."

Geist snorted and held back a laugh. Her sudden grunt and stifled chuckles silenced Varnish and the guards. Then the Russians motioned them forward. Geist didn't delay—she walked straight in and found herself stumbling through a haze.

The entire tent, from the floor to the roof, had a stagnant cloud of cigarette smoke. The three Russian officers inside, including General Volkov, stood around a wooden table, a map of the Eastern Front laid out before them. They stopped their discussion, folded up their paperwork, and then turned their attention to the newcomers.

Geist and Varnish saluted. Heinrich pushed up his glasses and took a step back, hiding himself somewhat in the shadow of the corner.

Varnish said a couple words in Russian. General Volkov held up a hand.

"Americans?" Volkov asked in perfect English. "I didn't think many American sorcerers had joined the war yet. Especially since your country has yet to join."

"Sorcerers sometimes act outside of their nation," Geist replied, relieved she could speak directly to the general. "But that's not important. I have serious business within the Russian Empire. I must make it to Petrograd as soon as possible."

Volkov lifted an eyebrow—one as red and bushy as his beard and hair. "Petrograd?" He waited a long moment as he looked Geist up and down.

His expression wasn't like a soldier looking over another soldier. It was… something else. Geist grew hot in the face, uncertain of how to bridge the conversation.

"Sir?" she asked. "We were summoned by your cavalrymen. If you can spare us, I need to leave."

"I sensed you coming," General Volkov said. "So I sent my men ahead to fetch you. All I want is to ask a few questions, then you can be on your way."

His voice had a low rumble to it, like the roar of a lion made into human words. Geist found herself getting tenser by the second, if only because she wasn't certain what would happen next. She couldn't reveal her operation to the general—it was top secret. What else did he want to know?

"What's your name, soldier?" he asked.

"Geist," she replied without thinking.

"Have you come to assassinate the tsar?"

She caught her breath, taken aback by the sudden escalation of seriousness. "N-never, sir. The Russian Empire is a trusted ally. I'm here to protect—"

"I know why you're here," General Volkov said with a dismissive wave of his hand. "You just told me." He tapped at his temple. "My sorcery does more than sense people. I can hear your inner thoughts, clear as the birds in spring."

The exact opposite of *communis* sorcery.

"That's an assault against a fellow sorcerer," Geist said. "We're allies."

Wartime rules between sorcerers dictated that friendly magic wouldn't be used against another without permission. By reading her mind without telling her, General Volkov had essentially stripped her privacy away.

"Times are desperate," Volkov replied.

Geist held her breath. Could the general hear everything? Two questions and he already knew? For a moment, no one said anything, not Varnish, not the other officers, not Heinrich. What would the general do if he understood the nature of their mission? Or if he knew her true identity? Even thinking about it added anxiety—what if he were listening now?

"I just needed to know if you were a threat to the tsar," General Volkov continued. He tensed and took a step back, a deep frown on his face. "You and your squad are free to continue to the capital." He stroked his mane of a beard and then motioned to a box set at the edge of the table. One of his officers handed it over. "Here. Take this. A sign of good will."

Hesitant, and still a bit shaken, Geist took a step forward and took the box. It had a brand burned into the top and weighed more than she expected.

"You're American," he said. "So you might enjoy the contents. Cigars and fine whiskey."

"Thank you, sir."

"The roads from here to Petrograd are rough and do damage to vehicles. You can take horses, but the fastest route is by train. East of here is a supply station. If you hurry, you can make the next departure. The train usually leaves after sundown."

Geist exhaled and allowed her stress to leave with her breath. Although Volkov had a gruffness to his voice and mannerisms, she couldn't help but feel his charisma.

No wonder all the soldiers love him.

"Thank you so much, sir," Geist said. "I appreciate the gift and the insight." She motioned to Heinrich. "But before we go, there is someone I'd—"

"That won't be necessary," Heinrich interjected. "You heard the general. We should leave right away."

Varnish nodded. "I agree. I know of the supply station of which General Volkov speaks. Ve'll need to hurry."

The other two Russian officers added their nods to the conversation.

Convinced it would be okay, Geist nodded. "Very well. God speed, General Volkov."

He smiled. "Good luck with your mission, Geist."

TEN

Train Ride to Petrograd

It took longer than expected to board the train. It was scheduled to leave at sundown, but it took several hours longer for it to even arrive. Once aboard, Geist and her crew took up seats in a cargo boxcar.

Supply trains didn't make for comfortable passenger vehicles. And the twenty-four-hour trek would surely take its toll.

Geist sat atop a crate as the train clacked along the tracks, the occasional rumble a problem for her stomach. She gripped on the edge of the container, her gaze on the grime-coated floor. What if their enemies were heading to Petrograd as well? Would they have a few hours' head start? She couldn't stop thinking of the possibility.

Hours passed, and night settled over the train.

A lantern, hanging from a hook mounted to the wall, swayed back and forth. The others didn't seem to mind the jostling of the boxcar. They continued conversations as though they were nobility on a luxury liner.

"So, here is my plan," Blick said as he scooted closer to Varnish. "You teach me some simple Russian phrases. Something women would like."

Varnish took a long drag on his cigarette and lifted an eyebrow.

Blick continued, smiling, "When we rush in to save them from this enemy threat, I will be the dashing Englishman who carries them to safety. I need something to say in that moment—something to steal their heart."

After exhaling a line of smoke, Varnish said, "Mothers in Russia tell their daughters, *date a man who looks like a chimpanzee. He appreciates it more.*"

Others in the boxcar chuckled, but Blick rubbed at the back of his neck and frowned. "What's that supposed to mean?"

"You don't understand?" Heinrich asked as he cleaned his glasses off on his vest. "He's saying you're so good looking that ladies will know you're a womanizing lout."

Blick brushed back his dusty blond hair, his smile widening. "Is that a backhanded insult or a secret compliment?"

With a huff, Heinrich replied, "When in doubt, always assume I'm insulting you."

The statement sent chortles throughout the group. Vergess and Varnish couldn't stifle it long. Both men laughed aloud, much to Blick's noticeable irritation. He shot them glares as he leaned back against the side of the boxcar.

"Who said Germans don't have a sense of humor?" Varnish asked as he shook the ashes of his smoke onto the floor. "I'm starting to like you. Ve should come up with a good codename for you to use."

"Says the man who picked the word *varnish* as his codename," Heinrich said.

Blick smirked. "I can think of a few colorful codenames."

Without acknowledging the statement, Heinrich continued, "Have any of you considered that I'm too prominent of a researcher to have a codename? The enemy will recognize me straight away. An alias won't save me."

"Oh, c'mon," Blick scoffed. "You think the average soldier knows what their nation's researchers look like? Get over yourself. Unless *your mum* is a part of the enemy, you'll be fine."

"I personally know some of our enemies."

Dreamer, his nose in his notebook, a pencil in hand, glanced up.

"Reports sent to Major Reese use a sorcerer's codename just in case our messages are intercepted. We don't want to alert spies that you're traveling in our group. Additionally—"

"Stop." Heinrich shook his head. "I don't need your lecture."

The end of Dreamer's explanation ushered in a long period of silence. Everyone went about their own business. Varnish smoked. Blick stared at the roof, his eyes and expression indicating he was deep in thought. Vergess remained standing, only a foot or so away from Geist, his gaze down.

Battery and Victory sat at the front of the boxcar. Battery held up a small mirror while Victory patiently shaved the stubble from his chin. While the train occasionally bumped and rocked, at no point did Victory cut himself. He always paused for a moment whenever something would cause him to slip. Normally he handled the task without Battery's help, but his right arm remained in a sling.

His injury gnawed at her.

If it had been anyone else with such an injury, Geist would've commanded them back to base, but Victory's sorcery was too useful to just send away. Plus, it was the type of sorcery that didn't need to be on the battlefield. He could stay behind and still be useful.

The longer Geist stared, the more she wanted him to look over and start a conversation. She had never been one for small chat, but she wanted to know things were okay between them.

Instead, Battery was the one to glance over and catch her eye. Then he glanced to his older brother and then back to her, half glowering.

Geist turned her attention to the wall of the boxcar, pretending it was interesting.

The dynamic of her team had felt different since she revealed her true identity to the group, many months ago. It wasn't negative, quite the opposite, but certain actions were seen... through a strange lens now that they knew she was a woman from Austria-Hungary.

Dreamer stood, walked over, and took a seat on the crate next to

Geist. He held out his book and pointed to his notes—his neat writing precise and legible, despite being tiny.

"This is a report of our status and known enemy capabilities," he whispered. "Once we stop, I'll send this off to Verdun. Is there anything you specifically want to relay to command?"

Geist stared at the report. It read:

DEAREST MOTHER,

THE BATTLES HAVE NOT GONE as expected. Each day we linger in the trenches, another dozen men become sick. Some have a rot of the foot. Some are bitten by rats that hide amongst the shadows and mud. Others cannot stomach the meals.

GEIST STOPPED READING. She didn't know the cipher to decode messages that masqueraded as letters to home. She pushed the book away and returned her gaze to the floor.

"Tell them about the ancient sorcerers of the Russian Empire," she murmured.

"Are you feeling well?"

"Yes."

"You've been quieter than normal since our visit to House Kott."

For a long moment, Geist mulled over the comment. Leaders had the extra burden of handling their problems themselves—she couldn't allow the others to know she feared the future or that she didn't trust herself not get dominated by the Eyes of the Kaiser a second time. Her dread would seep into them, like rain soaked up by the roots of plants.

If she was weak, they were weak.

"I said I'm fine," Geist stated.

Dreamer shut his book. "War is unpredictable. Even brilliant lights can be snuffed out. There's no shame in worrying."

Although they had spoken in hushed tones, Blick sat forward and sighed. "Bloody depressing, this conversation. There's also no shame in needing a drink. Didn't General Volkov give you something?"

"I'm fine," Geist said.

"*You* might not need a drink, but *I* do."

"We're not going to drink in the middle of an operation."

"How long do we have until our destination?"

The train operator had said the trek would take twenty-four hours. How long had they been traveling? It already felt like days had gone by, but Geist knew it couldn't have been long. They had yet to sleep.

"We still have nineteen hours," Battery chimed in.

He held up his arm, showing off his fancy wristwatch. He had become the technological one in the group, with his camera, compass, and timepiece, and Geist was thankful. She hated the idea of carrying around so much equipment.

"Nineteen hours is a long time," Blick said with a shrug. "We should enjoy things while we can."

Dreamer nodded along with his words. "Blick makes a compelling argument. It is written in Ecclesiastes, '*There is nothing better for a person than that he should eat and drink and find enjoyment in his toil.*'"

Swayed by the simple arguments, and by the fact they would have time to sleep off any problems, Geist picked up the box General Volkov had given her. She cracked open the top.

Old No. 7 Tennessee whiskey and Cabanas cigars.

The good stuff.

She pushed the cigars aside and picked up the bottle. There was enough for everyone to have a few drinks, but no glasses. Although fine whiskey wasn't meant to be swigged straight from the container, she threw back a mouthful regardless. To her surprise, a hint of caramel and toffee played across her tongue. The smell of whiskey stung her sinuses and dried out her saliva, leaving a campfire taste. She shook her head, shivering from the mild sensations of numbness.

No wonder soldiers lap this up, Geist thought.

The numbing continued through her lips, to her teeth, across her face, and even down her neck. If she consumed the whole bottle, she was certain it would eliminate all feeling, including her restless nerves.

Then she passed it to Blick. He downed two mouthfuls and handed it to Vergess. Once Vergess had his share, he held it out for Heinrich. Much to Geist's surprise—she figured he would never partake in such a "crude ritual"—Heinrich downed a mouthful before sending it over to Battery.

"Is it good?" Battery asked as he swirled the amber contents. "I've never had American whiskey."

Everyone exchanged chuckles and quick glances. Sometimes Geist forgot how young Battery was. A man barely aged eighteen. He hadn't seen much of the world.

"Just drink it, ya ninny," Blick said.

Battery took a sip and then passed it to Victory. After a mouthful for himself, Victory awkwardly handed it to Blick with his good arm. To no one's surprise, Blick took another mouthful.

"Englishmen drink like this?" Varnish asked. He inhaled his cigarette to the end and then stomped it out on the boxcar floor. "Give me the bottle. I'll show you how a real man does it."

"Hey. You stick with floor cleaner and leave the good stuff to the rest of us, got it?"

The screeching of metal, and the shaking of the boxcar, ended the conversation. Geist jumped to her feet. The lantern swung around and left its hook, but Vergess caught it before oil and fire could shatter across the floor. They were nowhere near a scheduled stop.

"Varnish," Geist said. "Speak to the train operator."

The Russian headed toward the front door. When he opened it, a rush of frigid air blasted into the car. A second later, he closed the door, but the chill remained.

Geist turned to Victory. "Why didn't you warn me about this?"

He shook his head. "I… didn't see this."

Nothing? He saw nothing about this? That's not like Victory.

The train continued to rumble until it came to a complete stop, its engine hissing in protest as it worked to stop the motion it had tirelessly built up. Battery braced himself against the wall until the last of the shaking subsided.

A few minutes passed before Varnish returned. Again, the brief second the door opened dropped the temperature another few degrees.

"The train operator says there have been problems with the track at this point," Varnish said as he shook off the cold. "Sabotage happens a lot out in these parts. They're sending a crew to investigate the railway."

The news bothered her. Austria-Hungary and Germany hadn't broken through the Eastern Front. Enemy soldiers couldn't be in the Russian Empire. Was it the enemy special forces unit who had tampered with the tracks in the past? Unlikely, but the possibility existed. If a train operator and his mundane engineers attempted to bother a group of trained sorcerers, it would be a bloodbath.

Her team stared at her, each tense and silent.

Geist took a deep breath. "Varnish, go tell the operator to stay in the engine room. We'll handle the investigation."

Varnish shrugged. "As you say." Then he disappeared through the door a second time, quicker than before.

"Battery, Vergess," she said. "You two are with me. We're going to investigate the tracks. The rest of you protect the train crew."

"Wait," Victory said. He stood and held his injured arm close. "Take Varnish with you. I… don't know why… I can't see much about this. All I know is that Varnish will return if he investigates beyond the tracks… but no one else will."

The statement chilled the boxcar more than the night air.

Something *was* waiting for them.

Geist reined in her pounding heart and replied with a curt nod. She, Vergess, and Battery waited for Varnish to return. Once he did, she motioned for him to join the team. A small bit of solace came from the fact that Victory saw them all returning. *We can handle this threat*, she assured herself. *We've handled far worse.*

Right before Geist exited the boxcar, she stopped and grabbed Battery's arm.

He flinched, his nerves plain to see. "W-what? Do you need my empowerment?"

"No. Empower Blick. If Victory sees anything unusual, I want him to use his telepathy to contact us."

"Wait, telepathically? Blick doesn't know *communis* sorcery. He chose his sorcery based on how little effort he could exert and still be considered a sorcerer."

Blick shot him a glare. "Didn't you have an operation to help you focus when you were younger? I don't think you have room to comment."

"Battery, empower him," Geist commanded. "We don't have time to dilly-dally over trivial details."

The two brothers exchanged odd looks. Battery offered Blick his hand, and once Battery had used his sorcery, Geist opened the boxcar door and jumped off the train. She landed in the mud, ice, and snow, a foot away from the tracks. Vergess landed second, followed by Varnish. Battery stepped out of the train next, shivering the entire time, despite being the only member of the squad to have brought a scarf.

A thick fog blanketed the area.

A terrible fog.

And it didn't help that it was the dead of night.

As a group of four, they trekked alongside the tracks. Once far enough away from the train, Geist glanced over to Battery.

"Are you okay?" she asked.

She never talked about his operation. The opals embedded on his back helped him focus his complicated magic, but it also left him a little smaller than the average man and scarred more than men shredded by barbed wire and shrapnel. And the one time they did discuss it, it obviously pained the man.

"I've had to live with older brothers my entire life," Battery said. "It doesn't bother me. I promise."

Vergess offered a half smile. "Want me to beat him up?"

Everyone shared a brief chuckle.

"No," Battery eventually said. "He only gets like that when he's upset. I think he might not be well."

The observation quieted the conversation. Geist kept her attention on the fog, hoping her *apex* sorcery would allow her to catch any sign of movement. But her thoughts kept returning to the Eyes of the Kaiser. Every tiny movement made her tense.

"Vergess," she muttered. "If I'm dominated again… you'll stop me, right?"

He didn't look at her when he nodded. "Of course."

"I mean it. If I… well, if I was responsible for killing any of the others…"

Geist couldn't bring herself to finish the sentence. Her chest tightened, and it was hard to breathe. She could kill the others—it wouldn't be hard, not with her sorceries. She'd never be able to wash their blood from her hands.

Battery rubbed the length of his arms and then turned to Varnish. "Do supply trains get stopped often?" He asked so loud that Geist knew he was trying to steer the conversation away from the wretched topic it had been on.

Varnish shook his head. "People tamper with the train tracks regularly. All to stall supplies to the front lines."

"Why would anyone do that?"

"Lots of people are upset by the var. Ve've been losing some engagements."

"So this is the work of Russian revolutionaries?"

"Right. The *Bolsheviks*."

The way Varnish said the last word—it came out with a hint of venom and pure disgust. Geist knew the Bolsheviks had caused social unrest, but she didn't know they resorted to such dastardly tactics. Harming the supply train didn't hurt the tsar. It hurt common, everyday soldiers. It was a coward's method of getting attention.

On the other hand, she was happy to hear it was the Bolsheviks. At least then it wasn't the Eyes of the Kaiser.

"We should quiet down," Vergess said as he glanced around.

The fog seemed to get denser, and Geist couldn't help but

remember the way GH Gas always moved toward people, never away. But she knew the fog wasn't magical—she would've been able to sense it then—yet it still unnerved her.

Geist pulled out her pistol and held it close. *Blick will inform us if Victory sees anything… We'll be fine.* Then again, the enemy could be lurking in the fog. Their glowing eyes would pierce the damp weather and steal their free will.

Focus, Geist. Focus.

They walked on the railway, keeping clear of the sleepers and spikes. No one wanted to get their boot caught on the tracks, though Geist knew she could always ghost out of the situation if it became a problem.

Walking around warmed her from the inside out. And the harder her heart beat, the more her breath steamed the air.

Vergess gave her a sideways glance and lifted an eyebrow.

"I'm fine," she mouthed.

Battery placed a hand on his Lancaster pistol.

"That's fancy equipment," Varnish said. "Most Brits don't carry that model."

"It was custom made," Battery replied.

"Is that right?"

"It was my grandfather's. It's more like a good luck charm."

The evening winds brought the smell of gunpowder and a biting chill that pierced even the thickest of uniforms. Fortunately, it took some of the fog, clearing more of the environment and revealing a field of stumps. Beyond them, perhaps half a mile away, Geist spotted trees. The forest would make for an excellent hiding place.

No wonder the train operator stopped here. The Bolsheviks likely hid in the trees, and that's why they've been cutting them back.

"There," Vergess said as he pointed. "Do you see it?"

Geist stared. Her nose stung with each inhale, but she maintained her concentration regardless. Her sorcery sharpened her vision, yet it wasn't enough. She rubbed at her eyes and shook her head.

"I see nothing," she said.

"You need to practice your sorcery more."

Varnish readied his rifle. "Vhat did you see?"

"Something on the tracks," Vergess replied. "Something metal. Not marked. Most likely civilian made."

Geist glanced up. "Is it magi-tech?"

"Not that I can tell. No opals or signs of sorcery."

Without any other words between them, Geist motioned forward. The group stayed close together as they advanced on the strange device placed between the rails. Geist took note of the silence.

The Bolshevik revolutionaries must've planted this here, she reasoned. *But where have they gone? Back to the forest?*

Vergess stepped over the rail and walked up to the metal device strapped to the track. Geist recognized two aircraft bombs strapped together. They were no longer than an adult arm and only as thick as a person's neck, but they could do a considerable amount of damage when dropped by fighter pilots. All markings had been scratched off, but Geist suspected they were Russian.

"The Bolsheviks would do something like this to their own countrymen?" Battery asked. "I didn't know the Russian Empire was in such turmoil."

Varnish grunted but otherwise didn't respond.

"Vergess," Geist said. "Destroy them."

He nodded and then knelt down. With a simple graze of his fingertips, the bomb shells rotted away before their eyes, seemingly trapped in a bubble of rapidly accelerated time. The metal rusted, decayed, and turned to flakes. The rot spread to every inch of the shell, destroying the weapons in a matter of seconds.

Runia sorcery had its uses.

"What else should we do?" Battery asked.

Varnish shrugged. "So I'm the only one who lives if I walk around here, is that it?"

That was what Victory had implied. And he was never wrong. But why could Varnish traverse the unknown? Was he working for the enemy as a double agent? Or would he even investigate at all if she sent him? What other explanations could there be?

Vergess and Battery stared at the man with suspicion. Varnish answered them with a huff and straightened the belt around his waist.

"Vhat? It's probably because I can speak vith my countrymen and you Englishmen can't."

The single suggestion got Geist chuckling. *Of course*, she thought. *That's logical. He could prevent a fight by explaining the situation.*

Geist waved her hand toward the forest. "Varnish, you investigate. Come back within five minutes. Vergess, you check the rails for a bit up the track. Make sure nothing else is there. Battery, you're with me."

The others nodded.

Before they headed off, Geist added, "Wait—what if one of us runs into the Eyes of the Kaiser? We should have a word or phrase we can give each other for safety."

Vergess shook his head. "People tend to act out their dominated commands with a single-minded focus. I've seen it hundreds of times when I trained with Hans and Otto. We'll know if they're dominated because they'll shamble back into the group and ignore any attempt to sway them off the course they're on."

"Still… I would feel safer knowing we had a phrase. Just in case. Why not the word *beachfront*? We'll say it to each other when we meet back up."

Again, the others nodded in agreement.

Geist used her sorcery to become invisible and watched from her incorporeal state as the others did as she commanded. Varnish headed off into the distant fog, his breath leaving a noticeable trail. For a moment, Geist wondered if she could follow him in her invisible state.

No. Victory said only Varnish wouldn't be harmed. I should wait until he reports back.

Vergess searched the tracks, disappearing into the fog for only a few seconds and then returning a moment later. He remained tense, his eyes searching the area with an intensity that Geist had only ever seen in battle.

Battery held up his Lancaster when Vergess drew near.

"Beachfront," Vergess snapped. "I was close enough you

could've heard the commands the enemy would've issued me." He backhanded Battery's shoulder and shook his head.

Battery huffed as he lowered his weapon. "Safety is important."

"Heh." Vergess glanced around. "Keep your eyes open. People were here recently. At least two."

"How can you tell?"

"I can smell them. I can also smell blood… but I don't see it."

"Maybe someone killed to get those aircraft bombs."

"Perhaps."

The more Geist knew about the situation, the more she wanted her entire squad with her. *Victory is never wrong*, she assured herself. *Everything will be fine. Nothing here will get us. We'll be returning to our trek in no time.*

"W-well," Battery muttered, his teeth clattering. "What if I empowered Vergess instead? Maybe he c-could use his bloodhound skills and find something."

It wasn't a bad idea. Enhanced *apex* sorcery would be useful.

But she didn't want to risk losing contact with Victory. Half the reason she left him behind was to make sure he wouldn't be in harm's way. What if the Eyes of the Kaiser had taken *him* over? They would use his future-sight for their devious plans. She couldn't risk him out in the open when they didn't know their surroundings.

"Don't," Geist said. "We'll wait for Varnish."

The two nodded and ended the conversation.

Four minutes passed. The longer they remained standing in place, the more the warmth left Geist's body. By the time she spotted Varnish exiting the fog, she realized she couldn't feel her fingers. And Varnish took his sweet time ambling over, glancing around as he went.

The moment he drew near, he said, "Beachfront."

Battery exhaled. "C-could you have been any slower?"

Varnish shrugged.

"So? Did you see anything?"

"Nothing. Ve're alone."

Odd.

Geist turned in a complete circle. No one was here? But then why had Victory warned about only sending Varnish? Shouldn't he have seen someone?

"Let's head back to the train," she muttered. "If there's nothing on the tracks and no one here, we should be on our way."

They headed back to the train, loaded into the boxcar, and informed the operator they had cleared away the dangers. Once the train started back up, Geist settled in for another long ride.

ELEVEN

Dangers in Petrograd

Geist awoke with a jerk of her leg. In an instant, she was standing, the rumbling of the boxcar just confusing enough that she stood froze for a long moment to take everything in. The others slept in sitting positions, some with their heads down, other with their caps over their faces. Geist ran a hand down her face and cleared away the sweat.

Her head hurt.

It had hurt for a while, ever since Vergess clocked her straight across the chin. She had figured it was the blow that left her dazed, but something didn't feel right about the current throbbing.

Dreamer stirred from his sleep. He stretched, took in a deep breath, and then glanced in her direction. In her groggy state, Geist found herself obsessing about his appearance. He wore illusions to hide his true nature as an Arab Crow, even going so far as to wear pale skin, blue eyes, and blond hair.

"You can sleep without breaking your illusions?" she whispered.

The thought had never occurred to her—since it was easy to forget he even swaddled himself in illusions—but sorcerers had to concentrate to use their magic. How could he focus while asleep? It was impossible!

Dreamer brushed off his tunic. "You can master a sorcery to the point it becomes a process the body does for you. Like breathing. I need to focus to remove my illusions, or if I'm injured, then they drop. But otherwise, I have sustained it long enough to keep indefinitely."

"I see…"

She had never heard of such a level of mastery. *Maybe if I weren't focusing on learning a second sorcery, I could've kept my invisibility going without thought.* The advantages of maintaining stealth, even while asleep, intrigued her, but did it beat improved physical prowess? The pros and cons only added to her headache.

The clacking of the train slowed. The change in speed woke everyone else.

Vergess groaned as he rolled from his side. "It's like my headache intensified the longer we went."

"Same," Blick responded. He stood and rubbed at his temples. "I don't feel right."

Vergess took a moment getting to his feet, his eyes squinted shut. Heinrich didn't complain like the others. He brushed himself off and stood near the boxcar wall, not a peep out of him.

As the train came to a gradual stop, her team readied themselves by the car door. The moment they stopped, Vergess pulled it open, allowing the early evening winds to slap them all into full wakefulness.

With a shiver, Geist jumped onto the platform. Bells rang, men shouted, and horses pulling carts of supplies added to the cacophony of the train station. Packed snow and icy walkways made everything slippery, but that didn't slow anyone. Russian soldiers rushed to unload the boxcar, some of which barked out questions.

Varnish stepped in and barked answers, his anger enough to startle the soldiers into backing down. Geist allowed him to handle the situation as she followed Victory to the gates. The moment they were even slightly separated from the others, he placed his good hand on her shoulder and leaned in close.

"Something is wrong," Victory muttered. "Everyone is ill."

"What do you mean?"

Her head hurt—more than before—but that wasn't the same as sickness of the gut or lungs. None of the others coughed, none of them pissed more than usual, and they ate fine. Perhaps it had been the alcohol?

Geist shook her head. *No. Blick and Vergess both complained about their head hurting before we arrived at House Kott. This isn't new.*

"I think this may be sorcery," Victory said.

"Why?"

"Heinrich is the only one of us who nullifies sorcery, and he's the only one without symptoms. I would bet my life this was magical."

"Okay. But then who is doing it?"

"Maybe our enemy has been targeting us," Victory said with a shrug.

"But we've been suffering from it since we've entered the Russian Empire," Geist replied. "Long before our enemy knew we were here."

This isn't them. It's something else...

"It's been much harder to see anything with my sorcery," Victory muttered. "If this continues, I don't know how much help I'm going to be."

But should she dedicate time to the mystery illness? They didn't have the luxury of costly experiments or recovery. They had already been delayed twice with their train ride to Petrograd. What were her other options?

Battery hustled to her side, stepping between her and Victory. "Are you discussing the plan? The others want to know where we're heading."

"The Winter Palace," Geist said. "That's the home of the Royal House Romanov. We'll head there at once."

"Even though it's the evening?"

"Our information is too important to wait for morning."

Battery rubbed at his neck. "But we're dealing with a Royal House. You know how they can be."

"Appearances sometimes trump common sense," Victory muttered.

Geist immediately thought of her ex-fiancé—Prince Leopold of the Royal House Habsburg-Lorraine. His ego demanded everyone genuflect before any proper conversations could be had. *Why must these spoiled monarchs be so detached from reality? We don't have time to adhere to formalities!*

"We'll risk upsetting them," she said.

She exited the train station courtyard and walked past the gate guards to enter the city proper. The main road through Petrograd, wide enough to accommodate four carriages if they rode side by side, was clogged with people and animals. One glance revealed the popular trends of the region: thick mustaches and newsy caps. Geist had a hard time differentiating one man from another, as everyone fought the cold with a long black or brown jacket that went to their ankles. If a woman had her collar up high enough, Geist couldn't differentiate them, either.

Wind rushed along the road like it had somewhere to be. Snow came down by the boat load, covering everything in a foot of ivory. The horses snorted and shivered, but the Russian denizens shrugged off the chill with a scowl.

Vergess, Blick, Dreamer, Heinrich, and Varnish caught up as a group.

"Take us to the Winter Palace," Geist said as she tapped Varnish on the arm.

He jerked away from her touch. "I spoke to the soldiers at the gate. The Vinter Palace has been converted into a hospice for vounded soldiers. Tsar Nicolas has moved his family to Alexander Palace."

Damn. "Where is Alexander Palace?"

"Near Tsarskoye Selo," Varnish said. "Ve can take a passenger train there, but it's almost an hour's travel, and I'll have to secure tickets first."

The icy air burned her nose. Geist shivered. "Is there a beer hall we can stay in while you arrange accommodations?"

"All of the Russian Empire is under prohibition. The beer halls are closed."

Goddammit. "Any place, then," Geist said, holding back all number of curse words. "Anything to get out of this blasted weather!"

"I d-didn't know the world c-could get so c-cold," Dreamer said, his teeth chattering nonstop.

Varnish glanced around. "I can take you to a dining hall for soldiers."

"Do it," Geist snapped.

Without another word, Varnish took off down the road and the group followed behind, careful not to get lost in the sea of bodies. Although they were dressed different, wearing the uniform of their respective homelands, the Russian citizens paid them little attention. Most were rushing to get into long lines—lines that extended down four blocks—and others were shouting and holding signs. Unrest filled the air.

A pack of three children ran up to Geist and held their bluish hands out.

"Rubles," they each said. "Rubles."

Geist motioned them away. "I have nothing for you."

The children spat out words and kicked up snow.

Battery reached into his backpack and withdrew two cans of *bully beef*—meat that had been brined and boiled to near flavorless conditions. He handed them to the children, who snatched them away and ran off without another word.

"Those were meant to be emergency rations," Geist said.

"I packed extra," Battery replied. "And I couldn't stand to think of them not eating." He rubbed at his arms and kept his scarf tight around his neck.

Varnish led them past dozens of four-story buildings, each built right next to the other, only allowing a few inches of space between. The windows had Russian words written across them in white paint. Geist kept an eye out for street signs, but most had been ripped down.

When they finally reached their destination, Varnish had to yell at the guards blocking the front door. The Russian soldiers had their rifles held tight and shouted at anyone who got near. Once Varnish convinced them to let everyone in, they gave Geist and her team odd glances but otherwise remained silent.

Geist entered the building after Varnish and traveled down a dark hall until she entered a dining room with a dozen long tables. At least fifty Russian soldiers sat around eating beetroot borscht and puff-pastry pirozhki. The sour smell of the borscht didn't help Geist's headache. She rubbed at the bridge of her nose, hoping to find a corner of the room where the scent would be weaker.

"M-much better," Dreamer said with a sigh of relief.

A fire raged in a gargantuan fire pit near the back of the room. That, coupled with the many bodies, almost made the place too warm. Geist didn't care. It was better than the snow outside.

"Wait here," Varnish commanded. He turned and left before Geist could even acknowledge his statement.

The dining hall seemed a safe place to rest while they made arrangements for the last bit of their trek.

TWO HOURS of waiting and the night brought with it another foot of snow.

Did acquiring train tickets really require two hours? One more and Geist had every intention of going out to search for him.

In the meantime, she sat next to a window, watching the last citizens of Petrograd rush down the road, despite the terrible hour. The people waiting in lines eventually got bread, but those who didn't make it before sundown were denied. The fights that broke out afterward lasted an hour before the soldiers got involved.

While Geist couldn't speak Russian, the Russian soldiers in the dining hall still insisted on talking. Several walked over and struck up conversations that no one could understand. They pointed to Victory's injured arm and then a gnarled scar on one of the infantry gunners, and the Russian all had a good laugh. Victory and Dreamer managed to continue the "conversation" through pointing and laughing and even mimicking scenes of a fight, but Geist couldn't bring herself to socialize.

Blick, Heinrich, and Vergess sat around her, each looking more miserable than the last.

"We should've saved some of that whiskey," Blick muttered.

"We should've brought lice powder," Heinrich quipped.

The door to the dining hall opened. Varnish pushed his way in, a long jacket wrapped around his uniform. He brushed the snow out of his mustache and walked over to Geist.

She stood and placed her hand on her pistol. "Varnish?"

"Beachfront," he said.

Blick and Heinrich exchanged puzzled glances.

"The trains haven't been running properly," Varnish continued. "I think I have transport, but it might be suspicious. I vas hoping you vould investigate."

Even he was on edge?

Geist exhaled and stared at the floor. She didn't like the idea of traveling out in the cold, but if there was no other option, she wouldn't complain.

"All right," she said. Then she turned to Battery. "You're with me. First, empower Blick, but if anything happens while we're out, I'm going to need your help."

Battery nodded. "Of course."

"Allow me to accompany you," Heinrich said as he stood. "I would like to visit the Winter Palace, if at all possible. I have messages to relay to individuals who were supposed to be stationed there. I suspect they left with the tsar, but just in case."

"Do ve really have time to be vandering around the palace grounds?" Varnish asked with a glare.

Geist waved away the comment. "First we'll deal with the transportation. If we have time, Heinrich can relay his messages. Come on, then."

Before they exited, Varnish snapped his fingers and said a few things in Russian. The soldiers in the dining hall managed to put together a set of three extra coats and hats. They handed them over but also got a chuckle when the bottom of the coat hit the ground for both Battery and Geist. Her shortness didn't typically bother her, but it felt as though the Russians were taunting her about it.

"Come," Varnish said. He opened the door and marched out into the snow.

Geist and Battery walked side by side while Heinrich trailed behind. The streetlights lit them a path, but the flurry of snow kept everything shrouded in a thin veil of white. Fortunately, the many people earlier had packed down the sidewalks. A few times Battery slipped around like he was in the middle of slapstick routine, yet he always managed to keep his footing.

They rounded a corner, past a cobbler and a shirt factory. Most of the boarded-up windows had red words painted on signs outside.

But when they neared the warehouses for the train depot, Geist glanced around. She jogged to Varnish's side as he knocked on a warehouse door.

"Th-this isn't the t-ticket booth," she said, her voice quavering.

"There is someone who specializes in moving things," Varnish said. "He moves them fast and vithout notice. That's what you vant, right?"

"Y-yes."

Varnish motioned with a jerk of his head. "Follow me. He's in here."

He opened the door, and Geist stepped out of the cold.

The dark room had a single lantern set on top of a box in the corner. Two purple eyes stared through the darkness, their color and glint immediately noticeable—and the first thing she looked at.

"Don't move."

It all happened in an instant. She knew the danger, her body even tensed long before her mind registered the threat, but it was already over.

Geist couldn't move.

TWELVE

Dominated

Varnish struck an unsuspecting Battery across the face with his pistol. Blood wept from Battery's busted eyebrow as he pulled his out sidearm, but he wasn't fast enough. Varnish slammed him head-first into the doorframe. When Heinrich went to back away, Varnish pointed his firearm straight at his head.

"Get inside," he growled.

Heinrich swallowed hard and walked into the warehouse. Varnish kicked Battery's Lancaster to the side and then dragged him to his feet.

The moment Battery got into the warehouse, he turned his half-lidded attention to the bright purple eyes in the corner.

No!

"You will cooperate with us," the man said in English.

Battery's gaze went vacant, and he nodded along with the words.

"Pick up your weapon and stand guard at the door."

And without any protest, Battery did as he was told. With his Lancaster back in hand, he closed the warehouse door, a pained expression on his face, but otherwise no indication he would leave his post without instructions.

Varnish stumbled over to a stack of cargo boxes. He grabbed at his gut as he ran into a crate, his eyes scrunched shut. He groaned and rubbed at his face.

"Otto," Varnish said through clenched teeth. "Hurry and kill them. My head… it hurts too much to maintain this disguise. It'll start slipping soon…"

Otto—one of the Eyes of the Kaiser—stepped out of the shadows. He wore a typical Russian outfit, complete with a long coat and newsy hat. But his eyes… Geist saw them imposed over her own vision, like an afterimage of glancing at the sun.

Don't move.

It was only then that she realized she wasn't breathing. She couldn't bring herself to inhale. She just stood still, staring at the one spot in the warehouse room with an unblinking intensity. How long could she maintain her stillness? Would she pass out from lack of oxygen? What would happen then?

Otto walked over to Heinrich and gave him the once over. "I almost can't believe it. Another traitor traveling through Russia? And here I was hoping for Wilhelm."

He reached into Heinrich's jacket and withdrew his sidearm. Heinrich flinched back, his hands trembling.

"Worried?" Otto asked in German. He slowly took Heinrich's glasses off and tucked them into his coat pocket. "As long as you cooperate, you'll live long enough to see your uncle. He's here in the Russian Empire as well."

"That's… impossible," Heinrich said. "My uncle, he's sick and—"

"Like Amalgam? No. We fixed that. Both Amalgam and your uncle are doing fine. I'm sure he'll be happy to see you."

Heinrich didn't respond. He took a step back and hit the wall, his jaw clenched hard.

Geist's chest burned, lungs filled with trapped air.

Don't move.

"*Otto*," Varnish hissed. "Why're you waiting? I told you I don't have time!"

"If you can't maintain your form, drop it," Otto said.

With a long groan, Varnish clawed at his face. Although Geist couldn't see the full extent of his actions—she couldn't move her head to see or avoid the situation—she could make out the sick rip of skin. Varnish tore enough to throw bits to the floor. He took in gasps as though surfacing from water.

Geist's vision darkened at the edges.

"Fleshcraft sorcery?" Heinrich muttered. "Disgusting."

Otto smiled. "Pavel does good work. And no one ever finds the bodies. It's the mark of a good spy."

Although her thoughts faded with each slam of her panicked heart, Geist tried to think of how someone masquerading as a Russian ally could deceive them. Had he been with them since the beginning? *No,* she thought, every second a painful torture. *It must have been the train. And the fog. This spy was the one waiting for us. The one Victory saw.*

The Russian traitor agent, Pavel, ripped another layer of stolen flesh from his neck, revealing his true skin underneath. Otto glanced over, an eyebrow raised as his ally took in sharp breaths, but that was all Heinrich needed.

With one touch to Otto's face, Heinrich nullified the magic of Otto's eyes. The shine of purple ended, and Geist gasped.

In the next second, everyone leapt into frantic action.

Geist whipped around and held out her hand. She didn't have the breath needed to shout instructions, but Battery didn't need them. He grabbed her hand, his empowerment near instantaneous. Otto aimed his weapon and fired. His bullet went straight through Battery's chest, but it didn't touch flesh.

When empowered, Geist's sorcery effected more than herself. It extended outward, and in the past, it had made other objects incorporeal. Could she use it on other people?

She rushed to Battery, and the two of them stumbled through the warehouse door, ghosting to the outside and tumbling through the snow. In the next instant, Geist was on her feet, dragging Battery up to his, thankful her sorcery had worked as she had hoped.

In the next moment, she made them both invisible, fearing Otto and Pavel would be in hot pursuit at any second.

"Run," Geist said, breathless. "Get the others!"

Although she couldn't see him, she heard Battery take in a nervous breath. "R-right. But what about you?"

"I'll get Heinrich."

"Keep my empowerment."

"Go, dammit!"

The moment he ran off, her sorcery left him. He reappeared as he ran toward the main road and took a hard corner. Ice and snow made it difficult for him to gain traction, but he pushed forward as fast as he could regardless.

No one exited the warehouse door. Geist pulled out her handgun and waited a second. Nothing. Then she realized—they would likely exit out another door of the warehouse and perhaps even flee with their one kidnap victim.

Fuck.

Geist ghosted through the door and entered a pitch-black warehouse. Otto and Pavel had doused the lantern, but the echo of their boots rang between crates. They were heading to the opposite side of the warehouse.

After a moment of focus, Geist could see through the darkness. She hesitated, though, unwilling to go running through the warehouse toward her targets. *Vergess said they would use the shadows to their advantage.* She closed her eyes and took a few steps forward. With her *specter* sorcery, she could move through the crates, but how could she fight two enemy sorcerers while blind? And how could she hope to defeat them while rescuing Heinrich?

I can't leave him, she reasoned. *I have to go.*

Keeping her eyes shut tight, Geist ran forward. She felt every object as it passed through her body, though she couldn't determine exactly what they were. Crates? Barrels? The physical sensation left her shivering.

The sounds of strikes and kicks, and the splatter of wet blood slowed her run.

"Do it again," Otto growled in German. "And I'll happily explain to our new magi-tech general why I had to end your life."

Geist heard someone spit—no doubt in her mind it was Heinrich. *He's too damn defiant for his own good!* She stopped once she could hear them breathe. Invisible and undetected, she inched a bit closer, still trying to think up a plan of attack.

Another punch, this one followed by a short grunt of pain.

Outside the warehouse, the hiss and whistles of trains rang out into the night.

"We can't stay here long," Pavel said, his voice much different than when he imitated Varnish. He no longer had an accent, and he spoke as though he had smoked since birth. "I didn't leave the Ethereal Squadron far behind."

Another punch and someone hit the floor.

"Carry him," Otto said in English. "We'll leave via the train. It should be here by now."

Geist opened a single eye, squinting long enough to get her bearings. She spotted Otto opening the back door while Pavel scooped up Heinrich's limp body from the concrete floor. Satisfied she had enough visual information, she rushed forward, her heavy footfalls echoing.

"Look out!" Pavel barked.

"Surrender," Otto commanded.

But Geist kept her eyes shut. She ran straight for Otto's voice and swiped wide. She heard him stumble back, and although she hadn't connected, she knew she was close. Geist swung again, hoping to clip his chest and drag flesh straight out of his lungs.

"*Get away from me,*" Otto hissed.

His commands did nothing.

He fired his Luger, and Geist jumped back—not because the bullet struck her, but because the bang shattered her eardrums. For a long moment, all she heard was the dull ringing of a gunshot.

Geist held up her weapon and fired it in Otto's direction. Someone yelled, but right as she was about to lunge, a gauntleted first struck her in the back of the neck. For a brief second, Geist's vision went black. When she opened her eyes, she was on the floor of the warehouse, the whole world spinning.

Someone grabbed her by the shoulder. Geist jerked free and rolled to the side. When she jumped to her feet, she almost gasped.

Amalgam—dressed in his full magi-tech armor—reached for her. She stumbled backward, taken aback by his presence. Her back collided with the boxes, having failed to ghost through them in her panic.

"Stop running," he said through his sinister gas mask. "It'll be easier if you surrender now."

During the commotion, Pavel exited the warehouse with Heinrich over his shoulder.

Otto searched the area, his purple eyes glowing bright in the darkness. Geist immediately closed hers.

"Give yourself up!" he commanded.

Regaining her focus, Geist went incorporeal, ran through the warehouse wall, and came to a halt outside. She didn't need to kill Otto or Amalgam or Pavel—all she needed to do was retrieve Heinrich and make it back to her team. Once she had them at her side, she knew she could handle the threat, but until then, she was at a disadvantage … and blind.

She chanced opening her eyes.

The snowy evening greeted with a blast of frigid wind. Geist didn't care. She could barely feel her own breathing. Adrenaline iced her veins, dulling her to all sensations. Her gaze fell to Pavel, who pushed himself through a small group of Russian train workers. He said some things in Russian and then waved them away. The workers took off in different directions, panic written on their faces.

Geist ran after him. Seconds later, Otto and Amalgam burst out of the warehouse.

I'll never be able to hide with Amalgam here.

She turned her attention to the trains in the area. None of them were passenger cars. Most didn't even have boxcars. They were flat beds piled high with crates, no doubt carrying munitions.

Russian soldiers on the opposite loading platform caught sight of Pavel and shouted something. They ran to get around, but Geist knew it would take them a few minutes at the very least.

She picked up her pace. It wasn't hard to catch to a man carrying a full-grown adult.

The second she neared Pavel, Geist grabbed at his side and

plunged her hand deep. When it became solid, her fingernails raked fleshy organs. Pavel screamed and hit the platform on both knees. Geist ripped out her hand, now soaked in blood, and shook away the bits of flesh she tore from his body.

Pavel released Heinrich and cradled his injury. Heinrich rolled to his side and held a hand over his gut. Bruises and cuts covered his face. Red marks dotted his arms. He shivered as Geist grabbed his shoulder and attempted to pull him up.

"Stand!" she barked in German. "Goddammit, *stand*!"

Heinrich struggled to get to his feet.

Gunshots rang out in the train station—the crack of the pistol mixing with the screech of the trains on turntables. A bullet clipped the side of Heinrich's knee, and he half fell on Geist. She held him, but she knew it couldn't last.

Otto stopped and pointed his Lugar. Geist avoided looking him in the eye. Her heart beat hard against her ribs when she heard Amalgam stomping up to her. If it were just Otto, she could've stayed incorporeal the whole time, but Amalgam would break through her sorcery.

She lifted her pistol and fired. Amalgam took the shot, ripped the weapon from her grasp, and then backhanded her with it.

Again, Geist hit the ground. She gritted her teeth, hating how her head felt as though it would burst in half, torn apart by pain from outside and within. Her sorcery failed, and each breath stung her throat.

When she briefly opened her eyes—just to piece together a plan —she caught Otto aiming for her chest. Right as he was about to pull the trigger, Amalgam moved in the way.

"What is your problem?" Otto asked through clenched teeth. "Move."

Otto stepped forward and attempted to move Amalgam aside, but he wasn't nearly as large, and his dominating eyes had no effect on a man without them. Amalgam reacted by grabbing Otto's arm.

"Lieutenant Cavell said he wanted to handle his daughter," Amalgam stated.

"This isn't the time for vendettas! This is for survival. We kill her now, before this gets out of hand."

Geist got to her feet.

Otto shoved Amalgam and lifted his firearm. It wasn't enough. Amalgam kept his grip on the man's arm and unleashed a burst of sickly green flames from his palm. It burned the sleeve of Otto's jacket and singed the skin beneath.

"*Cretin*," Otto hissed as he attempted to jerk free. "What kind of traitor are you?"

Focusing as much as she could, Geist lifted Heinrich up. Although she hadn't mastered *apex* sorcery—not by a long shot— what little she had gained helped her drag the researcher to the side of the platform. She leapt down while Otto and Amalgam fought each other and then headed for a train leaving the station. Without glancing back, she hopped onto another platform and then half threw Heinrich onto the last flatbed.

"Release me!" Otto shouted.

A small piece of Geist almost wanted to laugh. Otto probably wasn't accustomed to people disobeying him.

To her surprise, Amalgam did. He let go of Otto and turned to face her, his mirror-like gas mask goggles reflecting the station as Geist jogged alongside the moving train. She leapt onto the flatbed as it left the last portion of the platform. To her horror, Amalgam reached into a pouch and threw a handful of buttons.

Geist knocked them away, frantic to keep any from landing on the flatbed.

Then her legs gave out and she fell forward onto her knees. A small stack of ammunition broke her fall, but the corners of the boxes dug into her skin. Breathing deep, she kept her gaze on Amalgam as the train picked up speed, taking her farther and farther away.

THIRTEEN

Traitor

_____

A malgam "watched" the train pick up speed. The faint sparkle of Geist's aura created a beacon he could sense long after the vehicle had pulled out of the station. It drifted from his detection, but he knew where she was headed.

Again, Geist had been _so close_. Then Otto had almost killed her. Geist—the one person in the world that still made Amalgam feel alive—and Otto had come within seconds of erasing her existence.

Russian soldiers ran onto the platform with their rifles ready. They yelled orders, pointed their weapons, and motioned with their bayonets. Amalgam ignored them as he climbed back onto the platform. Animalistic rage clawed at his thoughts, preventing him from even considering the soldiers as threats. It took all his willpower not to rend Otto's throat and toss his body onto the tracks.

Otto turned his sorcerer eyes on the soldiers.

He said something in stilted Russian. The soldiers, their auras dimming, turned and marched off. Knowing Otto, they would throw themselves in front of a moving train. An effective way to deal with a problem.

Otto turned to face Amalgam. "And _you_," he said through clenched teeth. "Dogs will be made to heel, understand? Germany has fixed you and created a god of war. You owe the Kaiser everything." He rubbed at his arm—where Amalgam had held him—his skin still intact, though red.

"The girl has information," Amalgam said, ignoring the threat. "You almost wasted a valuable resource."

He knew killing Otto wouldn't go over well. He didn't want to be stalked by Lieutenant Cavell while he hunted for Geist, nor did he want to be without a base of operations if he broke away from Germany.

Otto pulled his coat tight, unharmed from the fight.

Pavel remained on the ground, curled in a tight ball, his blood pouring onto the platform. It was a show, though. A way to look nonthreatening. Amalgam could sense the sorcery in Pavel's body slowly fixing all the damage.

"We could've gotten information from Heinrich," Otto muttered. Then he turned to Pavel. "Get up or I'll force you to get up."

Amalgam chuckled, just to irritate Otto. "Heinrich resists your sorcery. We would've gotten nothing from him."

"But he doesn't resist knives and bullets. Sooner or later, he would break."

A chunk of Pavel's intestines sat cold on the train platform. Pavel scooped up the organ with a bloodied hand. As he stood, he held the flesh against his wound. Like sugar dissolving into water, the bit of intestines melted back into the man.

Russian sorcerers had all manner of bizarre sorceries. Fleshcrafters—disgusting spies—stole skin, bone, muscle, and organs from others to use as their own. If they killed someone, they could wear their skin, take their windpipe, and imitate someone without flaw. They were perfect sorcerers for infiltration. Unlike invisibility and illusions, perceptive sorcerers couldn't see through a fleshcrafted disguise. Pavel slipped by even the golden-eyed Ethereal Squadron members without a problem.

Pavel straightened himself and lost some of his stolen flesh. Without his disguise… he was thin. Skeletal. Disturbing. Most found him unsettling.

"I can't maintain my disguises," Pavel muttered, his real voice a harsh rasp. "Damn headaches make it impossible. My face almost melted away on the train ride."

Otto exhaled. "Headaches... The Russian Empire is a hellhole."

A powerful sorcery hung in the air. When Amalgam listened, he could faintly make out the whispering. It got more powerful the closer they got to the Alexander Palace, and he knew it was somehow the source. What was there? Something that wanted to keep enemy sorcerers away.

It affected Pavel terribly, preventing his sorcery. Otto, however, came from the Kaiser's Guard. They trained the sorcerers ruthlessly to withstand attacks on their focus. It was no wonder Otto remained mostly unaffected.

"You," Otto said, his contempt enough to tell Amalgam he was talking to him. "Lieutenant Cavell thought you could handle this whole mission on your own. Yet they got away a second time. Because you stopped me."

Amalgam turned away, his heated breath trapped in his gas mask and agitating him further. "We know where they're heading. It won't be difficult to corner them again. We still have the advantage."

"Your monster body doesn't feel the cold like the rest of us, does it? We can't afford to dally through the snow when we've come here to collect."

Otto and Hans both saw Amalgam as a dog—a *monster*. It made sense. They only ever had appreciation for each other and the Kaiser. But Amalgam hated hearing it from them, for some reason. *Does it matter?* he thought, a cruel smile on his twisted face. *I am a monster. Perhaps I shouldn't take such offense.*

"We should regroup with the others," Otto said.

"You think Lieutenant Cavell will accept our failure?" Amalgam asked.

It took Otto a few long seconds to mull over the question. "No," he finally muttered.

Amalgam hated hearing Otto's thoughts.

... brother... where are you? ... we could've accomplished this together...

The two brothers thought about each other nonstop, to the point it grated on Amalgam's patience. He turned away and focused his thoughts on Geist. All he wanted was to goad Otto into continuing the pursuit. Perhaps with both the Eyes of the Kaiser, she wouldn't have gotten away. Then again, she probably would've been killed had Hans been around to shoot at her as well.

Which was why Amalgam argued for their group to split up. Lieutenant Cavell, his son, and Hans were continuing with the collection, only because Amalgam had convinced Lieutenant Cavell that he would be successful.

Pavel patted his bloody coat. "We should leave this place. More Russian soldiers will come through here."

"We should return to our pursuit," Amalgam said. "We should target the weak members of the Ethereal Squadron—the ones without combat sorceries. We can weaken their force."

Pavel snapped his fingers. "One of them is injured from the last encounter. He has some sort of future sight. Lieutenant Cavell would love to get his hands on him and take his blood. And that researcher won't be walking right for a while, not after the gunshot to his leg."

"We can't let up. The more pressure we apply, the harder it'll be for them to escape."

Otto nodded along with the words. "Very well. We can catch them in Alexander Palace. I doubt they know of the rot within."

Although Amalgam gave serious thought to heading out on his own, he went along with the plan. He knew Geist. She wouldn't leave a member of her team behind. Hell, she even risked returning just to save the researcher, and he wasn't an official member. If Amalgam managed to pluck a few from the herd, Geist would come for them.

FOURTEEN

Tsarskoye Selo

Geist huddled behind a large crate of munitions and rested her head on the wood. Battery's empowerment only worked if he was in range. After a few minutes, his wellspring of power left her. Exhaustion settled in afterward, along with the terrible pounding of her never-ending headache.

Twice Geist had fought with the Eyes of the Kaiser, and twice she had been dominated. If it weren't for her team, she never would've escaped.

What if they caught me alone? she wondered. *I have to deal with this somehow.*

The harsh evening winds brought with it a fresh sprinkling of snow. Heinrich pushed himself up into a sitting position and shivered. Then he moved to her side. Without his glasses, and with his clothes bloodied and torn, he almost looked like someone completely different. His hair, often kept tidy and combed, had become disheveled during the fighting. He ran a hand through it, but that didn't help.

"Where's this train going?" Heinrich asked.

"I don't know."

Geist had seen signs at the train depot. Russian signs. They hadn't been informative.

When Heinrich shivered again, Geist inched closer. Blood oozed from his busted lip and nose. It was obvious Heinrich had been hit with the butt of a gun more than once. He reached up a few times, as if to adjust his glasses, but then he must've realized he didn't have them and instead cursed in German under his breath.

"You didn't have to anger them," Geist said as she pulled her knees up against her chest. "Getting yourself killed because you didn't follow a few simple instructions is foolish."

"I followed instructions my entire life," Heinrich snapped. "And look what happened. My research and creations will be tools of war for all time." He shoved his trembling hands into his coat pockets. "I'm not going to make the same mistake again."

Geist half-smiled and dropped the conversation. If Heinrich wanted to adhere to some sort of personal code of defiance, so be it. He knew the consequences and went with it anyway.

His knee, injured by the sideswipe of a bullet, would have to be examined by a medical professional. If Cross were available, she could heal it up, but without her sorcery, it was imperative they prevent anything from becoming infected.

"Do you have any medical supplies?" she asked.

"No."

Of course not. That would be convenient. She rubbed at her eyes, wishing Battery were here. *He's always prepared.* Although she didn't like to share her medical supplies—men didn't bleed once a month, after all—she reached into a belt pouch and withdrew a small amount of bandage and cellucotton.

"Try not to put weight on this leg until we get to a medic," Geist said as she pulled his injured knee close and wrapped it.

Heinrich didn't fight her impromptu treatment. He closed his eyes and continued to shiver.

Once finished, Geist returned to her comfortable position, fighting to ignore the clack-clack of the train as it sped down the rails. Every little shake and jostle irritated her head. She, too, closed her eyes and breathed into her hands, trapping the warmth.

I'll rest for just a bit, she told herself. *Then I'll figure out how to get us back to the group.*

WHEN GEIST AWOKE, it was still dark.

At some point, she and Heinrich had huddled together to conserve heat. Being smaller, it had been easy for Geist to tuck herself under his armpit and keep comfortable. Heinrich, still asleep, leaned heavy on her, his shoulder bonier than she would've expected.

Warm and somewhat rejuvenated, Geist pushed away from Heinrich and stood. The evening winds whipped around the crate and shocked her into a full state of wakefulness. She shook off the sudden chill and turned her attention to the front of the train. Somehow, she would speak with the operator and figure out their destination.

Maybe I'll get lucky and he'll know English.

She went to step around Heinrich, but he held up a hand. Then he struggled to get to one foot.

"Don't go," he said.

Geist lifted an eyebrow. "I'll be right back. You can rest here."

"I'd rather accompany you."

"We shouldn't risk harming your injured leg."

"I don't care," he snapped.

The heat in his voice took Geist by surprise. She narrowed her eyes into a glare. If the enemy masqueraded as Varnish, could they do it with Heinrich? But code words didn't work before. How could she make sure this was Heinrich?

"Hold out your hand," she commanded.

Heinrich did as he was told. Geist touched his fingertips with her own.

"Use your sorcery on me."

Although Geist had only felt it a handful of times, *nullis* sorcery had a certain feel that was unmistakable. Like Battery, it soaked into her very being. Unlike Battery, it drained her of any sense of magic, leaving behind a hollow sensation.

This was, without a doubt, Heinrich. From what Geist understood, fleshcrafters didn't take the sorcery of the corpse they wore.

And at least her headache faded for a moment.

Unless the enemy can somehow mimic sorceries as well, she thought with a dry sense of sarcasm. She had never heard of such a feat, but she wouldn't start doubting her team now. That was the one thing she could always rely on.

"I'd rather stay as close to you as possible," Heinrich said. He removed his hand and shoved it into his pocket, ending his sorcery. "You're the only one I trust to keep me safe."

Heinrich *had* been distrusting of the others, going so far as to make enemies of them—confrontational, even in quiet moments.

"I'm the same as any of the others," Geist said. "They'll protect you just as I would."

Heinrich leaned on the crate. He rested the side of his head against the wood and exhaled a stream of warm breath.

"They weren't the ones who dove into the basement of the OHL and dragged me out of a war zone," he said. "And I was there when you risked everything to neutralize the Paris Gun." He chuckled. "And it's not like that little one—what's his stupid name? —*Battery* came rushing back through a warehouse of enemies to protect me. It was *you.* Obviously, you're willing to take more risks. You're determined to succeed. That's a quality I want in a protector."

Geist hadn't thought about any of that. She recalled when she first met Heinrich. He wanted to defect, and she managed to get him out of the OHL—enemy headquarters—even if the escape had been messy. But she didn't know he thought of her as someone who was determined to succeed. It was a compliment she had never received before.

"Ya know," she said with a smirk, "you've saved me a good number of times, too. Back in that battle with the Paris Guns, I thought Prince Leopold would kill me, and if you hadn't been there to nullify his sorcery, he might've." She turned away, grappling with thoughts. "And back in the warehouse, with the Eyes of the Kaiser... I think I would've suffocated. Or at least passed out and been helpless. If it hadn't been for you."

Heinrich slid back down into a sitting position. "Amusing."

"I'm trying to thank you."

"Well, I should tell you something personal."

Geist turned back around, half expecting him to reveal himself as an enemy or double agent.

"I never had to speak with General Volkov," Heinrich said. "Nor did I have anyone to see in the Winter Palace. I fabricated it all so I could continue to stay close to you."

It took a moment for Geist's heart to return to a steady beat. "Because you wanted me to protect you?"

"Yes."

She laughed. "Okay. Anything else?"

He stared up at her, his green eyes a little more vibrant without his glasses. For a moment, Geist thought he was about to say something, but at the last moment he glanced to the floor of the flat bed and turned away.

"I want to get out of this damn cold," he said.

Geist nodded. She knelt and offered her shoulder. "C'mon. Let's go."

After a moment of thought, Heinrich forced himself up enough to lean his weight on her. After the rest, Geist knew she could handle it. And it wasn't like he was particularly bulky.

"I don't think you know the others as well as you should," Geist said as she helped him to his one good leg. "Battery was there at the Paris Guns, after all. He risked his life for the mission, too. And Vergess helped pull you out of the OHL. And he stood toe-to-toe with Prince Leopold. Every member of the Ethereal Squadron has been tested by the fires of war. And they're still here."

Heinrich didn't reply.

"I trust them with my life. You should as well."

For a long while, Heinrich said nothing. They walked together across the flatbed of the train, Geist ensuring they wouldn't fall. When they reached the connection point, she helped Heinrich across first before crossing over the tiny steel walkway herself. Together they made their way up another flatbed.

"Give me a codename then," Heinrich finally said. "I doubt the others will really see me as an ally until I have one."

Geist smiled. "You want me to pick it?"

"The others will accept whatever you choose. Just don't embarrass me."

"You can pick a name and I can tell the others it was my idea."

Heinrich growled something under his breath. "Pick the damn name."

She laughed as she reached the end of the flatbed. Within a few seconds, she knew the name that suited him most.

"Defiant," she said. Ever since he rejected the title of Magi-Tech General. It was how he was.

"Really?" he asked. "Out of all the English words you could've used?"

"Even now." Geist chuckled. "Or maybe we should go with *Trotzig*? If you want the German version, that is."

"No. I said I would accept whatever you picked."

A light powder of snow wafted over them as they made their way into the third flatbed. And although Geist couldn't articulate what had changed, she felt a little lighter in step. Like some sort of wall between them had come down.

Defiant rubbed at his eyes. "Maybe you should've given me the codename *Blind*."

"Is it bad?"

"Everything is just a shape. These crates. You. The train. Colors and shapes."

"Are you sure this isn't just another excuse to stick close to me?"

He chortled. "We both know that when we regroup, you'll just have your man drag me around."

My man? Geist's face heated to the point she swore it melted snowflakes before they even reached her. She had never heard anyone refer to Vergess as *her man*. Then again, it wasn't like anyone outside of her team knew about her relationship with Vergess. *Is that how they refer to him to each other?*

The train clacks came at slower intervals as Geist helped Defiant across the next flatbed. Using her *apex* sorcery, she leaned to the side and attempted to view the destination of the train. Sitting in the distance, a little more than a quarter of a mile, was a large railway station, decorated with pillars and frescos of angels.

"We're nearing a town," Geist muttered.

"Are there any distinguishing buildings?"

She turned her gaze to the far distance, beyond the railway station. Trees blocked most of her sight, but one feature stood out above the rest. Even at night—it glittered with a fine polish.

"I see this golden onion dome," she said. "It has a cross on top. It's the tallest building I can see."

Defiant nodded. "It's probably the Fedorovskiy Cathedral. It's famous for its onion dome roofs. That means we've arrived in the town of Tsarskoye Selo."

"Home to Alexander Palace."

"Catherine Palace as well."

Geist half smiled. "The Winter Palace. The Alexander Palace. The Catherine Palace. How many damn palaces does Russia have?"

"Enough to cause civil unrest," he quipped.

Instead of heading for the train operator, Geist moved to the edge of the flatbed. Alexander Palace was her real goal. If she could avoid pantomiming with Russian soldiers, it would be for the best. They could leave the train and make their way to the palace by foot.

"Do you know a lot about the Russian Empire?" Geist asked.

"I know enough. I studied the Rococo architecture of both Alexander and Catherine Palace during my general studies, as well the history that led to the current state of the tsars. The Kaiser has a distaste for Russia, after all. He wants to see them fall, so he made sure everyone close to him know the nation's weaknesses."

"I see."

Once the train had slowed enough, Geist held Defiant close.

"We're going to jump."

He sighed and then twisted his fingers into the fabric of her coat. "Do it."

She leapt off, trying to keep balance—and not to hurt Defiant—

but it didn't work quite like she had in mind. Both Geist and Defiant tumbled through the snow until they slid to the bottom of the tiny hill, each soaked in freezing water. The impact and roll hadn't hurt, but the shock of losing her balance had caused a slight amount of panic.

She rested in a ditch of snow, staring up into the dark sky. *At least it had worked.*

"Beautiful," Defiant muttered from inside his snowy rut.

Geist couldn't help but laugh as she got to her feet. After brushing off the snow, she jogged to Defiant's side. "Admit it. The last twenty-four hours have been the most excitement you've had in your entire life."

"Excitement doesn't equate to *good*."

She held out her hand and helped Defiant stagger to his one good leg. He shivered something fierce, and Geist was tempted to offer him her coat, but she knew it wouldn't matter, not when they were both soaked. Soon the cold would take its toll on her as well, even if she had *apex* sorcery.

The glint of lights caught her attention. Vehicles crept along snow-covered roads. The cars turned in Geist's direction, careful not to drive through snowbanks.

A part of her wanted to run, but she knew Defiant would never make it. Without Battery, she couldn't make both of them invisible.

"Don't look threatening," Geist said. "And let me do the talking."

"I don't even have a weapon."

"Good. Keep your hands visible."

The military cars pulled up—each of the passengers had glowing golden eyes, just like Blick. They hefted rifles and barked orders in Russian. Geist lifted her hands and took a single step forward.

"I'm American," she said. "*American.*"

The soldiers exchanged confused glances.

"I can't see a thing," Defiant murmured.

Not only was he missing his glasses, but the evening sky made it impossible for most people to see, even with perfect vision. The sorcerer soldiers, with enhanced vision, no doubt had seen Geist and Defiant on the train long before they jumped off.

I should have known the town with the tsar would've had plenty of sorcerer security.

One Russian stepped forward.

"You come vith us," he said in broken English. "Under arrest."

FIFTEEN

Grand Duchess Anastasia Nikolaevna of the Russia Empire

G eist didn't resist.

The Russian Empire was an ally against Austria-Hungary and Germany, after all. Fighting with Russian sorcerers would only hurt their chance of moving throughout Russia freely.

The Russian soldiers must have felt the same way. They grabbed Geist and Defiant, but they didn't use overt force or shout any orders. They gestured and motioned, confused looks on their face as though they hadn't been expecting an American.

It made sense. The United States hadn't joined the war, even if American sorcerers had.

Geist and Defiant were loaded into the car and driven to the town of Tsarskoye Selo. A short ride. The cold air, mixed with the ever-increasing pressure in Geist's head, made the trek a blurry one. She closed her eyes, counted her heartbeats, and tried to remain focused. As it stood, she didn't know if she'd be able to ghost away. Her damn headache raged so terribly that it would require all her willpower to maintain any of her magic.

The Russian soldiers stopped at a military building within the palace grounds. Geist allowed them to take her to a cell underground. The one who spoke broken English attempted to tell her something, but it was clear he didn't know the words.

"Wait," he repeated several times. "You American."

She nodded to the words, hoping he would understand, but since she spoke *no* Russian, it was all she could offer.

Defiant was taken to a different cell. It was clear he wanted to stay with her—he half resisted the Russian when they started dragging him away—but Geist shook her head and urged him to cooperate.

"Now isn't the time to be defiant," she muttered with a smirk.

He rolled his eyes and complied with the gentle gestures of the Russian soldier.

Left alone in a tiny five-by-five room with no windows, Geist took a seat on the sole bench and stared up at the ceiling. Someone who knew English, German, or French would eventually arrive, and then she would be able to explain the situation. And, if she was lucky, they would take her straight to the tsar.

The frustration of being so close to an important goal, yet somehow so far away, ate at her ability to sleep.

ALTHOUGH GEIST COULDN'T SEE the sky, her internal clock told her at least five hours had gone by. Considering how much ground her enemy could cross with just a few hours head start, the timing bothered her. What if something happened while she was locked up?

She had a contingency plan. If, in the next three hours, no one came to speak with her, she would attempt to ghost out of the building. She wouldn't be able to go far, not with the headaches. Perhaps she might even lose focus halfway through, but she had to try.

I can't stay here forever.

Just as Geist was about to stand and attempt a few uses of her sorcery, the door opened. She squared her shoulders and stood straight, surprised to see a member of Russia's Imperial Guard. He stood in the doorway, a white coat on his shoulders, his bluish-black trousers and tunic crisp with pressed folds. He even wore a hat with feathered frills.

And, like all Russians, it seemed, he maintained a thick mustache.

"I am Sorcerer Captain Uthof of the Palace Grenadiers Company," he said, his English stiff.

Geist saluted the captain and then took a step forward. "Sir, I'm with the Ethereal Squadron. I go by the name *Geist*, and I'm a commander of a small squad."

"I see," Captain Uthof said. "Well, then I have good news. Sorcerer General Volkov sent word you would be arriving. And I believe your squadron is already at the palace. They arrived a few short hours ago."

The news took a great weight off Geist's shoulders. She figured the others would arrive in Tsarskoye Selo of their own accord—it was their official destination—but she had worried they would opt to stay in Petrograd instead.

Captain Uthof stepped aside and ushered Geist into the hall. "I will be escorting you to Alexander Palace."

"What of my companion?" Geist asked. "I was brought here with another man. He's a researcher with the Ethereal Squadron. An important individual meant to help the Russian Empire with their magi-tech research."

"He was already taken to the palace to receive medical attention."

"I see. Thank you."

As Geist walked by Captain Uthof, she couldn't help but note the difference in their height. The captain must've stood a good foot taller than her, and even he seemed to raise an eyebrow when she passed.

"Most American sorcerers I've met were... larger," he said. "They always boasted about their fine beef upbringing."

Geist rubbed at the back of her neck. "I'm more of a spy. It's advantageous to go unnoticed."

"Hm."

Together they walked into the hall, Captain Uthof moving with a march in his step. Geist kept her normal gait, but his formal movements did tempt her to follow suit. It felt unusual to walk differently when next to other military personnel, but her fatigue was already dragging her down. She didn't know how much longer she could function without rest.

When they exited the building, the large expanse of the Alexander Estate lay before them. Perfect stone walkways, trees planted around the perimeter—and the building itself was a massive U with white pillars, two stories, and a balcony rooftop. Captain Uthof led her straight through the gates. The soldiers standing guard flashed their golden eyes for a moment before returning to their posts.

"Captain," Geist said. "I need to warn you about enemy sorcerers in the area."

The captain made a *hmm* noise, but otherwise said nothing. He kept his gaze forward as he marched along.

"These Austrian-Hungarian and German sorcerers are masters of infiltration. There was a fleshcrafter among them. And the Eyes of the Kaiser. These aren't threats to be taken lightly."

"You needn't worry," Captain Uthof said. "They will be dealt with in due time."

"But—"

"I wouldn't expect an American to understand. The Royal House Romanov has ways of dealing with intruders." He smiled as he stroked his mustache. "Why do you think Russia has never successfully been invaded? Our sorcery is far greater than the other European powers."

Although Geist didn't know what the Royal House Romanov had in the ways of sorcery, she didn't care in that moment. "One of your sorcerers was already a victim. An agent by the codename of Varnish. He was killed and his body used as a disguise for the enemy."

"We will inform Tsar Nicholas."

It was the first sentence that really struck a chord with Geist. She held her breath, and her energy returned in full force. She desperately needed to speak with the tsar. He had to be informed. He had to know what the Abomination Soldiers were plotting.

Soldiers at the entrance of Alexander Palace saluted as Geist and Captain Uthof approached. They threw open the double doors and allowed the captain entry without question. Geist gave them quick glances. Their Imperial Guard uniforms were blue, white, and accented with yellow—striking colors that could be seen from a great distance. How many were on the palace grounds? Were they all sorcerers? Geist didn't know, but she hoped there were plenty nearby.

"Geist!"

She returned her attention to the palace and stopped dead in her tracks. The massive entrance hall, large enough to be a ballroom, had staircases on either side of the room. Pillars stood in the middle, and the golden trim of the wallpaper glittered under the electric lights. It was almost too much to take in at once. Who had called her name?

Then she spotted them. Blick, Victory, Battery, and Vergess stood around one of the pillars, obviously waiting for someone or something. Battery waved—the one who had shouted her name—but it was Vergess who approached her first. He walked over with a few quick steps.

"What happened?" he asked as he flashed Captain Uthof a sideways glower.

"I'm sure you have much to discuss," the captain said. "I'll speak with the sorcerers of the Royal House and return in a moment." He didn't wait for acknowledgement. He continued down the gigantic entrance hall, his dress boots clicking on the polished tile floor.

"Are you okay?" Vergess asked. "Victory said he can't see anything with his future sight. Were you harmed?"

"I—"

Vergess gripped her shoulder, his gaze intense, as if absorbing every tiny detail about her. It took Geist by surprise. Her breath caught in her throat as she struggled to even remember what she had been talking about.

"Stop sending me away," he whispered, the intensity of voice a little more than Geist had been prepared for. "It almost killed me to hear Battery say you had run off by yourself to chase the Eyes of the Kaiser."

"It… couldn't be helped…" she muttered.

His concerns weren't those of a fellow soldier, but those of a loved one. Geist knew it, and she feared it would interfere with Vergess's sense of duty, but she didn't know how to correct the problem.

"I'm okay," she said. "You can stop worrying."

Vergess's grip tightened. "You're my intended. I'll never stop worrying."

My intended. He had said it with such passion and sincerity. Geist lost her words and just stared up at him. What could she say? How she felt in that moment couldn't be described in words.

Battery jogged to their side, and Geist turned away, well aware of her flushed cheeks and fast heart rate. *At least Vergess is the only one who will detect such things,* she reasoned.

"Geist," Battery said with a quick sigh. "I figured you would come here, but… we also considered the possibility that you had been dominated." Then Battery turned to Vergess. "This isn't the fleshcrafter?"

"No," he said.

Although Geist knew he was correct, the statement took her by surprise. "How do you know?" she asked. "You didn't catch Varnish."

"I wasn't as … intimate… with Varnish," Vergess said as his face grew red.

Perfect, she thought. *I guess that means Vergess needs to get "intimate" with everyone on the team. That way we can prevent this in the future.* The thought almost caused her to laugh aloud.

Battery stared at her for a long moment. He narrowed his eyes into a glower. "Oh, don't tell me you're thinking what I think you're bloody thinking."

"I don't think it'll go over well," Geist said. "What we need are tests. I know my code word didn't work before, but we need to stay on our toes. Anything and everything to keep the enemy from using another member of the Ethereal Squadron."

"I agree," Battery said. "Absolutely. We should join the others, though."

Vergess, Geist, and Battery walked over to the group. Geist glanced between them. Victory was still injured, and Blick leaned against the pillar with a vacant expression, lost in thought.

"Where is Dreamer?" she asked.

Battery pointed to the corner of the great entrance, one of the few places shrouded in a bit of darkness. Dreamer stood with his back against the wall, his head down—his illusions completely gone. He wore a British uniform, but he carried a large assortment of weapons tied to his body. A scimitar—the curved blade from Saudi Arabia—was strapped to the side of his leg. Several janbiyas—short, curved daggers—had been tucked between his belt and his body.

"What happened?" Geist asked.

"His head hurts too much when he tries to use his sorcery," Battery said. "He had to let the illusions drop."

Dreamer kept his arms tightly crossed over his chest, his gaze glued to his feet. His darker complexion wasn't common in the snowy north of the Russian Empire, and twice the Imperial Guards at the doors snuck glances in his direction.

"Everyone acted all surprised when it happened," Blick interjected.

Geist was surprised he had even paid attention to the conversation.

Blick continued, "But that's how he looks to me every time I use my all-seeing sorcery. It's no big deal."

"It is a big deal," Victory said. "Dreamer has a mastery of his sorcery and yet this magical blight has prevented him from focusing enough to use it. It's deeply concerning."

"Er, well, that's not—"

Geist turned to Dreamer. "You're not ashamed of your appearance, are you?"

He always took the look of a British soldier—to avoid detection, she had always suspected, since he was a spy for the Ethereal

Squadron—but there was no reason in her mind he would be upset with his true appearance.

"God made me as I am," Dreamer stated. "In his image. I'm never ashamed of his gifts." He pushed away from the wall and walked over to the group. "I am, however, disappointed that I can't maintain my sorcery. Without it, what am I? It's the only sorcery I've learned—and I'm the master of it. I feel like a world class athlete stripped of all physical prowess and bound to a wheelchair."

Geist half-smiled. *It makes sense now.* Dreamer had pride in magic, and he wasn't keen on having it stripped away.

A large double door swung open, and silence descended over the entrance hall. All the imperial guards snapped to attention, their gazes hard set.

In walked Captain Uthof and four women. One woman—no older than sixteen—stood out among the rest. She wore a necklace of pearls, a fine white lace dress, and held her head high. Her strawberry blonde hair was tied back in a loose ponytail, and although she wore a fine layer of makeup, it couldn't hide the dark bags under her blue eyes.

"Introducing Grand Duchess Anastasia Nikolaevna Romanov of the Russia Empire," Captain Uthof proclaimed.

Victory bowed deep. Geist, unsure of the etiquette of the situation, followed suit. The others eventually caught on and did the same.

The grand duchess stepped forward and smiled. "I can hardly believe it!" she said in proper British English. "Members of the Ethereal Squadron have come to Alexander Palace? I never thought I would see the day." She ended her statement with a squirrel-like giggle.

The three other women, dressed in fine dresses of silk and ivory, stood back, their brows furrowed, but they said nothing. Two were attendants, and the last was a governess, though it mattered little. Geist didn't have time to speak with the youngest daughter of the tsar.

She stepped forward. "It's a pleasure to meet you. I'm here on urgent business, however. I must speak with Tsar Nicholas at once."

"You've come to meet with Papa?" Grand Duchess Anastasia held a hand up to her collarbone. "I'm dreadfully sorry. He has gone to the front lines and hasn't returned home in over month. He isn't here."

The news hit hard. "When will he return?" Geist asked, trying hard to keep the despair from her voice.

"I can send him a summons, but Papa is busy with important war efforts."

"My news is as urgent as it is dire. Please, if there's any way to contact him, I need to know. He may be in danger."

Although Geist didn't know that—she had no reason to believe the enemy was after the tsar's sorcery—it wasn't outside the realm of possibility. He could be targeted at any moment, and with fiends like the Eyes of Kaiser, it was better to be safe than sorry. Tsar Nicolas needed to be informed of the threat.

Grand Duchess Anastasia turned to the three women behind her. "Maria, Emmeline, Lenah. Quickly. Send word to Papa. Tell me how long it'll take him to return home."

The three bowed their heads and then hustled off without a word.

"We have a sorcerer here with *communis* mastery," Grand Duchess Anastasia said as she returned her attention to Geist. "Normally his range of telepathy is limited to a city or district, but you need not worry. My attendants are powerful practitioners of an ancient and useful sorcery known as *potentia*."

Battery perked up, his eyes wide.

Potentia was the sorcery he used to empower others.

"All three of them know *potentia*?" Geist asked. "And they all empower a single person?"

Grand Duchess Anastasia nodded. "Oh? You know of *potentia*? Most sorcerers have little experience with it."

"I'm familiar with it, but I've never seen multiple people use it at once."

"Each sorcerer who uses their empowering magic magnifies the last. The range of telepathy will surely increase to reach the edge of the Russian Empire. Perhaps farther."

"Damn," Blick muttered under his breath.

"Please be my guests in the meantime," Grand Duchess Anastasia said. She held out her hands and motioned to the palace around her. "We have spare rooms, and I'll order you a fine meal. It's the least I can do for members of the Ethereal Squadron who have traveled so far."

Geist turned her gaze to the floor. "I…"

"Please! I know that one of your members still needs treatment with my older sister, Tatiana. You must give him time to rest."

Defiant does need rest, Geist reasoned. *But I really can't allow the enemy to have the lead. I still need to warn so many of—*

But then it struck her. Someone in the palace had nation-wide telepathy. What if she could send a message to the remaining sorcerer houses who were in danger of having their blood stolen? *But I doubt the grand duchess will allow me the use of her sorcerer to convince Russian sorcerers to leave the empire.* Geist shook her head. *Maybe she'll allow me to send a warning. I can go to them afterward and help them escape.*

"Grand Duchess Anastasia," Geist said. "There's a favor I need to ask of you. Several sorcerer houses in the Russian Empire may be at risk. Enemy operatives have come to—"

"Are you American?" Grand Duchess Anastasia injected.

"Uh, y-yes."

Although her family came from Austria-Hungary, Geist always considered herself American first. It was her home—the one place she enjoyed and admired above all others.

"I can tell by your accent," the grand duchess continued. "I do adore the Americas."

"Er, okay. As I was saying, there are enemy operatives out to kill Russian sorcerers. Perhaps you could have your friend warn these houses as well. They need to be on guard."

"Yes. That would be prudent. How many houses?"

"House Solovyev, House Lungin, House Menshov, and—" Geist stopped herself before she could add *House Kott*. That house was already accounted for. "Just those three, Grand Duchess."

Victory coughed into his hand. Not a normal cough, like Geist had heard a million times before, but something forced and awkward. She knew what it meant. Somehow, she had gotten her etiquette wrong.

Why can't Victory simply handle this? she thought, but the answer came to her a moment later. It was the burden of commanding the squad. *She* had to be the one to interact with the Royal Houses.

Without warning, Grand Duchess Anastasia gasped. She fell forward, her face pale and hands shaking. Captain Uthof rushed to her side and caught her before she completely collapsed to the floor. With a gentle touch, he helped her back onto her feet.

"Forgive me," she murmured. "Without the empowerment... I feel so weak..."

A dead fish had more color than she did.

Geist didn't comment. She knew what it felt like when Battery wasn't around—especially if she had been relying on him for an extended period of time. But *three* Batterys? She couldn't imagine.

But then her headache faded.

Just... gone.

The clarity of focus took Geist by surprise.

"You should rest, Your Grace," Captain Uthof said as he ushered the grand duchess toward the door. "Please. I'll make sure the tsar is informed. You can leave everything to me."

Before the grand duchess could be guided away, she stopped and turned back around. "I will order the servants to make arrangements for you in the palace." Her voice, half of what it was, came out breathless.

Geist rubbed at the back of her neck. "I don't know if—"

"You will be my dinner guests for the evening," Grand Duchess Anastasia said, more forceful than before—no longer a request. "Papa never takes long to answer my summons. And you will need to speak with him about House Solovyev and House Lungin. I've heard him speak of them in strict terms."

Waiting around wasn't Geist's plan. She mulled over the new information and recalled her overall mission. She needed to get the last three houses out of Russia, and she needed to escort Heinrich to any and all research facilitates that required more technical assistance with magi-tech.

They could wait to speak with House Solovyev and House Lungin until they spoke to the tsar, but there was no reason to delay speaking to House Menshov. Wasn't it nearby? *It's in a city near Petrograd*, she recalled. *Perhaps we can visit them while we wait for the tsar.*

"We'll stay the evening," Geist eventually said.

Grand Duchess Anastasia replied with a weak smile. Then she and the captain disappeared through a far door, leaving Geist with her team.

Perhaps a single night's rest would do them all good.

"How embarrassing," Battery said, shaking his head.

"What're you talking about?" Geist asked as she turned around.

Battery, Victory, and Dreamer regarded her with shakes of their head. Vergess and Blick, on the other hand, merely shrugged.

"You should refer to a grand duchess as *Your Grace*," Victory said. "Only social equals—other members of Royal Houses—may address her as *Duchess*, and it's just, well, embarrassing to say the full *Grand Duchess*."

Heat filled Geist's face and she brought a hand up to cover her embarrassment. Her father had taught her all sorts of etiquette for dealing with German and Austro-Hungarian royalty, but never anything for the Russian Empire. The tsar and his family were "weak" and "pathetic," so why bother learning any sort of formalities?

Blick rolled his eyes and wiped away a fake amount of sweat from his brow. "I'm glad I didn't have to speak with the duchess."

"You took the same etiquette classes we did," Battery snapped. He rounded on his brother with a glare. "How did you forget Professor Winton's manners and customs guide? Our father was a good friend to Grand Duchess Anastasia's grandmother and on her mother's side! We practiced this, for Pete's sake."

"How can you remember all this?" Blick asked. "That old curmudgeon spoke with a monotone."

Servants from the palace hustled over to Geist, towels and warm water in hand. They bowed, said some things in Russian, and then motioned to the stairways. The promise of rest quelled all irritations with the situation.

SIXTEEN

The Tsar's Family

G eist leaned back on the couch and glanced around. The massive sitting room connected six bedrooms, almost as if there was a tiny house inside of the palace. Given the many pictures of foreign diplomats hanging on the wall, she suspected it was a common area used for high-ranking guests.

"I don't get the Russian Empire," Blick said. He stared down at a bowl of water left by the door in their room. The silver container, half full of hot water, wafted steam. Hand towels and ointments sat nearby.

"What don't you get?" Victory asked.

Blick crossed his arms. "Well, their insistence on giving us warm water, for starters."

"It's to wash your hands."

"Thanks, genius. I got that. I meant, why would they think we need to wash our hands while we wait for the grand duchess? Do they think we're blood-soaked? Or maybe they think I'll shake off my knob and then attempt to hold hands with the duchess."

"*Blick*," Victory snapped.

The two exchanged quick glances like only brothers could. Blick shrugged. "What? There aren't any Russian here." Then he turned to Geist. "And she's heard worse when we all thought she had a knob."

Victory placed a hand over his face to hide the growing shade of pink. He mumbled something to himself before taking a seat in one of the large loveseats next to Geist.

"You're not offended, right?" Blick asked Geist, one eyebrow high.

Geist narrowed her eyes. "We're in the middle of Alexander Palace—the home of the tsar and his family. We shouldn't risk offending *them*. It'll jeopardize the operation. Keep the chatter about *your knob* to a minimum."

Battery shook his head. "This won't be the last time you need to give that command."

With a long exhale, Blick motioned to the giant room. There were no threats, no enemies—not even any servants—it was just Geist, her team, and the amenities of a palace. The electric lights, hydraulic lifts, and modern architecture designs added to the futuristic and secure feel of their surroundings.

Blick gave up with a huff. "I need a drink."

Dreamer, who had yet to reapply his illusions, sat on a small couch seat, his gaze glued to an electric lamp. He switched it on, then off, then on again, observing the bulb. A few times he rubbed his eyes, but otherwise he took copious amounts of notes in his faux book.

"This palace must have been remodeled recently," he said. "It was built in 1792, long before any of these luxuries would have been available."

Victory—recovered from his embarrassment—leaned forward, his elbows on his knees. "Do either of you still have a headache? Mine has been gone since we've arrived, basically."

"Ever since the grand duchess collapsed," Geist said. "I've noticed it, too."

"Do you think it was her sorcery?"

Geist wanted to say *no* immediately—no way her powers had been affecting them since they arrived—but Geist stopped before forming the words. What if it was the grand duchess? But why would she do it? What was the motive to harm the Ethereal Squadron when they were allies?

The door to the common room opened, and Vergess jumped to his feet.

A servant girl stepped in, a stack of clothing piled high in her arms. Defiant walked in behind her with a slight limp. He straightened himself as he approached the group and took a seat next to Dreamer. Although Geist expected him to react with shock to Dreamer's appearance, Defiant said nothing—as though nothing were even out of the ordinary.

"Excuse me," the servant girl said, a fine British accent to her words. "But Grand Duchess Anastasia has requested you for dinner."

"All of us?" Blick asked.

"O-Oh, I apologize. She only requested the presence of your commander. Everyone else is to dine with Captain Uthof of the Imperial Guard." The servant girl walked into the room and placed the clothing on an empty couch. She separated each set with care. "These are formal evening attire, so that you'll have proper garb for this evening's supper. We have a seamstress who will fix the lengths."

Geist almost threw her head back and laughed. Only when visiting a Royal House would they think it necessary to make sure everyone was *dressed properly* for dinner. It was, for all intents and purposes, a complete waste of time.

"Try to look at the bright side," Victory whispered. "If we have favor with the grand duchess, I'm sure the tsar will be more willing to lend us his aid."

The servant girl bowed her head and left.

Once alone again, Blick turned to Geist with a coy smile. "The grand duchess wants to see you alone? You're a real charmer."

She shook her head. "Now isn't the time for games."

"I bet the duchess asks you for a dance."

"For both our sakes, I hope she doesn't," Geist quipped.

Battery turned to her, his brows knitted together. "Wait, you don't know how to dance?"

Everyone in the room stopped what they were doing and stared.

The collective silence bothered Geist more than the question. Of course she knew how to dance! It had been one of the many lessons taught to her by tutors from all around the world. That wasn't the problem.

"I'm sure the grand duchess will want a *man* to dance with her," Geist drawled. "I was taught the steps for a woman. You can see how this will go poorly."

"Oh," Battery muttered. "I hadn't thought of that." He tapped his chin for a moment before smiling. Then he stood and held out his hand. "Well, it should be a simple task to teach you the opposite steps. I can help."

Tempted by his offer, Geist got to her feet, though her whole body felt cold and distant. She didn't want to risk exposing herself for some recognition from the tsar. She just wanted to complete the operation and leave.

Battery kept his hand out, but Vergess pushed it aside. He stepped in front of Geist and held out his hands.

"I'll do it," he stated.

Of the two options, Geist preferred Vergess's instruction. Then again, she didn't want to learn how to dance in front of her squad. Stumbling around like a drunkard wasn't high on her list of *team bonding.*

Geist hesitantly placed her hands on top of Vergess's. He turned them around. "You hold the woman's hands," he said. "You control what's going on." Then he nudged her, as if urging her to start the dance.

The others got out of their seats, moved the furniture to the edge of the room, and then leaned against the wall. They watched with amused half-smiles—even Defiant, who squinted the entire time. It was enough to twist Geist's stomach into knots.

Please, God. What have I done to deserve this?

She started with a few slow steps. Vergess urged Geist to go faster, even though they had no music to work with.

Which meant everything happened in painful silence.

While Geist enjoyed her close proximity to Vergess—especially since no one could complain—she couldn't enjoy a second of the event. She stutter-stepped around, hesitated for a few seconds, and pulled Vergess along by the hands, knowing full well she looked like a childish amateur. *I'm such a fool*, she thought, unable to look Vergess in the eye for fear of ridicule and mockery. *Why am I even doing this?*

For the past few years, she had trained, killed, and fought in a bloody war, yet the thought of playing the man in a ballroom dance was the thing that crippled her confidence. She had no idea what she was supposed to do, and half the time she continued to slip back into the role of the woman, secretly hoping Vergess would just take over so she could be done with the "lesson."

"Relax," Vergess whispered.

So damn easy to say.

And it didn't make things better that the others were muttering amongst themselves.

Then Blick snorted. "You're terrible."

Geist ripped her hands away from Vergess and turned away. "Yes. I agree. We should stop this."

"What?" Blick said. "We don't want to risk offending the tsar and his family, remember?"

Victory wheeled on his younger brother, a scowl that could wilt plants. Blick chortled, in no way intimidated.

"You should practice," Vergess said. "Just try again."

"Why don't you try explaining what she's doing wrong?" Dreamer interjected.

"She can learn by doing."

"A proper teacher uses every tool to teach a student."

"Yes, well, perhaps *explaining the dance* isn't my forte," Vergess barked. "Why don't *you* tell her?"

Dreamer shook his head. "I don't know how to dance. That wasn't a skill taught to eunuchs."

"Then perhaps you shouldn't offer advice on matters you know nothing of."

The odd argument got the others tense. Vergess and Dreamer stared for a long moment, but after exhaling, both men turned away.

Vergess returned his attention to Geist and held out his hand, ready to practice again.

"Why don't I try?" Victory said.

He walked around his chair, one arm still in a sling, but he held himself like only a gentleman could. Then he offered his good hand and smiled.

With his aristocratic upbringing, Geist figured Victory would know best. She exhaled and took his hand. The look Vergess gave her when she passed—it was fleeting—was like he wanted to object, but couldn't.

"You don't need to worry about the grand duchess discovering your secret," Victory said. "She won't have her hands all over you. That's improper." He motioned to his hip. "You place your hand here. She will place a hand on your shoulder. And while you may come together in the dance, I doubt she will notice anything through the layers of formal clothing."

"Th-thanks," Geist muttered. The simple explanation did put her at ease.

Victory continued, "The key to leading a dance is to control everything from your torso—the core momentum coming from your center of gravity. The woman may be holding one of your hands, but she'll feel the way you shift from your torso first."

When Victory swayed side to side, Geist felt the movement. It dawned on her then, like someone pulling back the curtains to reveal the truth. Dancing did come from the torso. Why had she been trying to pull Vergess by the hands? It seemed so foolish now.

"You try," Victory said.

Although she still felt ridiculous, Geist attempted to lead Victory around the room. To her surprise, he began humming. Although she had never considered his voice soothing or lyrical, the pleasant melody he provided for their faux dance reminded her of a quiet evening in London she once shared with her mother and younger brother, Dietrich. It made it easy to keep pace and focus on the footwork. Much easier than silence.

The others whispered among themselves, but Geist didn't feel as ridiculous as before. *At least I'm actually dancing.*

Halfway around the room, Geist stared up at Victory, closer than she had ever been with him before. He had a slight scar over his right eye—one that altered the way his eyebrow grew and affected his eyelashes. He had gotten the scar when they fought the German U-boat. A decision Geist had made. During the fight, a piece of glass had dug its way into his face, and Cross didn't get a chance to heal Victory until weeks later.

Then Geist glanced down at Victory's arm resting in the sling.

That was my fault, too.

Victory paused his humming to say, "And if the lady makes a misstep, you apologize."

"Really?" Geist asked as she returned her attention to him.

"Of course. As the gentleman, and the lead, you take responsibility for all mistakes. Always."

Shaken by Victory's words, and the scars on his body—*all due to her mistakes*—Geist continued to keep his gaze. It took her a moment, even while they danced, to whisper, "I'm sorry, Victory."

She didn't say anything else, but the look Victory offered in reply told her everything. He knew what she meant.

Instead of saying something cutting or hurtful, he gave her smile. "A gracious lady will always accept the apology. Everyone makes mistakes."

"I didn't mean for you to get injured, and—"

"I've already accepted your apology," Victory said. "And it's considered rude to speak in the middle of a dance. You should focus on keeping the appropriate distance and making sure the lady is enjoying herself."

Damn Victory and his perfect responses, Geist thought as she completed the circle around the room. The words they exchanged put her more at ease than his instructions, and although she wasn't perfect, Geist felt much better about dancing with the grand duchess.

"You'll use your future sight to see if I make a fool of myself, won't you?" Geist asked.

Victory chuckled. "Don't worry. From what I've seen, you'll somehow make her an ally. And, well, in a few outcomes, you upset her beyond repair, but those are much rarer. Don't spill tea on her dress, by the way. It seems to end terribly for you."

"I'll try to keep that in mind."

They stopped the dance where they started, and Battery gave a round of applause. No one else joined in the celebration, though. Blick rolled his eyes and walked over.

"Maybe *I* should give you a few quick tips to get the duchess's heart beating fast." He motioned Victory out of the way and offered his hands. "The real key is to breathe softly on the lady's neck. I'll demonstrate."

Vergess grabbed Blick by the collar of his uniform and jerked back. Blick stumbled, tried to rip himself free, but ultimately couldn't.

"She isn't trying to bed the grand duchess," Vergess growled. "You don't need to give her any pointers beyond dancing."

Blick straightened himself and smiled. "What's wrong? Worried you can't compare?"

Vergess tightened his grip on Blick's tunic. If he wanted, his *ruina* sorcery would waste Blick in an instant, and Geist knew she had to come between them before anything escalated. She stood, in a mild disbelief that they were even arguing, but Defiant huffed loud enough to garner everyone's attention.

"As much as I would love to see Vergess hospitalize my least favorite member of this crew, I do think a fight will get us thrown back in the holding cells."

Dreamer shook his head. "The two of you are acting like school children. What's gotten into you?"

"Nothing," Vergess said as he released Blick. He turned and moved away, stiff.

Although she found it endearing that he wanted to save her from Blick's seduction lessons, Geist didn't know how to handle the argument. A piece of Geist blamed herself, since she doubted the situation would have occurred if she weren't a woman in a disguise, but there was no changing that fact. She was what she was. Now how would she handle the new dynamics that arose?

Uncertain of how to proceed, Geist grabbed some of the formal clothing and examined her options. She would have to meet the grand duchess first.

GEIST DIDN'T like men's formalwear.

She didn't like *any* formalwear outside of standard military uniforms. Not because they didn't feel comfortable, but because of what they reminded her of. Once upon a time, her father groomed her to be a queen—to marry the prince of Austria-Hungary. Now, whenever she saw dresses and coattails, it brought back the memories, spoiling her mood and eroding away her happiness, one ballroom song at a time.

The Russian outfit came complete with a stiff leather belt, white pants, a blue tunic, and golden tassels on the shoulders. Geist felt like an oil painting. She fidgeted with each step, irritated by the knee-high boots. Once she reached her destination, she knocked on the dining room door with a gloved hand.

The door opened a moment later, and the same servant girl bowed her head.

"Greetings."

Geist replied with a nod and stepped inside.

Extravagance poured from the walls and pooled across the floor. Ivory, gold, silver, and paintings as long as a cargo truck adorned every inch of space. A long table, complete with polished silverware and delicate china, was positioned in the middle of the room. The grand duchess, however, was nowhere to be seen.

"Am I early?" Geist asked.

The servant frowned. "Many apologies. Her Grace will be with you shortly. She's tending to her family at the moment."

Tending to her family? Geist didn't understand what that meant, nor did she get an opportunity to ask for clarification. The servant girl hustled from the room, almost as if avoiding any conversation as fast as she could. Once the door snapped shut, Geist stood alone in the gilded room, her thoughts wandering. She smoothed the sleeves of her borrowed uniform more times than she could count.

Minutes passed, with only the ticking of a mechanical clock to keep the silence at bay.

The absence of the grand duchess worried Geist. Perhaps she could go look? Although she didn't want to get caught—and create a diplomatic incident—she also wanted to know more about the Russian Empire and its ruling family. If she could gather information, wouldn't it be advantageous?

Geist sighed and resigned herself to investigation.

Even if the grand duchess arrives while I'm gone, I can say I just needed to use the restroom. No one would fault me for that.

Cloaking herself in her *specter* sorcery, Geist crept up to the wall and ghosted through. The hallway, lit with electric lights, was empty. No guards. No servants. Where were they? Geist pushed the thoughts from her head as she continued through the massive palace.

She didn't stop at doors or even use the normal route of travel. Instead, she slid through walls, examined rooms, and made her way through with an unconventional path. Bathrooms, storerooms, studies, and personal libraries littered the palace. A few times she spotted ladies-in-waiting and governess' going about their work, but she ignored them. When Geist got closer to the center of the palace, however, she found where all the Imperial Guards were stationed.

They waited at doors, by the hydraulic lift, and even patrolled through the rooms. Knowing that some of them could see through invisibility with their glowing golden eyes, Geist avoided them physically. She stepped through a wall and came to an abrupt stop.

Vergess, Blick, and Battery stood next to a kitchen island, each of them leaning on the nearby countertop. Their Russian formalwear, less fancy than Geist's, fit them all well enough. Blick's strained at his biceps, and Battery's had obviously been made shorter, but otherwise they all could have passed for Russians—had they grown mustaches.

"I just don't like him," Blick said. "He's a twat."

Battery shrugged. "Everyone else gets along with him fine."

"Oh, yeah? Vergess, you too?"

Vergess turned in Geist's direction, his eyebrows knit together.

He stared for a long moment, his gaze on the floor, but he eventually forced his attention back to Blick. "I think his codename suits him. *Defiant.* I have respect for a man who refuses to bend his morals."

"Is that true, though?" Blick asked. He snapped his fingers. "He *did* bend. He made all those weapons for the enemy. Then he hated himself for it. If anything, he's a coward for running from his problems."

"I defected from the Kaiser Guard after years of service. Am I a coward, too?"

Blick chuckled. Then he fumbled with his words for a moment, as though unsure of how to proceed. "It's different with you. You're a soldier. Raised to be that way. Defiant had to... study the best ways to mutilate people. He had to be *innovative.* Which means he gave his atrocities a lot more thought." Blick waved away the comment. "I just think it's different. I'm not keen on him."

Although Geist could've stayed and listened to their conversation for hours—if only to know their inner thoughts on the rest of the Ethereal Squadron—she felt guilty for listening without their permission. And she had to make her way back to the dining room eventually.

Leaving the kitchen, she ghosted through a small pantry and then into another hall. An ornate staircase caught her eye, and she went up, careful not to creak the wood or disturb the fine carpeting.

The second story hallway, darker than the rest of the house, had an aura of depression that oozed from the somber oil paintings and blood-red wallpaper. To Geist's fascination, opals were used in most of the accents—embedded in the corners of picture frames or decorating the vases—and they glittered with an inner intensity.

Opals resonated with magic, Geist had always known, but now she paid more attention to them than ever before. Defiant used them in his magi-tech. They were, in essence, a magical resource, and the Royal House Romanov used them as house dressings.

After wandering a few feet, she knew she had found the grand duchess. Whispering, all in Russian, echoed out of a lone room. The door sat ajar.

Geist moved closer and waited.

Sobbing.

More Russian.

The talking stopped. Geist moved closer to the open door, but didn't bother going in all the way. Instead, she ghosted through the wall, careful to go slow, and the moment she could see on the other side, she examined the room.

In every way, it was a personal sanctuary.

Wooden soldiers filled a wall-long bookshelf. The bed, larger than most rooms, had a thick canopy that provided privacy. A sitting area, complete with a small library of reading materials, occupied the far corner, but never crowded the rest of the furniture.

Geist had found the grand duchess and who she assumed was her brother. The duchess wore a gown of scintillating white, accented with velvet black ivy that "grew" from the back and wrapped around to the front. Her brother, the tsesarevich, no older than thirteen, sat on the edge of the bed, his whole body trembling. Blood dripped from his right palm, spilling onto his pants and soaking into the fabric. He wore a miniature version of a Russian officer's uniform, and the spots of crimson only added to the realism of the attire.

Two men, both wearing the uniforms of the Russian navy, stood back, deep frowns on their faces. Two ladies-in-waiting held towels and bowls of warm water. They hovered close, wiping up the young boy's hand whenever they could, but they hesitated when touching him.

It almost looked like... the injury on his hand widened with each tiny motion he made. His puffy face, covered in a slight shine of tears, hardened somewhat as he stared at the wound.

One lady-in-waiting attempted to use sorcery—Geist could feel the chill of her magic the moment she touched the tsesarevich's hand—but it only seemed to make the injury worse. Blood gushed from the palm, and the boy cried out.

"Shh, shh, Alexei," the grand duchess whispered.

Had the servant woman attempted *corpus* sorcery? It healed

others. Geist had seen it work numerous times when Cross healed the soldiers. Why hadn't it worked with Tsesarevich Alexei?

Satisfied she understood enough, Geist slid back through the wall. Before she went all the way through, her attention snapped to a poster on the nearby wall. A Boy Scouts poster. One from America. It confused Geist for a moment, just because she never thought she'd see one in Russia, but it had been signed by an Eagle Scout, welcoming Alexei as part of a troop.

Geist left the room, both curious and somewhat guilty. Whatever was happening with the tsesarevich, it wasn't her place to pry. She left the hall, flew down the stairs, and rushed back to the dining room without anyone ever noticing.

SEVENTEEN

Fog of War

An entire hour crawled by as Geist waited for the Grand Duchess to arrive. She had plenty of time to dwell on what she had seen. The tsar's son, Alexei, was ill. A type of illness not even sorcery could cure.

The far door opened, and Geist snapped to attention.

Grand Duchess Anastasia walked into the room, bags under her eyes, though covered with a slight hint of makeup. She forced a smile and gave Geist a nod of her head. "Commander. Thank you for joining me."

"Just us, Your Grace?" Geist asked as she glanced around. No servants had ever returned.

"Yes. I hope that's not inconvenient. Do you require servants?"

Geist almost laughed. She had eaten tin rations in the trenches —she definitely didn't *need* servants. *I just thought every member of a Royal House would demand them.*

Somehow more nervous than before, Geist walked to the table and pulled out a chair. The grand duchess accepted the invitation to sit and then motioned to the chair next to her.

"Please sit next to me."

Geist couldn't think of a reason to deny the request so took a seat next to Grand Duchess Anastasia. The long table felt emptier than before. It had been built with forty people in mind, and with two at one end, it was almost like dining on the bow of a boat.

"It's quiet," Geist said. "Do you eat every meal like this?"

"Papa wanted us to know the tranquility of a simple life," the grand duchess said. "We eat most meals like this, so we can better know each other through conversation."

"Very interesting, Your Grace." *Nothing like how my father handled dinners.*

Grand Duchess Anastasia wrinkled her nose, and Geist figured she had done something else wrong. *Did I say 'Your Grace' too many times or something?*

The grand duchess touched Geist's knuckles for a brief moment. "When we're alone, call me Anastasie."

"The French version of your name?" Geist asked as she rubbed the back of her hand. "Why?"

"I like it better than *Your Grace*. And it's what my sisters call me. It seems more… familiar. Better for conversations." Anastasie tilted her head. "My captain of the guard said your codename was Geist. What's your real name?"

"I'm in the middle of an operation. I'm sorry, but I shouldn't reveal those kinds of details, even if we are alone."

"Operation?"

"A covert mission conducted by special forces operatives. My team and I are here to help sorcerers who are being targeted by the enemy. That's why I need to speak with Tsar Nicholas. It's beyond important."

Geist added the last sentence to really hammer home the point. Did Anastasie even realize how crucial it was that they see the tsar? Geist wanted to make sure the grand duchess hadn't forgotten.

"And you command a whole team of special operatives?" Anastasie asked, her eyes wide.

"Yes."

"I'm impressed. Papa says short men breed weakness, but he's obviously not met someone of your caliber."

Geist opened her mouth to retort, but held back the comment.

146

I'm not supposed to cause a diplomatic incident. But something about the comment bothered her more than before. Not because she was short —she had never cared—but she hated the thought someone would think *Battery* was a man of weakness, simply because of his height. He was a fine soldier, and Geist couldn't imagine the war without him. How could the tsar preemptively judge him?

"I'm sorry if my sorcery hindered you." Anastasie turned away. She held a hand to the collar of her dress.

"Your sorcery? I'm not sure what it is."

"All members of the Royal House Romanov have access to *victoriam magnam*," Anastasie said. "It's the *Fog of War* of sorcery. It, well, harms the minds of sorcerers, and the longer they're affected, the worse it becomes. After a while, they lose focus, have pains in their head, and then they can't use their sorcery. I suppose, if drawn out, it would eventually drive them insane. And then kill them."

Geist caught her breath.

The headaches really had come from the grand duchess. But Geist couldn't believe it. She had experienced the headaches since crossing the border of the nation—hundreds of miles away from Alexander Palace.

"Your servants," Geist whispered. "The ones with *potentia* sorcery... They've been empowering your *victoriam magnam*. You've been using your sorcery to blanket all of the Russian Empire in your protection."

It was almost unimaginable—personal sorcery never extended so far! First telepathy, and now the ability to slow drain and kill one's enemies. And the grand duchess was only sixteen, perhaps seventeen. She had come a long way in mastering her magic, even if she had been empowered by three others.

"That's right," Anastasie said. "I protect my countrymen. But it's hard when I never get to see them."

"Why don't you travel your nation?"

"I... want to. But Papa doesn't want me to leave the palace. Mama and my little brother stay to the inner sanctuary. She's sick, and so is little Alexei. I'm supposed to help them instead of my nation." Anastasie met Geist's eyes, a tiredness in her gaze that seeped to the rest of her features. "The war has taken its toll on Papa. He isn't the same, and the many attempts on his life have left him paranoid. I wanted to help… so I've been practicing my sorcery."

"Does your sorcery affect your own soldiers?"

"No. I can control it, to a degree. Right now, I'm not targeting anyone who has sworn loyalty to the empire, which is why the Bolsheviks still operate without hindrance. They think they're *helping* all of the Russian Empire with their revolts." She forced herself to smile. "I can exclude you and your team, as well. Now that I know you exist and who you are—it shouldn't be difficult."

"I'm impressed," Geist said. "Genuinely."

Anastasie perked up. "It means the world to hear an American say that."

"An American?"

"Yes! Aren't all of you gallivanting across deserts and taming the wild? I've heard of American sorcerers bending the mountains to their will and even normal men building hundreds of miles of train tracks through barren wastelands."

"W-Well, I guess there is some of that."

"Please tell me!" She moved to the edge of her seat, her knees touching Geist's. "I've always fancied stories of the Americas, ever since I was a little girl."

Geist inched away, uncertain of what to say. Victory made it sound as though she would win Anastasie over, but this wasn't what Geist had expected. What good ol' American stories could she regale the grand duchess with?

The thought of weaving a fantastical tale bothered her more than anything else. Geist had never considered herself a "social" person.

"Uh," Geist rubbed at her neck. "Perhaps we can engage in a different activity? Would you care to dance?"

"Oh, no, no. Mama has me dance enough as it is. I rarely get to speak with an actual person from outside the palace. Please. Tell me about the Americas."

Damn.

It took Geist a solid minute to think of a few stories. "Have you heard of Betsy Ross?"

Anastasie shook her head. "Oh, yes. Many times. It's trite and boring. Tell me something *exciting.*"

"Well, er, there was a sorcerer by the name of Mike Flint. He was the *king of the keelboaters* because he used to brawl other men on a rickety keelboat. Does that interest you?"

"Were the fights gruesome?" Anastasie asked, covering her mouth with her fingers.

"They were rough and tumble."

"Fascinating. Please continue. In detail."

"Uh… why don't you tell me about your family? Your brother… you said he was ill."

The sight of Alexei wouldn't leave Geist's mind. He had bled, even when healed, and now it was apparent Anastasie couldn't leave the palace because she was his keeper. Could the bleeding have something to do with the Eyes of the Kaiser?

Anastasie fidgeted with her strawberry-blonde hair, her hands shaking.

"Is everything all right?" Geist asked.

"My brother is going through a bout of illness," Anastasie said, no emotion in her voice. "He has recovered from worse. I'm sure he will pull through. We must have faith."

Although she wore white, Geist saw no red smudges or stains. Somehow, she had interacted with her brother without coming into contact with his blood.

"Have you tried healing sorcery?" Geist asked.

"We… we have. Many times."

Her voice wavered, and Geist knew it was only a matter of moments before the grand duchess lost her composure. Should she push the subject? Geist wanted to press further.

"Does the magic not work?" she asked.

Anastasie shook her head. "You don't understand. A magical blood disease runs through the line of our mother, all the way from the first sorcerers. Sorcery makes it worse. Except… except for

Honorable Rasputin. His sorcery always made Mama and Alexei feel better, but without him, I don't know what we'll do."

Geist took her seat back at the table and then offered a smile. "One of my squad is a knowledgeable researcher of sorcery. Do you think Alexei would be comfortable with another sorcerer examining his illness?"

"You would order one of your men to help Alexei?" Anastasie asked, breathless. She reached out and grabbed Geist's hand. "I knew Americans were kind, but I never imagined you would play the role of guardian angels."

"Uh, well, I can't promise anything, but I trust Defiant to find some solution to the problem."

It was more than that. Geist didn't want to drag Defiant around the Russian Empire without his glasses. Alexander Palace was also one of the most fortified places within a few hundred miles. The Imperial Guard, run by a sorcerer, stalked the palace grounds, and the entire city seemed to have soldiers waiting in every corner.

Defiant would be safe while he recovered. And Geist could take her team to deal with House Menshov.

"Alexei loves the Ethereal Squadron," Anastasie said as she smiled. It was like she regained her strength and happiness—one moment she was melancholy and the next exuberant. "Ever since Papa made him a Lance Corporal, he's enjoyed issuing orders to sorcerers."

"Alexei? Isn't he too young to be a Lance Corporal?"

"All sorcerer men of the Royal House Romanov take officer rank in the military." Anastasie shook her head. "Since our sorcery revolves around the fog of war, it's a tradition."

"You say it like you're disappointed."

She shook her head. "No. I'm worried. Alexei has never taken well to *victoriam magnam* sorcery. And, well, neither has Papa. I fear they may rely on it in the wrong moment, and then—"

The door to the dining room opened a second time, and multiple servants walked in to present the food. They brought duck, steamed vegetables, a fine soup, and a tray of tea.

Geist jumped up and took the food immediately. The grand

duchess's hands still trembled, and Geist couldn't stand the thought of her pouring her own drink and spilling on herself. She took painstaking care to serve the grand duchess, including pouring her tea.

"You have a lovely dress," Geist said as she scooted the cup farther from the edge of the table.

"It was my Grandmama's. It means the world to me to wear it like this. Almost as if I'm a woman now."

Geist understood why spilling tea would have ruined the evening. *Victory is always right.*

Anastasie stroked the velvet ivy and smiled to herself. "It's so difficult, with this war, to really grasp what's going on. I just hope that I'm helping the people of Russia. I… sometimes feel like I'm too small to affect things, even if I'm a grand duchess."

The sentiment hit home with Geist. When she had lived under her father's rule, and in her mother's care, she had felt powerless. So many things were out of her control. But after joining the Ethereal Squadron, Geist understood what it meant to take the reins of personal destiny. Sometimes the weight of responsibility dug deep, but it was better than watching as everything was decided for her.

"Have you thought about joining the war effort officially?" Geist asked.

Anastasie sighed. "Papa says I must watch Mama and Alexei."

"What if Defiant, my squad member, can help them? Would you consider joining then?"

"I wouldn't hesitate." Anastasie scooted to the edge of her chair, her eyes wide, her posture straight. "I've tried to tell Papa—he doesn't listen to anyone, though—but I would love to help the people and do things with my own hands."

The desperation in her voice added to Geist's realization. Anastasie wanted to protect her country. She wanted to fight in the war. Maybe not like a special operative, since she was so young and frail, but perhaps as someone like Cross, Defiant, or Tinker. Someone who helped and mattered in the war effort. And with an ability like *victoriam magnam* sorcery, it could be very useful.

"Thank you," Anastasie said as she brought the teacup to her lips. "I appreciate your time. The moment I know when my papa will arrive at the palace, I will let you know. He's far to the south, however, and he seems preoccupied…"

"I have things to accomplish in the meantime," Geist said. "As long as you sent my warning, I think we'll be able to save all the Russian sorcerers who are in danger."

Anastasie nodded. "Yes. Of course, commander. I will make sure your messages are delivered." Then she saluted—with the wrong hand—which got Geist laughing.

An odd thought crossed her mind. Wouldn't Anastasie's sorcery be better with *four* people who could empower her? Would it help all of the Russian Empire to have blanket of sorcery that hindered all enemy forces?

"Anastasie, would you mind if I left a soldier to watch over you?" Geist asked. "Battery has *potentia* sorcery as well. Perhaps he can aid you in some way."

The grand duchess placed her cup on its saucer and answered with a squirrel-like giggle. "I would like that very much, especially if he can tell me stories of the front."

GEIST STOOD at the edge of the Alexander Palace, watching the harsh winds bringing with them another layer of snow. The morning breeze, although chilly, was refreshing. A single motorcar drove up the driveway and parked at the bottom of the stairs.

"You don't want to bring Victory?" Dreamer asked.

He had donned his illusionary disguise once again, masking his origins and resuming the identity of an Englishman.

"He needs to rest," Geist said.

Dreamer shrugged. "They have healers here, even if they aren't as proficient as the healers near the front lines in Verdun. He can get a bit of sorcery and be capable of moving."

"I'd prefer he rested."

And she already knew what Victory had to say. He said the trek would likely happen without incident and that they would return quicker than expected. With such good news, Geist almost couldn't wait until the operation was over. They had only two more houses to warn.

Vergess took his place by her side, silent as usual. He crossed his arms and kept his gaze distant, though anytime Geist looked over, he met her glance.

Blick stretched. "It's just us four, then? No one else?"

"I think we'll be able to handle House Menshov," Geist replied. "We'll take them to the Petrograd ports. If the boats aren't running, we'll take a train back to Riga, and then they can leave."

"How long do you think we'll be?"

"A couple days at the most. It should be a quick outing."

EIGHTEEN

House Menshov

Without the aid of someone who spoke Russian, navigating the streets of Petrograd proved troublesome. Ice coated everything. From her boots, to her pants, to her breath—it burned to breathe through her nose, and it stung if her eyes remained open too wide.

Fortunately, Dreamer found a carriage with a driver who understood enough broken English to take them to their destination, and the sorcerers of House Menshov were marked as speaking both English and French fluently. There was no need to have a Russian guide for their short trek.

They continued through the streets of Petrograd, one side of the road marked with white words and rude pictures—the opposite side marked with red in equal amounts of vulgarity. The frigid weather hardly bothered the denizens as they shuffled by, but Geist was certain she would never know warmth again. She shivered continually, even within the safety of her carriage. She glanced over at Vergess, who sat next to her, but she turned away, knowing full well it wasn't the time to engage in physical contact. Even if he would be warm.

"*Lean on him,*" Blick said, his voice straight to Geist's mind.

She snapped her attention to him—he sat directly across from her—and he replied with a coy smirk. Unable to respond with telepathic words, Geist shook her head and looked out the window. What was his game? To irritate her?

"Why wouldn't you?" Blick continued. *"Victory isn't here to talk about protocol. Defiant isn't here to get snippy. Dreamer and I won't mind."* He elbowed Dreamer and said aloud, "You have things to write down, right?"

"I suppose I do," Dreamer said. He brushed himself off like Blick had left dander and opened his book.

Geist didn't know why Blick was so insistent. He motioned for her to get it over with, and she responded with a slight shake of her head, hoping Vergess and Dreamer weren't seeing her bizarre mannerisms. *Why must everyone be so difficult?*

"Place your hand on his shoulder," Blick said. He mimicked the gesture with Dreamer—his hand half an inch from Dreamer's shoulder, so as to not disturb him. *"Then tell Vergess you're cold and you want him to cuddle you."*

Geist glared. *I'm not doing that. Not here. Not now.* She hoped her expression conveyed the message clear enough.

"C'mon. I'm trying to help you. I saw the way you both danced back at the palace. I've seen coatracks with better chemistry." Blick smiled wide as he leaned forward. *"I know. You can place a hand on his knee. Trust me. It's a clear indication a woman likes a man. The knee is one of the most intimate places a person can touch another. In public, I mean."*

"I'm not touching his knee," Geist mouthed. *What is his problem?*

"Is something wrong?" Vergess asked.

Geist shook her head and leaned away. "N-nope. I'm fine. You're knee. *I mean*—everything is fine. No problems."

The following silence twisted in Geist's gut. Why was Blick trying so hard? She knew she was awkward—she had been ever since she was a girl—and having someone point it out only made the situation worse. This wasn't the time for such behavior. *It never is,* she thought. *And it won't be until the war is over.*

Blick made a dramatic show of placing his own hand on his own knee. Geist narrowed her eyes into a glower. As if to extra make the point, Blick placed his hand on Dreamer's knee.

With a sarcastically slow glance, Dreamer turned his attention to Blick, one eyebrow cocked, his pencil poised on the page of his book. The two men stared at each other for a moment, and Geist knew Blick had to be explaining the situation with his telepathy. Dreamer let out a short exhale and returned to his book, unfazed by the bizarre interaction.

"*See?*" Blick said. "*We're all doing it. No need to get self-conscious.*" He motioned with his other hand, urging Geist to continue. She pursued her lips and glared, her face hot, her body no longer chilled from the Russian temperature.

How do Victory and Battery put up with this at home?

Vergess stared at Blick, then his hand. "Are you… touching Dreamer?"

"We were having a moment," Blick replied as he took his hand back. "No big deal."

"Uh-huh."

The bumpy carriage ride didn't help anyone's mood. The two men glowered at each for a long moment. After a few minutes, they turned away, and Blick became silent. Fortunately, the journey didn't take much longer. A couple hours and they arrived on the long road to House Menshov. A large fence and gate blocked the path to the estate. The carriage driver rode up, and men in heavy coats walked over from their posts, cigarettes held tightly in their mouths.

Geist opened the carriage door and stepped outside. It took all her willpower to keep her teeth from chattering. The grand duchess had given them a code word to use.

"American," she said and then pointed to herself. "We're here to see Lady Menshov."

The men gave each other quick glances before waving their hands. They walked back to their post and opened the wrought iron gates. The screech of the iced-over metal hurt Geist's ears, but she was glad they hadn't attempted to turn her away.

She hopped back in the carriage and then stared down the long road to the manse.

To Geist's surprise, every half mile there was another fence and iron gate, each manned with men. They carried rifles and open sidearms. Some even had a bandoleer of grenades. They conducted themselves not as sorcerers, but as normal men. There were enough to fill a whole company—and there was no way House Menshov had hired them all in the last few hours. Which meant they had already been on the estate long before Geist had sent her warning.

After the first gate, however, the men didn't require any more questioning. They opened each gate without any words exchanged.

"So, Victory predicted this meeting would be quick, huh?" Blick asked.

Geist nodded. "He said we would likely return to Alexander Palace after only a few hours here."

"Maybe they agree to leave the Russian Empire and they already have their bags packed."

"I have a bad feeling about this," Vergess said as he stared out the frosted carriage window. "Look at the decorations on the fences and walls."

Geist glanced outside. The midafternoon light streamed through thinning clouds and illuminated the Menshov estate. Each fence, made with iron bars and stone walls, had been meticulously crafted. The Menshov coat of arms—a man in heavy armor atop a two-headed horse—had been carved into the stone and twisted into the wrought iron.

"What about them?" Geist asked.

"Count the number of gates we had to pass through."

"Several. What's your point?"

"My point is that this house is somewhat entrenched in their history. We haven't even reached the front door, and already they've made it clear that they value their home, blood, and prestige. If I had to guess, Victory's vision was of us failing to convince them and returning without success."

Blick tapped the glass with his knuckles. "Maybe we discover they're well protected. The grand duchess did warn them, after all. If they aren't going to die, that's just as good as bringing them back to Verdun."

"I'm on Vergess's side," Dreamer interjected. "Out of all the houses we were supposed to visit, this one is the oldest and has been an aristocratic house longer than the rest. I figured they would offer the most resistance to moving."

The more Geist heard about the family, the more she agreed with the assessment. Did that mean House Menshov would send them away within the hour? The thought irritated Geist more than expected.

We already lost sorcerers at House Kott. I'm not going to let House Menshov fall to the same squad of enemies. The Eyes of the Kaiser, coupled with an infiltration specialist like a fleshcrafter, make everything unsafe—it doesn't matter how many fences they have. I'll have to force the sorcerers of House Menshov to see reason.

"We're not leaving until we convince them," Geist stated.

Dreamer, Vergess, and Blick responded with serious expressions. Each of them nodded.

The real question was: how would they go about persuading an old aristocratic family that they should move out of their home territory?

"Dreamer, do you think it would be possible to give us more noble appearances?" Geist asked. "Something high class, but not flashy."

"Of course," he said.

He touched everyone's knee, his fingers lingering for a few seconds before heading to the next. Magic spread from the location of his touch, weaving itself across the clothing. While Dreamer could make powerful illusions, he couldn't make them appear without a base. They acted like a paint—coating something in existence, and without a medium, they couldn't exist.

When his sorcery finished, Geist, Blick, and Vergess each had a new outfit. Geist wore an American uniform, specifically an officer variant from the union north. Blick wore a British design, bright red and crisp white. Vergess also sported the design of the Americas, but more modern, in a muted grey.

Dreamer changed himself faster than the others. Practically in an instant, he had the grand design of a duke. He even gave himself a thick mustache.

"Do you like it?" Dreamer asked.

Geist nodded. "Beautiful."

"But why?"

"I think I have a negotiating angle that will help us convince them to move."

The moment their illusions were complete, the carriage came to a stop. Geist held her breath as she slid out of the door and stepped into the biting cold. House Menshov—a manse with an icy exterior that rivaled the weather—had no color. Pillars surrounded the compound, but they looked more like bars on a prison. Statues of monsters, perhaps gargoyles, lined the edge of the roof.

Vergess, Blick, and Dreamer joined her outside. Together, they made their way to the front door. A pair of guards greeted them with a bow and then opened the door.

Warmth washed over her the moment Geist stepped into the building. With a shiver to dislodge any snow on her person, she made her way to the center of the entrance hall. The lavish frescos, carpets, and tapestries were starting to be common sights. The Russian Empire had taken care of its sorcerers.

"Ah, members of Ethereal Squadron."

A woman in a jade dress walked down the single massive staircase that led to the upper story. Her train fluttered down each step as she walked, creating a green waterfall effect. She brushed aside her auburn hair and stared down at the group with a forced smile.

"I'm Lady Menshov," she said. "It's a pleasure to meet you."

Geist couldn't help but note how thin she was. Almost skeletal.

It was then that Geist noticed the numerous guards at the top of the staircase. They didn't carry rifles, but Geist was familiar with the bulge of a hidden sidearm. The men spread themselves out on the second story balcony.

"I'm Geist. Commander within the Ethereal Squadron." Geist offered a deep bow. "I'm delighted to be here."

"Is that so?" Lady Menshov asked.

"Yes." Geist stood once more, hoping to look a tad bit taller. "Everyone has heard of the mighty capital of the Russian Empire. I wanted to see it with my own eyes before… well, before anything happens to it."

Lady Menshov walked the last few steps into the entrance hall, her head high, her chin slightly up. "Whatever are you referring to, my darling? Saint Petersburg—or Petrograd, whatever you want to call it—will stand for eternity. It's the heart of a nation that's never been destroyed."

"Lady Menshov," Geist said. "Forgive me, but that's not why I've come calling."

"I've heard you wanted to warn me about enemy agents."

"Yes."

"As you can see," Lady Menshov said as she gestured to her surroundings, "I've always put safety first. Any assassins in the middle of the night will be riddled with bullets. And if they live through that, they will taste my family's sorcery. Surely there is nothing to worry about." She tilted her head, her slender neck adorned with polished pearls. "I appreciate the concern, but you're unfamiliar with House Menshov. We're a sturdy people."

So, she is prepared, Geist thought. *This must've been what Victory saw—and Vergess was right. She's going to try and send us away.*

Geist smoothed her fancy outfit and took a step closer. "Have you been outside your estate lately, Lady Menshov? The city of Petrograd is embroiled in conflict. Each day the war drags on, it agitates the people. Tell me—do you think your tiny piece of property, located near the heart of political conflict, will weather a peasant demonstration? Or a full-blown riot?"

Vergess, Blick, and Dreamer gave her sideways glances, as though catching on to her plan all at the same time.

If Lady Menshov felt safe, she would never leave. But if her well-being was called into question, perhaps the idea of leaving wouldn't seem so repugnant.

"That's why I came here," Geist said. "There are many moving pieces in the Russian Empire. The front lines are moving inward, and the people are restless. Yes, there are enemy agents, and maybe your guards can protect you against them, but they're a symptom of the greater problem."

Lady Menshov held onto the ground floor banister of the staircase. It was a wooden carving of a bat monster, and she stroked the head of the creature for a long moment as she mulled over the details of the situation.

"You have the tsar's permission to speak with me on such matters?" she asked. "You're implying revolution. Surely the tsar would not take kindly to such rumors."

Geist took a breath and held it, her mind flashing through a million scenarios. Did she lie? *I have to. I can't let her stay here.*

"I have his permission," Geist said. "That's why I sent word from Alexander Palace. This is a serious matter that cannot be overlooked."

Out of the corner of her eye, Geist spotted movement upstairs. At first, she thought it was guards—overzealous and perhaps targeting her and the others—but when she glanced up, she noticed it was a pair of teenagers, one boy and one girl. They moved behind the guards the moment they met Geist's eye. Too fast for Geist to get a good look.

"Where would we even go?" Lady Menshov asked with a forced laugh. "I'm used to a certain standard of living. Not many places can accommodate sorcerers as great as the ones in my family."

"You be surprised by the accommodations of the United States." Geist stood proud, hoping her fancier outfit would speak for itself. "We might be a new nation, but we've learned from our European brethren. Aristocrats from all over come to the Americas to start a new life with vast estates."

Although Blick didn't normally speak in meetings of great importance, he stepped forward and offered a small bow. "If I can be so bold, my lady. Have you seen the paintings by Frederic Church?"

"Of course," Lady Menshov said. "Who doesn't know of Church's beautiful landscape paintings?"

"The war won't last forever." Blick smiled—he had an easygoing air about him—and then he continued, "Can you imagine the other ladies in court when you describe how you saw those breathtaking landscapes in person? You'd be the envy of the ball."

While Geist had seen many paintings by Frederic Church, the only one she could ever recall was titled *Cotopaxi*. The harsh red hues, stark shadows, and ominous sun reminded her of war, even though the painting was nothing more than a landscape. Something about the brush strokes called to her soul. The man was a brilliant painter, and if he could tempt Lady Menshov into visiting America, Geist promised she would hunt down one of his paintings and purchase it for herself.

Lady Menshov brought her fingers to her bottom lip. "Is this some sort of attempt by the Americas to steal Russian sorcerers?"

"I'm British, my lady," Blick said.

"As am I," Dreamer added. "The Ethereal Squadron only wishes to protect sorcerers who would be targeted by the enemy."

Geist could hardly believe how well it was going. Lady Menshov dwelled on the information, obviously taking it to heart. *Could we really sway her? Maybe Victory was just correct. Maybe we will help her and return to Alexander Palace in a matter of hours.*

"The tension has been thick," Lady Menshov muttered.

"Even the streets of Petrograd are marked with agitators," Geist added. "Surely that's proof enough."

"Very well. I will speak with the rest of the sorcerers and we will contemplate leaving for an extended vacation. Perhaps a cruise around the Americas to relieve us of the wartime stress." Lady Menshov said the last bit with the back of her hand to her forehead.

The lavish surroundings, separated from the fighting, made the last statement ring hollow, but Geist kept the comment to herself. She didn't care why Lady Menshov left, just that she *would* be leaving.

Thank goodness. Only two houses left to visit.

NINETEEN

Riots

"Victory is always right," Blick said.

He shrugged and leaned back on the carriage bench. He and Dreamer shared one side, but Blick took up more than his fair share. Dreamer didn't seem to mind. He kept to himself, writing notes and letters.

Vergess kept his arms crossed and his eyes on the floor.

While Geist still felt energized after their quick victory in House Menshov, she worried about the other houses. Why would the tsar have spoken to them already? Was he pressuring them into joining the military? It would make sneaking them out of the Russian Empire entirely too difficult.

Just House Solovyev and House Lungin remaining, Geist thought. *Perhaps there's even a way to proceed with this faster. If we had the heads of the house meet me together, then I could convince them both at the same time. It would save me the hassle of traveling and ensure I helped them as quickly as possible.*

The carriage came to a slow stop. Geist looked up from her musings and gave the others questioning glances.

They shook their heads.

"Wait here," Geist said. "I'll look around outside and report back."

Wrapping herself in invisibility, Geist exited the vehicle and stepped onto the icy road. To her shock, people clogged a nearby intersection and a large swath of the main road. Some people held signs; some waved torches. They shouted and pointed, and Geist couldn't help but note that they all wore something bright red on their person. A scarf or handkerchief—something.

The carriage driver, a thin Russian man with two coats, trembled on his seat, from the cold or fear, Geist couldn't tell. She crept closer to the crowds, careful to keep her footsteps on the packed snow, lest she leave an obvious hint to her presence.

A convoy of automobiles moved through the center of the crowd. They flew the flag of the Russian Empire, a three-band white-blue-red design with a double-headed eagle in the corner. The military personnel that marched alongside the convoy of automobiles had their rifles at the ready. They shouted at the crowds.

Geist couldn't understand Russian, but some things were universal. A ragged woman, face worn with hunger and sickness, shambled to the vehicles, her sign nothing more than a crude picture of bread. When she got too close, soldiers struck her across the cheek with the butt of their weapons.

Agitation spread through the protestors like the wind in a storm.

Someone threw a snowball and hit one of the soldiers. In the next instant, irritation shifted to full-on violence.

Soldiers opened fire on the citizens of Petrograd.

The crack of their rifles startled the crowd. The people broke apart like a flock of sheep beset by wolves, fleeing in all directions. Dozens ran by Geist, but she didn't move. She kept her attention on the soldiers and how their hands shook and their eyes lacked focus. When she glanced behind her, the carriage had already turned around and headed away from the violence.

Dammit, Geist thought.

The fleeing denizens ran into buildings and even the back alleys of the capital city. The violence escalated as people leaned out windows and opened fire with handguns. Two soldiers fell to the snow, dead. The rest returned fire on the attackers, showcasing their military training.

Glass and blood stained the road.

Although Geist had seen far worse—the terrors of GH Gas melting the flesh from sorcerers—the scene disturbed her more than that. Russians opened fire on their own countrymen. These weren't the enemies. These weren't the Austro-Hungarians, or the Germans, or the Ottoman Empire. They were starving women, workers without jobs, and disheartened nationals who didn't know how else to express their frustration with a war they were losing.

Once the citizens had fled from the road, the soldiers kicked the bodies out of the way of the vehicles. The convoy continued on its way, leaving only a dozen soldiers behind to clean up the mess.

Geist turned around and jogged down the street. Russian citizens were rallying in nearby buildings, some passing out crude rifles. She ignored them and continued along the backstreets, far from the main road. She spotted her carriage hidden behind a grouping of trees, the driver shaking from head to toe as he dabbed his handkerchief across his forehead.

Geist ghosted through the carriage door and took her seat next to Vergess. After a second, she dropped her invisibility.

"What happened?" Blick demanded.

Dreamer shook his head. "Vergess looked around when we escaped with the crowds. He said there was a riot."

"It was some sort of demonstration," Geist said. "Russian civilians were grouped around a line of vehicles. Everyone shouted at once. It got out of control faster than I thought."

"Was it the tsar?"

Geist caught her breath. The flags, the guards, the many vehicles—it made sense. Tsar Nicholas had returned to Petrograd. And the people were there to protest his military strategies.

"Would the tsar allow his soldiers to open fire on his citizens?" Geist asked.

Battery shook his head. "I don't know. Is that what happened? Soldiers opened fire?"

"Yes."

The grave news brought with it a solid second of silence. Although there had been warning signs, Geist didn't think the empire was on the verge of revolt and revolution, even if she had said as much to Lady Menshov. But if the tsar had to gun down his own citizens… in his own capital city…

We need to complete this operation as fast as possible.

"Let's get back to Alexander Palace," Geist said.

TWENTY

Disguises

A malgam dug his fingers into the throat of the Imperial Guard. The man struggled and thrashed, but each breath he took was wetter than the last. Amalgam couldn't see the details, but his mind painted a picture of bulging eyes and purple skin. His own lack of empathy—the deep disregard for humanity—disturbed Amalgam more than the mental images. For a split second, he almost let the man go. But what did it matter? One Russian. A million Russians. There was nothing but to move forward.

"He's dead," Otto stated. "Give him to Pavel."

Amalgam dropped the corpse to the guardhouse floor, alongside the other three.

A traitor, some Bolshevik revolutionist, stood by the door, his legs trembling. He babbled something in Russian, his voice shaking as much as the rest of his body. He had no magical aura, just the keys to the guardhouse they needed. One word about how they would harm the tsar and the traitor had given them everything.

Pavel rubbed at his temples as he moved over to the corpses in the room. "The headaches have started again," he muttered. "I don't know how long I can keep this up. It's... so much worse here."

Otto huffed. "Weak."

Sorcerers trained in the Kaiser's Guard were far more focused than others. Even Otto felt the headaches, but he could push them aside and continue with his magic regardless. That was the benefit of being raised as a deadly tool rather than a human being. Pavel, on the other hand, didn't have such an advantage.

"Look at me," Otto commanded. "If you can't do it, I'll do it for you."

Pavel shook his head, his gaze on the bloodstained floor. "N-No. Not that."

"Will your sorcery fail if I leave you to your own devices?"

"I can maintain it for a few minutes. Long enough to get into the palace."

"That's not good enough."

Otto grabbed Pavel by the collar and yanked him closer. The moment they locked eyes, Otto said, "Use your sorcery on Amalgam."

That was all it took. Otto's sorcery gripped Pavel, ripping away control. Perhaps Pavel had headaches, but while under domination, it would be Otto's focus that determined whether Pavel could maintain his magic. In essence, Otto's focus was so great that he overrode Pavel's with his own.

Pavel, his aura dim and his thoughts blurred, knelt down and shifted through the bodies. He removed the clothes—enough to create a clean Imperial Guard uniform—and then stripped flesh from bone.

The Russian traitor made the sign of the cross as he watched. When Pavel ripped off a strip of skin, the traitor gagged.

Amalgam rotated his shoulders and mulled over his plans in his head. Geist had left Alexander Palace. He knew it the instant it happened. But he needed to have patience. Everything was working perfectly, and soon the tsar would arrive, creating a whole host of new opportunities. Bolsheviks infested the royal grounds. There were other forces at play—forces who wished the Russian Empire harm—that would aid him in his plans.

"Hurry," Otto said. He motioned to the traitor. "Our new friend won't be able to keep his pants dry for much longer."

Pavel made no response at the joke and instead quickened his pace. This seemed to amuse Otto more than anything else, like a child delighted with his toys. Amalgam suspected Otto would prefer to control everyone all the time. Easier to deal with then. Easier to comprehend.

Otto turned in Amalgam's direction. "Bring us one of the Ethereal Squadron."

THE CITY of Tsarskoye Selo swarmed with soldiers, both sorcerer and standard. Civilians crowded the streets, some holding red banners, everyone shouting and throwing their fists in the sky. The soldiers kept them away from the main road, but that was all they could muster. They were too outnumbered to corral an entire city.

The tsar had returned. Amalgam could feel his aura. And soon he would return to Alexander Palace.

Wrapped in the flesh of another, Amalgam pushed his way through the angry mobs. If one looked close enough, they would see his eyes didn't move and never blinked. Pavel had simply scooped out the jellied orbs of the dead guard and squeezed them into Amalgam's empty sockets. The sorcery kept them from melting off his face, but that didn't make them functioning organs.

Dressed as an Imperial Guard, and without his gas mask, he breathed fresh air. He didn't like it. Too crisp. Too thick with the scent of gunpowder and snow. It reminded him too much of his life before he became a monster. The gas mask kept all the memories and sensations away, like a wall between him and the world.

Amalgam preferred the barrier.

When he reached the fence of the palace ground, he threw a button over and willed himself to teleport to it. The distracted soldiers—too caught up in preventing the citizens from flooding into Alexander Palace—didn't catch his entry, and when any glanced over, all they saw was an Imperial Guard, even with their golden eyes.

Amalgam continued his way into the palace, leaving a trail of buttons hidden in the snow. Escaping would be a quick and effort-less affair. Although a headache plagued him, his warped body didn't absorb magic like the rest. He didn't need the Kaiser Guard's training to keep his thoughts from dissolving into agony.

The place teemed with magic. Like streams of water, he sensed the flow and followed the pull of those familiar. He had interacted with the Ethereal Squadron enough to know when they were close.

Three were here.

The small one. The one with future sight. And… the researcher.

Amalgam didn't care for Heinrich von Veltheim. His whole family was devoid of aura. The lack of sensation, both magical and mind, made Amalgam feel as blind as he actually was. The sorcery was useful, and the new magi-tech general—Heinrich's uncle—had done extraordinary things with it, but it still irritated Amalgam.

He could at least sense the "hole" in his vision, however. He knew where Heinrich was. He knew how to avoid him. Although Otto was keen to get him back, that wasn't what Amalgam was after.

While servants and governess' rushed to prepare the house, Amalgam stepped around them and headed straight for the room with the Ethereal Squadron. No one bothered him or questioned his presence. They ran around, flustered and muttering in Russian.

When Amalgam approached the door, he tensed and placed his hand on his sidearm. Even if it came to a fight, he could teleport from the palace in the instant. He placed his hand on the doorknob and stopped for a brief second. He listened for the thoughts of the individuals in the room. What were their names? Battery and Victory.

"It will be nice to meet with the tsar," the younger one, Battery, said. "Hopefully he'll be as understanding as his daughter."

The older one, Victory, had an odd sensation to his sorcery. His thoughts rang loud, as though urgent in his own head. … *he's already here … much faster than I envisioned* … And then he said, "Battery, you should check up on Defiant and the grand duchess."

"Right now?" Battery replied. And his thoughts, louder than

before, mixed with the conversation. … *Victory has been … strange lately …*

"Yes. I get the feeling the grand duchess could use your help."

"*My* help? As in, my sorcery? Do you, uh, think she would appreciate my presence? I mean, she has attendants, and I'm a foreign national, so maybe she wouldn't want—"

"Trust me," Victory said with a laugh—a laugh that sounded natural, even if his thoughts were panicked. "She'll appreciate your company."

"*My* company?" Battery inner musings shifted in an instant. … *my goodness … I've never held the attention of …*

"You two will have plenty to talk about. Besides, I'm your older brother. Would I lead you astray?"

"Blick would lead me astray."

"I'm not Blick."

Battery paused for a moment, his thoughts too blurred and fast —Amalgam didn't bother to make sense of them. He tuned them out and focused on the tension he felt from Victory. Why hadn't Victory mentioned anything? If he knew there was danger, why hadn't he called for the guards?

"I'll g-go right away," Battery said.

"Good," Victory replied. "Use the other door. It's a faster route to the grand duchess."

"Right. Thank you."

A door opened and closed, and Amalgam sensed the aura of the smaller one disappearing deeper into the palace. An odd silence settled on the room. Victory didn't leave. He didn't even move.

Amalgam stepped into the sitting room and closed the door behind him.

"This isn't going to work out like you want it to," Victory said, his voice solemn.

Amalgam stepped around the couch and pushed a side table from his path. He wouldn't be manipulated by the likes of some soft Ethereal Squadron support sorcerer. It didn't matter what he said.

"Geist won't be caught by these traps," Victory added.

The statement gave Amalgam pause. Maybe the man *did* know

what he wanted. But did it matter? He would say anything. Then again, he also should have seen this coming and prepared.

"You're not fighting," Amalgam whispered. "Why?"

"I've seen a million outcomes. If I went straight for the others, you would kill the grand duchess. If I fled the palace with Battery, you would find and kill Defiant. But in this scenario, I stay here—calm and collected—and no one will get injured."

Victory reported as though it were a cold fact. Amalgam chuckled. The *destiny* sorcery had always been a thing of legend. Could this sorcerer really see what would happen in the future? Had Victory chosen to let the others leave, so that they wouldn't get caught up in a fight they would ultimately lose?

"Seems an odd decision for a soldier," Amalgam said. "Or do you see an eventual rescue? Is that it? Maybe I should defy all your future sight and simply leave you dead in this room. It would make our operation easier."

"Then you wouldn't have someone to lure Geist." Victory stepped closer and slowly pulled his weapon. Then he tossed it on the nearby couch. "And if I allowed you to capture two of us, one would be drained of blood the moment we met your squad."

Amalgam didn't need magic to know the last statement was true.

Perhaps Victory did know everything.

But it didn't matter. Victory wouldn't help him capture Geist, so at a certain level, he couldn't trust what the man had to say. Amalgam grabbed Victory's injured arm and twisted it to the side.

Victory gritted his teeth and sharply inhaled.

"Just for fun," Amalgam said, "why don't you tell me the chances you'll make it out of this alive?"

"You don't have to do this. I can help you get out of the situation you're in. You've seen only a fraction of my predictive abilities. I know there's a way you can escape the life you lead."

The phrase—*you don't have to do this*—harkened back to when Amalgam and Geist had been locked in the research basement of the OHL together. She had said the same damn thing. Why couldn't they see there was no going back? He was a monster. It couldn't be undone. Now all he wanted was company. Someone who understood.

Amalgam let go of Victory's arm. After a few calming breaths, Victory relaxed.

"Thank you. We should—"

Without warning, Amalgam punched Victory across the face, the blow powerful enough to break some of Amalgam's knuckles. Victory hit the floor unconscious, blood pouring from his ruptured nose.

"Didn't see that coming," Amalgam quipped.

Then he knelt down and placed his hand on the man's back. His teleportation extended to people who couldn't fight back—anyone sleeping or incapacitated. With Victory stunned, there would be no problem returning to Otto undetected.

Amalgam hesitated for a moment, right before using his sorcery.

Obviously, Victory's powers weren't absolute or else he would've known about the punch. But he had still been right about a great many things. Had he been trying to convince Amalgam to defect? Geist had. But she was different. She was always different. She was the only one Amalgam even wanted to hear from.

He shook the doubt away and left the palace with his prize.

TWENTY-ONE

Tsar Nicholas

G eist, Vergess, Dreamer, and Blick arrived on the edge of Tsarskoye Selo and were placed in a queue of other vehicles. Armed guards inspected each automobile, cart, and carriage from top to bottom. At the same time take, they shouted at the protesting citizens, trying to keep them at bay. Geist watched the proceedings with a keen eye, worried someone might put their hands in the wrong place on her body when searching. Fortunately, the soldiers seemed the most interested in belts and boots—and the physical compartments of the vehicles—rather than any areas Geist would be worried about. The golden-eyed sorcerers did sweeps of the passengers, but they didn't linger on her long, not when they had to turn their attention to the protesting Russians.

Once the soldiers were satisfied with their search of the carriage, it proceeded to Alexander Palace. The protestors threw snow and rotten food, but most aimed toward military vehicles. The carriages didn't feel the brunt of the attacks.

"These guards don't look happy to be fighting the citizens," Blick muttered. He closed the curtains on the carriage windows and turned back to the group. "I don't blame them."

"It's more than that," Dreamer said.

"How so?"

"You can't taste the murder in the air? Russian blood running in the streets of the capital city will ignite anger as quickly as a bonfire will burn a dry forest. We're just seeing the beginning. This won't end soon."

Geist scooted to the edge of her seat. "You make it sound like we're in immediate danger."

"We are."

"But *we* didn't attack the Russians. We're not part of this."

"It doesn't matter. We're on the same side as the tsar, headed to his palace. People will see us as *his* allies, not the Russian Empire's."

Vergess leaned back and huffed. "I'm sure the tsar will quell this. I've heard multiple reports of the tsar firing on his own soldiers— and it already happened in the capital over a decade ago. A bunch of peaceful demonstrators were gunned down. I'd say this tsar is either brutal or incompetent, but either way, he answers these problems with violence."

Blick chuckled. "No wonder Varnish wasn't pro-tsar."

The mounting pressure to leave the Russian Empire weighed heavily on Geist's thoughts. The Royal Houses tended to have a firm grasp of their nations and wouldn't tolerate upstarts. How did the situation become so unstable? What had led it to becoming so rotten?

"Dreamer," Geist said. "How long do you think we have before the violence gets out of hand?"

"A few hours," he replied.

"Even though Vergess said the tsar quells revolution with violence?"

"The world isn't what it used to be. Even in my homeland of Saudi Arabia, there is revolt against the Ottomans. The old ways are dying, and people no longer want to be kept in the dark. The more this violence spreads, the more the citizens will believe they have nothing to lose and everything to gain. I think the tsar is sowing his own problems in blood and mayhem."

Geist rubbed at her arms, her stomach twisting in a knot. She knew the world wouldn't be the same after the war, but she had imagined some things would always be constant—the world of magic and sorcerers wouldn't change. It couldn't. It was secret and different from anything else. Sorcerers had vast powers the mundane could never imagine.

Yet now sorcerers had created magi-tech. And they were stealing schools of magic from the blood of others. And modern weapons wielded by normal soldiers could kill in an instant.

Nothing would be the same after this war.

Would being a member of a Royal House even matter? What if their sorceries were stolen and given out to everyone? What if—

Geist turned to Vergess. "Do you think…?"

"What is it?" he asked.

Can the blood of sorcerers be given to anyone? Could it make non-sorcerers… sorcerers?

Geist hadn't even considered it before, but what if the GH Gas could warp a person so thoroughly it gave them access to magic when they previously had none?

"Never mind," Geist muttered. She didn't want to focus on the hypothetical when she had real problems staring her in the face.

The carriage stopped in front of Alexander Palace, but there was a commotion at the front doors. The Imperial Guard pushed people back—servants and diplomats alike—refusing anyone entrance. Geist and the others exited the carriage only to be greeted by rifles.

"I need to speak to Captain Uthof," she said. "*Captain Uthof.*"

Perhaps some of the soldiers recognized her, because they grabbed Geist by the shoulder and pushed her through the line of soldiers. Vergess and Blick argued with the Russian soldiers, speaking in different languages and gesturing to the palace, but Dreamer stayed back, an air of British politeness about him, even when being manhandled by the Imperial Guard.

The guards didn't take Geist through the front doors. Instead, they took her to the security tower just beyond the marble pillars. It was separated from the building, but clearly the heart of the Imperial Guard operations. Captain Uthof stood amongst a group of shouting guards. One guard threw down his rifle and stormed from the building. Another pointed his rifle at the deserter, but Captain Uthof shoved the barrel to the floor.

Geist jumped in, her teeth gritted. "What's going on here, Captain?"

"Geist," Captain Uthof said as he snapped his attention to her. "You should take your men and return to Petrograd. At once."

"Half my men are still in the palace." She glanced around. The tense soldiers turned her curious gaze with harsh glares. "What's happening here? I thought the Imperial Guard was—"

"I'm ordering you and your men to leave the palace grounds," Captain Uthof interjected.

Geist caught her breath. Although soldiers tended to pay respects to higher-ranking officers in foreign armies, it wasn't standard practice to follow their orders unless they were in a direct chain of command. However, the Ethereal Squadron was different. Sorcerer soldiers and sorcerer officers in allied situations tended to form their own secret hierarchy.

But Captain Uthof wasn't in the Ethereal Squadron. He was a sorcerer of higher military rank. He didn't have the authority to order her to do anything, especially not when she was on special assignment by Major Reese.

Geist didn't want to cause a diplomatic scene, so she replied with a quick bow of her head. "I'll get my men and leave."

Get her men included the ones in the palace.

I won't leave them, she told herself as she stormed out of the security tower. *Especially not when the chance of riot is so high.*

Geist ran back to Blick, Vergess, and Dreamer. They turned to her, hard looks as though they understood they needed to act with urgency. They couldn't force their way into the palace. Geist could sneak in—and with Battery, could attempt to sneak the others out of the palace—but she didn't want to separate any more than they already had. Especially given the circumstances.

She motioned to the edge of the palace estate, and her three teammates followed her away from the commotion.

ONCE THEY WERE out of sight of the Imperial Guard and the protesters, Dreamer disguised them as members of Russian military. Geist ghosted through a wall, into a grand study, and crept to the window, and opened it from the inside. Blick, Vergess, and Dreamer climbed inside.

They moved as a group of four into the main hall of the palace and blended into the gathering that congregated near the entrance. Geist feared someone might call them out—the Imperial Guard was close-knit—but no one had eyes on them. Everyone kept their attention on a single man giving a speech to the palace.

Tsar Nicholas Romanov II.

Although Geist had never met him personally, she recognized the medals on his bright blue coat. One fact amused her—outside of the decoration on his chest, he had no prominent features. He grew a beard and mustache, like most Russians. His hair line receded in a U fashion, like any older man. He wasn't even notably tall. He had plain features, a slow drawl to his voice, and a weaker posture.

Blick turned to her with a lifted eyebrow. With his telepathy, he asked, *"Do you want me to use my eyes on him?"*

She responded with a curt nod.

Using his golden eyes, Blick stared over the crowd and gave the tsar his full attention. A second later, he turned away, his eyebrows knit. He shook his head.

"It's not him. A disguise. Like Dreamer's sorcery."

Geist exhaled. She wanted to speak with the tsar, but at the same time, she didn't want to be anywhere near the tsar. The situation was too tumultuous. Too uncertain. And much too close to actual violence.

"Is he here?" Geist asked.

"Yes," Vergess stated.

She turned to him. "How do you know?"

"It's the smell."

"You know what he smells like? Have you met him before?"

"I know what his daughter smells like. And their blood is unique.

He's here. His stink is in the room, even if someone has taken the role of duplicate for him."

The crowd of Russians cheered at the end of his speech, but Geist couldn't help but notice some of them did it with frowns under their thick mustaches. The air smelled of sweat and anger. Even inside Alexander Palace, discontentment infected the walls. How could Vergess detect the scent of single man through the rank smell of a small army?

Dreamer stepped closer to her and muttered, "What should we do?"

"We'll use your illusions to disguise our squad as members of the Imperial Guard, not just normal soldiers," Geist said. "And then we leave this place."

"We don't speak with Tsar Nicholas?"

"No." But Geist thought better of her decision. "We'll speak with the grand duchess, but only if we can get a quick audience. Otherwise, our priority is escaping Petrograd before any more violence takes place."

The others nodded along with her sentiments.

Under the cover of Dreamer's illusions, they made their way through Alexander Palace. Although Geist didn't know the interior as well as she would've liked, it was simple enough to return to the sitting room where she had left her squad members. When they arrived in the room, however, there was no one to greet them.

"Vergess," Geist said. "Can you… sniff out our teammates?"

Blick snorted.

"I can," Vergess said.

"Good. Round them up and bring them here."

He nodded and headed out without another word. Dreamer and Blick glanced around the empty sitting room. There were enough chairs and couches for a whole battalion to take a seat, but they opted to stand. The tense atmosphere didn't lend well to relaxation.

Something metal reflected the electric lighting of the room. Geist turned to stare at a couch, her chest tightening as she recognized a

Webley Revolver—the standard-issue service handgun for British soldiers. It didn't belong to any of the Russians. And none of her squad would just *leave their weapon on a couch*. Although Geist couldn't articulate it right away, her mind already jumped to the worst possible conclusion.

It belonged to someone in her squad. And he had left it for her to find.

Because he was in trouble.

TWENTY-TWO

Base of Operations

A malgam flashed into existence within a wine cellar.

He rubbed at his twisted face, making sure to get every piece of false flesh from his body. He had never been a fan of fleshcrafting, and he hated it more now that it reminded him he didn't even have normal flesh of his own. It was like he was pretending to be a man. It felt pathetic and disgusting. Like his very existence.

Teleporting left Amalgam feeling seasick, and he wobbled a bit before he steadied himself. It took him a second to remember he held Victory by the back of the tunic—Victory's unconscious body barely above the floor, blood running from his busted nose, completely limp.

Amalgam dropped the man. Victory hit the cold stone floor and groaned.

"Wait here," Amalgam said with a laugh to himself.

He stomped out of the wine cellar, up the stairs, and made his way to a small room designated for his purposes. Inside, next to the tiny bed and nightstand, was his pack of equipment and magi-tech. Amalgam donned a new gas mask straight away, strapping it around his head as tight as he could get it without cutting off blood flow.

He had hated the mask as first, but…

Something didn't feel right without it.

Once secure over his face, Amalgam straightened his shoulders and picked up his weapons. The familiar echo of his breath caught behind the mask was a pleasant melody. It relaxed him. Restored his confidence. He knew what he needed to do.

The empty halls of Lavvit Monastery suited Amalgam just fine. He walked into the main corridor, back down the wine cellar stairs, and straight to the cold subterranean level without meeting a single other person. There had once been a whole family running around the monastery, but they were either dead or restrained even further down below the house. The silence that followed allowed Amalgam to rest easier. He entered the cellar and left the door open behind him.

Victory, slowly regaining consciousness, rolled to his side with a grunt.

Before Amalgam could do anything to the Ethereal Squadron member, he sensed the approach of powerful magic. He knew the sorcerer in a matter of moments—Lieutenant Cavell. The man liked to remain invisible, even when in friendly territory, if only to keep his subordinates on their toes.

The lieutenant walked down the stairs, quiet and careful, a level of masterwork to his steps. Amalgam smiled. Even after all this time, Cavell thought he could sneak up on him. *He's a fool if he thinks he'll ever be more than a beacon.*

"I have one," Amalgam said, his voice muffled by the mask yet somehow more *right* than without it.

Lieutenant Cavell stood on the last step and released his invisibility. "Where are Otto and Pavel?"

"I told them to meet me here. It shouldn't take them long."

"Tsar Nicholas has already returned to Alexander Palace."

"I'm aware."

The lieutenant strode into the cellar and stopped once he reached Victory's side. Amalgam knew the lieutenant well—if their new prisoner made even the slightest attempt at defiance, Cavell would delight in shredding him to the edge of death. But Victory didn't get up, or even move, and instead kept a hand under his nose, stifling the blood. He even kept his gaze on the floor, in every way passive.

Lieutenant Cavell sneered. "Which one is this?" he asked, his German laced with a strong Austrian accent.

Could Victory understand German? Amalgam didn't know, but he also didn't care.

"The one who can see the future," Amalgam said.

"Good. Drain him. I want the blood."

"Not yet."

The silence that followed could unsettle the dead. Lieutenant Cavell turned around, his jaw clenched. Perhaps he was a mystery to some, but not to Amalgam. He heard Cavell's thoughts louder than others—almost as if the lieutenant were growling them straight into his ear.

... *damn monster doesn't know his place ... I thought they said it was trained ...*

"I need him," Amalgam continued. "To lure the rest of the Ethereal Squadron."

Lieutenant Cavell glared. "Don't be a fool. How will they even know he's still alive? We should kill him now and send the body parts home one piece at a time."

The lieutenant's aura—the hue of magic only Amalgam could "see"—flared a bit, twisting like a fire after it popped with embers. The occurrence was unnatural and only began after the lieutenant started adding blood to his body. Was it a negative effect of taking someone else's magic? Currently, there was no way to tell.

"The Ethereal Squadron may have a way to detect if he's alive," Amalgam said. He had no evidence to think that, but it was a real possibility. Many sorceries could be used to determine if Victory was alive, and Amalgam didn't want to risk losing Geist over the lieutenant's thirst for blood. "Besides, don't you want your daughter back? Once we've eliminated the Ethereal Squadron, you can drain them all of their blood. It would be foolish to waste this opportunity."

The amount of blood required to transfer magic was more than just a tiny drop. And the process of extracting it, even if done care-fully, tended to kill the sorcerer within the hour. The loss of blood was too much. If Lieutenant Cavell even attempted to get enough blood from Victory, it would be the end of the man, and Amalgam refused to give up his one avenue for bait.

Victory was right. If I had brought two, the lieutenant would've gone straight for the jugular.

"Why didn't you capture Florence when you were at Alexander Palace?" Lieutenant Cavell asked. "She should've been simple to apprehend—a mere girl in a soldier's uniform."

I wouldn't be here if I had her, Amalgam thought with a hint of sarcasm.

When he listened to Cavell's inner musings, however, Amalgam realized the man harbored a twisted purpose.

... the girl has cost me so much ... I'll take it straight from her skin ... and then offer her magic to the prince ... before he takes it from me or my sons ...

Cavell wanted to offer up his daughter to the prince of Austria-Hungary. No qualms. No second guessing. He just wanted to avoid anyone coming after him for *his* sorceries.

The future is looking bleak, Amalgam mused to himself. *If sorcerers hunt each other for their magics, we'll have another damn world war in no time.*

"Well?" Cavell barked. "Or did you miss that? Your gas mask on too tight?"

Amalgam shook his head. "Your daughter wasn't around when I snuck into the palace. Besides, we both know she isn't the easiest of targets. Anyone with *specter* sorcery would be difficult to pin down without sufficient surprise. This support sorcerer, though... not so much."

"Tsk." Lieutenant Cavell waved away the comment and turned his attention back to Victory.

During the entire conversation, Victory hadn't moved. What was his end game? Amalgam figured he would've fought—couldn't he envision a way out of this?—or perhaps he was biding his time until he had some opening for attack. Best to keep careful track of him.

"Take this piece of shit to the basement," Cavell commanded.

"Keep him with the others. If the tsar has already returned to Alexandra Palace, it's only a matter of time before the entire Russian Empire is ablaze with revolution. We need to make sure everything here is secure."

Amalgam nodded.

They couldn't afford for anything to go wrong during the uprising. The goal was to sweep up as many Russian sorcerers during the fighting, but that wouldn't be possible if they had problems inside their base of operations. Victory had to be chained down like the rest—like livestock before the slaughter. He was already a carcass.

Amalgam grabbed Victory by the upper arm and dragged him to his feet. Victory swayed and then balanced himself enough to walk. Again, he said no words, and made no attempt to fight. Together they walked out of the cellar, with Cavell close on their heels until they made it to the hallway. Then the lieutenant turned in the opposite direction, no doubt to slip out the front door.

"What's in the basement?" Victory whispered in English.

Amalgam didn't bother answering. He tightened his grip on the man's arm and led him away from the door—away from any exits—and headed straight for their long stairway down.

It wasn't a basement, per se, but more of an underground bunker. Lavvit Monastery was run by a family of sorcerers known for their sorcery to mold unworked stone. They created tunnels, underground workshops, and interesting subterranean rooms, all to keep themselves safe from outsiders. Perhaps it would've worked a hundred years ago, but the world was modernizing. They hadn't protected themselves well enough when the Eyes of the Kaiser came calling, and they didn't have anything in place to deal with GH Gas.

The history of the monastery didn't interest Amalgam, however. All he knew was that the family had been killed so he, and the others, could use the monastery's warren as a base of operations while they stole blood from Russians. And it had worked out beautifully, especially with Pavel nearby to fleshcraft anyone into looking like an actual member of the church.

"What's in the basement?" Victory asked again, this time with a shakier voice.

"Scared?" Amalgam taunted. He slammed opened a door that led deeper underground. Perhaps it was dark, he couldn't tell. Perhaps the shadows were playing tricks with Victory's mind.

"I can't envision any future beyond the basement. There's something there… preventing any magic. It's just blank."

"You'll get a good look at it soon enough."

"Fechner, it doesn't—"

Amalgam dug his fingers into Victory's bicep and then slammed him against the rough stone wall. Victory grunted and then slouched, his shoulder and back bloodied from the jagged edges of the natural rock.

"My name is Amalgam," he drawled.

Victory placed a hand on top of Amalgam's tightening grip. "You can be the master of your own life. You can choose your own values. You don't have to hate your own existence."

What did he know? He was just trying to be manipulative.

He's an enemy—no matter what he says he can see. He'll always be untrustworthy.

Amalgam slammed him into the wall, albeit weaker than before.

"Enough," he said. "The basement isn't what you think it is. We have a researcher ourselves, after all. Did you really think you were the only ones with someone who could nullify magic?"

Victory's breathing shorted as the information sank in. "You have a sorcerer from the von Veltheim House here?"

"That's right. Our new *magi-tech general*. A genius innovator. He's here to help us use all the sorcerers we're going to gather."

It took a few moments, but Victory eventually whispered, "Why are you telling me this?"

"We've made him an impromptu lab. And that's where we'll be keeping you."

The dead sorcerers of Lavvit Monastery had been lucky. They didn't have to suffer through the experimentations of Helmuth von Veltheim, the Second Magi-Tech General of Imperial Germany. The man had no empathy—detached from humanity in order to further his research. Much like his detachment from magic. Nothing got through.

Well, except for when he had an accident with the GH Gas. He hadn't been the same since then. That was why Heinrich was originally given the title of magi-tech general—his uncle was a monster, as far as everyone else was concerned.

Like me.

Amalgam yanked Victory from the wall and continued down the stairs. Victory's words did eat at him, however. But choosing one's destiny was for the role of a man, not a deformed creature. Amalgam buried the thoughts and instead focused on when he would see Geist next.

TWENTY-THREE

Rescue

—————

"What're we going to do?" Blick asked.

He spoke with a terse edge that betrayed what he really wanted to do—burn all of Tsarskoye Selo to ground until they found his brother. Geist could understand, to a limited degree, but her concerns were more with the logistics. They had searched Alexander Palace and found nothing. No forced break in, no hint of struggle, and the only person missing was Victory.

Where was he? Geist had no idea where to begin looking.

And they didn't have time to search the Russian Empire for one lost soldier. Not to mention the Russians were agitated and on the verge of civil war. At any second she could see a riot overtaking the city.

This is the worst time something like this could happen, she thought, glaring at the floor.

Blick paced the sitting room. He ran his hands through his hair.

Soldiers with rifles ran up and down the halls. Shouting filled Alexander Palace. The anxious atmosphere spilled over into everyone's mood, Geist could feel it coursing through her own veins.

Like holding a lit stick of dynamite, just waiting for the punchline.

"Is there any way to check if he's alive?" Battery asked. He had handled the situation better than Blick, but not by much. With shaky hands, he rubbed his tunic and fiddled with his belt. "Maybe there's a Russian sorcerer we could turn to? I spoke with the grand duchess. She seemed willing to help."

If Victory were here, I could just ask him. Goddammit, why did it have to be him?

Vergess crossed his arms. "We have to face the reality of the situation. Our enemies are hunting sorcerers for their blood. And Victory... well, he has plenty of interesting magics in his blood."

Battery turned on his heel. "What're you saying?"

"You know what I'm saying."

"Vergess," Geist snapped. "Now's not the time. I refuse to believe he's dead."

Dreamer stepped between them, his hands up. "Listen, if Victory is in the hands of the enemy, there's little we can do for him. Our best bet would be to continue with the operation and ask the Russian Empire to handle his rescue."

Blick clicked his tongue with a harsh 'tsk' and waved away the comment. "We know who took him. It's the same bastards as before. I'm sure the Eyes of the Kaiser controlled him right out the front door."

Geist's heart stopped. She continued to stare at the floor, the conversation drifting away as she focused on an odd detail. It took a prolonged moment to regain her breath.

A single button—shiny black and blending in with the dark carpet—caught her attention. She knelt down and picked it up, her fingers trembling. The only person she knew with *itinerant* sorcery, the sorcery of teleporting from one similar object to the next, was Amalgam.

But even knowing who took Victory didn't help.

"I thought we were leaving the palace," Dreamer said. "The protestors aren't deterred by the increase of soldiers."

Geist glanced around. "Where's Defiant?"

"He's finishing up his treatments for Tsesarevich Alexei. He thinks he can cure him of his *curse*, but it's taking longer than expected."

Blick shook his head. "Tell him to stop. It's not our mission to save the tsar's son from some ancient blood disease. We should be worrying about Victory long before the kid."

"Wait," Geist said. "I'll go see Defiant. Where is he?"

Vergess lifted an eyebrow. "He's with some of the doctors and governesses in their medicine room. What're you thinking?"

"Defiant knows the workings of magic better than anybody." Geist closed her hand tight around the button. "He might have a way to find Victory."

WITHOUT HIS GLASSES, Defiant brought everything within inches of his face before setting it back down on the desk and moving on to the next object. Geist waited as Defiant crushed up a series of white opals and poured them into a glass bottle.

The medicine room—more opulent than any grand ballroom in Berlin—shone with the luster and polish of smooth silver, gold, and opals. The walls, almost gaudy, had gold leaf swirled through the wallpaper and up onto the ceiling. The desks and shelves, all covered in bottles and medical tools, glistened with a cleanliness that was only achieved through two full-time workers.

"I don't understand why people shun modern research," Defiant said in German.

Three governesses, each waiting by the side of the desk, furrowed their brows, no doubt confused. They spoke Russian and some English and not a word of German.

"Defiant," Geist said. "Will this take much longer?"

"It depends. I need to test it first."

Geist tossed the button on the desk. It spun in a circle before landing near one of the empty bottles. Defiant squinted at it.

"It was Amalgam," Geist said. "He was here."

Defiant continued working, his eyebrows knit together.

Geist continued, "I need your help. I have to find Victory."

"My help?"

"You're the only one I know, and trust, to get this done. I can't think of any sorcery that would find him, and I thought you might have some *trick* or *clever idea* to locate things. Or maybe you just know the enemy better than us." Geist placed her hands on the deck. "You know Amalgam personally. Maybe that could—"

"I'll do it," Defiant interjected.

It took a moment for Geist recover. She asked, "What's your plan?"

Defiant picked up the button and placed it in front of him. "You said you trusted me, didn't you? Give me time. A few hours. I'll think of something."

Although she wanted to leave it at that—Defiant seemed sure of himself, after all—she knew they didn't have the time.

"The Russian Empire is on the cusp of a revolution. Can you do this somewhere else? Alexander Palace isn't safe so long as the tsar is here."

"If the Russians allow us to take some supplies, then I can do it anywhere. But I need opals. And perhaps Battery's assistance."

Geist nodded along with his words. "I'll speak to the grand duchess. Thank you, Defiant."

He didn't answer. He simply turned back to his work, his focus unparalleled.

"YOU HAVE MY FULL SUPPORT," Anastasie said.

Although the entire palace was up in arms, and there were soldiers with rifles at every door, the grand duchess had managed to find a small tearoom and clear it of anyone else's presence. She held her cup with a delicate grace befitting royalty and sipped the hot liquid with a distant look in her eyes.

"Thank you," Geist said. She pushed her cup away, not caring for tea as much as hard liquor. "We'll leave as soon as Defiant has a remedy for your brother."

Anastasie perked up. "Do you truly believe it'll work?"

"Defiant can do amazing things with magic."

"Fantastic. Papa has been agitated since arriving, but I know he'll feel better once Alexei is well." Anastasie placed her cup back on the saucer and then smoothed her white frilly dress. "I, uh…"

Geist stood. "Thank you again, Your Grace. But the instant Defiant is ready, we'll be on our way."

"W-Wait."

Although Geist wanted to deny the request and leave the room without another word, she hesitated. The grand duchess had been nothing but helpful since their arrival. The least she could do is hear out her last request.

"Yes?" Geist asked.

Anastasie stared up at her with a furrowed brow. "What's it like in the empire? Are *all* the citizens like the ones here in Tsarskoye Selo? Papa said that only the Bolsheviks were upset, but the people in the crowd… they're not all Bolsheviks. Why are they so furious?"

"Well…" Geist rubbed at the back of her neck. What was she supposed to say?

"Don't they know I've been trying?" Anastasie asked. She stood from her chair and shook her head. "We've all played our part in the war. My sorcery has been used to protect them since Papa joined the battlefield. And he's led our troops into battle, like any proper tsar should. What more do they want?"

I don't have time for this.

"I'm sorry," Geist said. "I don't have answers for you." She turned to leave, and Anastasie took a few steps closer.

"You've traveled through the empire, right?" Anastasie asked.

"Yes."

"I want to speak to the citizens myself. I want to know why they're upset. If the Ethereal Squadron is heading for the ports to leave, perhaps you could escort me for part of your trek."

Geist gritted her teeth. The last thing she wanted to do was protect a grand duchess while in the middle of an operation.

"I'm sorry. We can't."

"But—"

"We aren't your Imperial Guard. Or even standard soldiers. We're special agents. We have an operation to complete. I'm sorry, but this isn't something we can do."

Anastasie stared for a moment, her eyes wide. She opened her mouth, caught her words, and then glanced to the floor, caught up in a silent argument with herself. Royal House sorcerers often got their way; Geist knew that. She risked upsetting a powerful ally, but what else could she say? There was no way they could take her.

"Papa and Mama refuse to let us leave the palace," Anastasie muttered, never looking up. "Despite my efforts to help, I'm trapped. The Imperial Guard won't be my escort because, in the end, they're loyal to Papa first and me second. I thought... since you're the commander of your own squad... you could make a decision without consulting anyone else."

Although Geist already knew the answer, she mulled over the comments. Not too long ago, it had been *her* trapped in her father's house. Unable to leave. Unable to find the answers she craved. Anastasie's plight was exactly her own.

But what am I going to tell the grand duchess? she thought dryly. *Should I tell her to disguise herself as a man and join the Ethereal Squadron, like me? I don't have any other solutions.*

"It's dangerous out there," Geist said, grasping for any reason to dissuade her. "Especially with the revolutionaries. They'd recognize you in an instant. My team wouldn't be able to—"

"I've seen the illusions." Anastasie glanced up, pleading with her saucer eyes. "I know your squad could handle it. And they'd listen to you."

"No. It can't happen. You're safer here than with us."

"I don't care about my safety. I care about the Russian Empire."

Her voice heightened with each word, as passion fueled her anger. Geist didn't want to argue with her—she wasn't the grand duchess's keeper—but here she was, telling her that some things were impossible.

Geist walked to the door and placed her hand on the handle. "I'm sorry. I can't help you." Then she left before the grand duchess could concoct another argument to go.

"WE'LL NEVER MAKE it out of this accursed city," Blick growled.

Even with illusions, it had taken them half an hour to make it through the crowded streets via carriage. Then another hour to find a place near Petrograd for Defiant to do his research. Every minute that passed was another minute Victory had to suffer at the hands of the enemy.

Blick stared out the window as it began to snow, his back to the rest of the dining hall. Battery, sitting at one of the long tables, organized his backpack with a single-minded look of determination, as though he would find his missing brother at the end of the clutter.

They were alone. Technically, the dining hall was closed, but Geist got them in regardless. She needed a space for Defiant to work, and she wanted to gather her thoughts before searching through the Russian Empire.

Dreamer sat on a wooden chair, writing his encoded reports. His hand trembled, and Geist couldn't help but notice. Everyone was fraying at the edges. How long could they last?

"We can't sit around," Blick said. "We have too much to do, and we're running out of time."

"Defiant needs to find Victory," Geist replied. "And for that, he needs time."

"We still have to convince those Russian sorcerers to flee the country. House Solovyev and House Lungin are both here in Petrograd. Some of us should deal with that while Defiant is busy." Blick turned around and glared. "It's the only way to get everything done."

Geist crossed her arms and then uncrossed them. "Which house is closer?"

"House Solovyev, though House Lungin is in the same district. They're both on the western estate, on the outskirts of town. Solovyev is closest to us, and Lungin is at the other end."

She hated the thought of splitting up—especially after what happened to Victory—but she knew Blick was right. *We are running out of time.*

Then a thought struck her. Amalgam made it clear in House

Kott. He was after *her* and no one else. So why did he take Victory? She already knew the answer.

To get to her.

She turned to the rest of the group.

"We're going to finish the operation," she said. "And listen. Victory isn't dead. I have a strong hunch he's going to be used as bait against us. I think, right now, the best thing to do is to prepare for our final flight from the Russian Empire."

Battery glanced up. "What makes you think he's alive?"

"Trust me," she said.

"O-Okay. Then what should we do?"

Geist motioned to Vergess. "You and me. We'll be the fastest if it's just us. We're going to these last two houses and we're going to get them to flee the Russian Empire come hell or high water."

"And the rest of us are waiting here?" Blick asked.

"That's right."

Everyone looked around the empty dining hall devoid of guards, walls, and weapons. The drafty hall had thick curtains for the windows and a large kitchen filled with giant pantries, but not many spots to hide.

"Alexander Palace was a place rife with confusion," Geist said. "But with Defiant and Blick, nothing should confuse you here, not even that fleshcrafting bastard." *And Amalgam will be coming for me anyway. I'm sure of it. He's going to dangle Victory around until I take the bait.*

Vergess stepped to her side. "Then let's do this."

TWENTY-FOUR

Revolt

The streets of Petrograd were clogged with people. Crowds upon crowds—filling the pathways from shoulder to shoulder—prevented any sort of fast travel. Geist and Vergess shoved their way through, but even that took time. Everyone was out looking for a fight. Even the slightest agitation caused a shouting match.

"I can ghost through the buildings," Geist said. "And you can push your way through the crowd. We can meet up at the end of the street."

Vergess met her gaze, his eyebrows knitted. "Why don't we take the roofs? We can stay together and get a better perceptive of the rioting if we're above it all." He pointed to the multi-story buildings.

"Will it be faster?"

"You wanted to train your *apex* sorcery, right? Might as well run over the roofs at full tilt."

Geist smirked and nodded.

They pushed their way to the ladders on the side of the building. Vergess hefted himself upward. Geist followed suit. Once on the roof, Vergess sprinted to the edge and leapt the few feet to the next building. He then turned around and motioned for her to follow.

Geist dashed and then jumped. She landed with an ease she hadn't been expecting and attributed that to her *apex* sorcery as well. *I really need to master this,* she thought. Then she ran and made another leap, aiming to clear the gap between buildings with another effortless motion.

"*Commander Geist,*" a woman said, speaking straight to Geist's mind.

The midair communication startle Geist enough that she landed and stumbled forward, but she recovered with the grace of a combat expert.

"*Grand Duchess Anastasia has asked me to relay a message. She says her brother has felt well since taking the medication your team provided.*"

Geist held still, intent on listening to the unspoken words. She knew Defiant would deliver. He had a way with magic, and if he thought he couldn't handle it, he would've said so from the start. *Which means he'll probably find Victory.* The one thought helped eased the mounting stress. Having dependable people on her team—whether they were combats or support—was comforting.

"*Grand Duchess Anastasia would like you to return to Alexander Palace before you leave the Russian Empire, both to reward the Ethereal Squadron, and to procure more medication.*"

Although she couldn't answer, Geist shook her head. Could they afford to return to the palace? It would be a risk. *I can deal with it later.*

"Geist," Vergess said.

She glanced up.

He stood on the next building over. "What's wrong?"

"I'm coming," she said as she ran and leapt to the next building over.

Vergess nodded once she landed, and the two of them set across the rooftops of Petrograd. Unfortunately, not every building was the same height. While they made good time through one block, the next required jumping down onto roofs with hidden dangers. Piles of snow obscured a stack of wood, which Geist hit and tumbled though. When Vergess glanced back, she got to her feet and waved it off. She wasn't about to complain over a few scrapes. War in the trenches had been far worse.

When they made it to buildings several stories tall, Vergess effortlessly scaled them—gripping the bricks and windowsills and hauling himself upward. Some streetside citizens glanced over and marveled, but it wasn't like his athleticism screamed *magic*. He could get away with his feats so long as he kept it in the realm of plausible.

Not that it matters much here, Geist thought. *They all believe in witches and curses anyway.*

Not to be outdone by Vergess, Geist forced herself up the wall. She could've used her *specter* sorcery to get inside and climb the stairs, but Vergess was right. Once she mastered *apex* sorcery, she would be an unrivaled sorcerer of war.

Like her father.

After Geist reached the top—her fingertips bleeding from the rough brick walls—they ran a few more houses before jumping down into a wide road and continuing toward the large estates that dotted the hills on the edge of Petrograd. House Solovyev was amongst the lavish homes.

The street was snow-covered and mostly empty. A few carriages rolled by, followed by a rare automobile. The run didn't bother her, and Vergess hadn't even broken into a sweat.

"You've been practicing," Vergess said in German, speaking between controlled breaths.

Geist smiled and matched his pace. "Next time, I'm just ghosting through all the buildings. Probably would've beaten you here."

He smirked. "Is that a challenge?"

Although she hadn't meant it as such, she enjoyed the playful edge to his voice. "Maybe it was." Vergess increased his speed. She matched it.

"I'm not the type that would allow someone else to win," he said. "Even if they were my intended."

"I wouldn't want it any other way."

Running around a carriage and turning a corner, Geist could almost live in that one moment. But the realities of war refused to be ignored, even for a few seconds. The evening darkness, coupled with the cloud cover and groups of trees, made it difficult to see far, even though Geist could see through most gloom. However, the longer she inhaled, the most she tasted the char of burned materials.

Something was on fire.

A sickening sensation slid down Geist's spine. The running kept her warm enough as they traveled, and her *apex* sorcery kept her from slipping across the ice. Vergess kept pace, his intense gaze set on the street ahead of them. Groups of Russian citizens gathered at corners, some shouting, others yelling.

After a short distance, the source of the burning became apparent—houses were on fire. Geist caught her breath as she dashed by one manse and then another. Flames, fueled by some chemical source, raged across the wood and cloth of gigantic homes. When people ran from the burning buildings, there were citizens waiting with Mosin-Nagant rifles, Russian military standard. Shots were fired, even at children.

Geist slowed her run and almost jumped the fences to stop what was going on, but she knew she had to make it to House Solovyev without delay.

Military rifles? Mass burnings? What's going on?

Vergess motioned to her as he ran by, and Geist resumed her run. The long road between estates would've best been traveled with a horse. She felt no fatigue as she pushed herself to the limits of her sorcery, though magicless men and women pointed or stared.

"There," Vergess called out.

House Solovyev sat in the distance, a great pillar of smoke rising from a bonfire bursting out of the manse's windows. Angry citizens stood nearby. Some pointed, others scowled, but none moved to douse the flames or offer aid.

Corpses littered the front yard. Most shot. Some burned. All mutilated.

Without waiting for Vergess, Geist shrouded herself in *specter* sorcery and ran across the massive lawn to the manse, avoiding the bodies of Solovyev sorcerers. She ghosted through a wall and entered the dining room. Fire blazed throughout the room, the smoke snaking up the wallpaper and clouding at the ceiling. Geist covered her mouth with the collar of her tunic and glanced around.

More bodies littered the floor. Not charred bodies or people who had passed out from smoke, but bodies riddled with bullet holes and deep lacerations. Pools of crimson spotted the white carpets, and as Geist made her way to the opposite wall, the sick squish of her footsteps disturbed her more than the fire.

This wasn't Amalgam and the Eyes of the Kaiser. They wouldn't have left the blood. This was the Russians outside. The Bolsheviks? Revolutionaries? She shook her head. *It doesn't matter. I need to save anyone I can.*

Geist dashed through the house until she came to a library far hotter than anywhere else. The moment she ghosted through the door, she cringed back into the hall. The heat—it felt like boiling water splashed across her body—and then the sensations became an icy numbness, something Geist had never experienced before.

Damn.

A wooden beam, half burned, collapsed from the ceiling, sending embers swirling into the smoke. Geist coughed, beat at her chest, and then closed her eyes.

It's too much.

She turned around and dashed through the burning building, careful to avoid the flames. While she was perfectly capable of going through solid material, that didn't mean she was immune to the heat or destruction of fire. It would catch her, even while incorporeal, and it would burn.

Geist made it out of the building and dropped her invisibility.

"Are you okay?"

She glanced up and found Vergess rushing to her side.

Before he could protest, she grabbed his arm and then pointed to the manse. "There. We need to go back in." She wheezed for a moment and then forced a deep inhale. "I need to clear things. I can't make it alone. Come."

Geist ran through the wall and back into the blood-soaked dining room. Vergess went to the wall, placed his hand on the side, and rotted away the wood with his *ruina* sorcery. The rapid aging of the wallpaper, support columns, and carpet gave the room a sickly appearance, even beyond the fire and corpses. Vergess stepped through his blackened hole and then motioned to the far door.

Without Battery's power, Geist couldn't extend her invisibility and ghosting abilities to another person, which meant she had to guide Vergess through the wreckage. He gritted his teeth and pushed forward, shielding his eyes with one arm. When they made it to a door blocked by flame, he rotted away another hole and stood back.

Someone shouted from deeper inside the building.

Geist pointed, and Vergess understood. They rushed forward— Geist going through the boundaries while Vergess created a new path. The *ruina* sorcery would eventually come back to bite them as the structure of the house continued to deteriorate, but they needed a way to get people out.

Deep in the back of the house, in a room reserved for private study, Geist found a teenage boy and two children. They were on the floor, the teenager shouting things in Russian between heavy coughing. He kept the kids down, and even though they cried—both no older than five—they didn't move or run around.

The study wasn't as bad as the rest of the house. No fires, but smoke had filtered in from under the door. Geist jogged over to the three Russians and knelt down.

"Come," she said in English.

The teen snapped his head up, his eyes watery and wide. Although he replied in Russian, it was clear he understood a rescue had come. He stood, his legs shaking, and then urged his child wards to their feet.

Geist ushered them across the room. The children—one girl, one boy—trembled and swayed. The little girl fell back to the floor and cried, her face red. Geist scooped her up, held her close, and rushed the three to the door. When the teenager reached for the handle, Geist grabbed his forearm.

"Wait."

The teen knitted his eyebrows, but did as he was told.

Seconds later, the rotting of Vergess's *ruina* sorcery carved a hole through the door. He motioned the teenager out and then picked up the little boy. With the children secure, they ran through the many holes in the walls of House Solovyev. Geist dodged and weaved through the flames, careful to shield the child as much as possible.

The moment they exited the building, Geist took a deep breath of air and slowed her pace. The far side of House Solovyev collapsed in a blaze of embers and flames, sending more smoke into the darkening sky.

Russian citizens pointed from the streets, their rifles ready.

"Vergess," Geist called out. "Can you take them?"

Citizens fired, and the teenager flinched at the crack of gunshots. He shouted something and grabbed for the children. Vergess took the girl from Geist—one child per arm—and ignored the frantic panic of the teenager.

"I'll take them out of the district," he said.

Geist nodded. "I'll handle the revolutionaries."

"What about House Lungin?"

"I'll head there afterward... If there's anything left, I'll fight for it."

Bullets whistled by. Those that hit Vergess tore his clothes but left him unscathed. Those that "hit" Geist went right through her incorporeal form. Vergess grabbed the teen by the hand, keeping himself between him and the angry mob, and then took off for the next estate.

"I'll find you afterward," he shouted in German.

Hardened to combat and filled with a lust to destroy those who wanted to take her life, Geist turned her attention to the Bolsheviks. Perhaps they were legitimately upset. Perhaps they had been wronged. But that didn't matter. They wanted to destroy. Kill. Ruin. And now they had set their sights on innocents.

Vergess had once said that it was far easier to destroy than create. Geist agreed. She had no love for destructive thugs who thought they could wreck everything around them and consider it a "just cause." Whatever their grievances, it didn't require the death of children, the uninvolved, or the passersby.

When Geist entered the crowd, she was invisible. The first man with a rifle, carrying a red scarf, aimed for Vergess. She reached out, thrust an incorporeal hand into the man's body, and then became solid as she ripped out a chuck of his insides. The gooey—and slick—innards of a human body still sent goosebumps down Geist's spine every time she gripped them with her fingers, but she had gotten good at pinpointing the most debilitating spots on the human body.

When one man fell, Geist turned to the next. She could waste a whole army of mundane soldiers. They couldn't deal with her sorcery. They couldn't harm her. And she gained confidence from knowing she was a god among the terrible revolutionaries.

After she ripped the spleen out of a third man, the crowds began to shout and point. Normally, soldiers panicked after witnessing such terrible things. Geist was invisible, after all. All the Russians saw were men exploding outward with blood and mutilated body parts. Yet the Russians didn't act like normal soldiers. They pointed and fled, but they kept their guns up and even fired in Geist's direction, as though they knew magic were involved.

Makes sense, Geist thought with a smile as she attacked the fifth Bolshevik in her path. *They must've seen something like this before.*

It didn't matter. Even if someone in the crowd knew it was *specter* sorcery at play, they couldn't do anything. Geist continued her assault, distracting the crowds and injuring the best riflemen, knowing that Vergess would be long gone.

Once satisfied that Vergess had gotten enough of a head start, Geist broke away from the mob and rushed down the road. She gave House Solovyev one last glance. She hadn't had enough time to search the place properly. Had there been others? It didn't matter anymore. One more wall collapsed, sending the whole thing to the ground.

Invisible, incorporeal, and faster than normal men, Geist dashed through the posh estates of Petrograd, not bothering to dodge fences, gates, walls, or buildings. She headed in a direct line for her destination, the sights blurring by her on either side. She knew roughly where the last house was. She just had to get there.

The destruction engulfed the neighborhood as Geist sped

through. Men and women, anger in their eyes, lit fire to houses, paintings, tapestries, and landscaping. They chanted things in Russian, but Geist didn't need to know their language to guess their motives. Tired of the social order and ruling class, the people of Petrograd decided they would burn everything to the ground and start anew.

Just like the Kaiser wanted, Geist mused. *That was why he shipped so many troublemakers to the capital. And that's why the Eyes of the Kaiser are here. They were banking on social unrest so they could seize blood from Russian sorcerers. Not only that, but if the tsar loses power, the Russian Empire will have no choice but to withdraw from the war.*

If the Russian Empire fails, Germany and Austria-Hungary won't have to fight two fronts. They'll be free to focus on France and Britain.

Lost in her realizations, Geist almost missed her final destination—House Lungin. She slowed when she came to the iron-wrought fence, her heart stopped for a moment as she gazed through the bars. The house had been ripped apart. Not with fire, but as though the hands of God had reached down and pulled the walls in opposite directions.

What happened here?

The estate had the warmth of a ghost town, devoid of life. Not even the protestors ventured onto the property. They marched around it, their torches and signs far from even the grass of the lawn. When Geist went to ghost through the bars—just to check the wreckage—a sharp pain filled her chest.

She couldn't bring herself to get any closer. The chill of magic lingered like a barrier.

Is this their sorcery? she wondered. *Some sort of protection? But what happened to their house?*

It occurred to her they may have already gone. Perhaps the damage was from them activating a powerful barrier of magic in an instant. It wouldn't surprise Geist if that were the case. The family likely left after that.

For the sake of optimism, I'll mark them as having escaped on their own.

Geist turned around and ran back through the west hills of Petrograd.

"*Geist.*"

The word straight to her thoughts almost jarred her out of her *specter* sorcery.

Blick.

"*You need to come back. Defiant came through. He's found Victory.*"

TWENTY-FIVE

American

Geist headed straight for the road back to her squad. Vergess would be there, somewhere, and she was bound to catch up to him. The longer she ran, however, the more she realized just how bad the rioting had become. Men and women threw buckets of oil across lavish buildings and then struck up a match. When soldiers came to stop them, they would either get into a fight or join in the destruction.

Geist had never seen so many people keen on the devastation of their homeland. Had they no love for their country? She shook her head. There was no way to prevent the disaster—it had already started—so she kept her sights set ahead.

I can't lose focus now.

GEIST AND VERGESS made it back to the dining hall in record time. Geist ghosted through the wall, and Vergess slammed the front door open, busting the wood on the doorframe where the lock had been secure. The others flinched and reached for their weapons, but they held back a moment later.

"You're back," Blick said. "Finally." He hefted his rifle and stomped toward the front door. "We shouldn't wait a second longer. C'mon, Battery."

His younger brother jumped to his side with a nod. Together they made it to the busted doorframe and then waited.

Geist dropped her invisibility. "Where are we headed?"

"A place to the north," Defiant said. He stood from his seat at a long wooden table, dark bags under his eyes. He held his coat tight across his body as icy wind flooded the room. "It isn't far. I estimate within the boundaries of Petrograd."

Still within the zone of riots. No matter where they went, they would be hounded by protesting Russians. It would be dangerous, but Geist didn't want to leave her team any more than she had to. Once she had Victory, she wanted to escape the Russian Empire as fast as possible. But how would they all travel without getting harmed?

"Vergess," she said. "You take point. If anyone tries to stop us, I want you to stop them."

He replied with a curt nod.

"Blick, I know you want to get Victory back more than anyone, but I want you to stay in the middle of the group. Keep everyone updated with your telepathy."

Although it took him a moment longer to reply, Blick did so in similar fashion.

"Battery—you empower me. I'll protect you and Defiant. Dreamer, you'll make us look like Bolsheviks. If any Russians try to muscle their way into our group, I'll rip them apart from the inside out, got it?"

With a plan in place, they left the dining hall and entered the city. The evening sky, blotted out with the smoke of a dozen burning buildings, still sprinkled the city with a flurry of snowflakes. The cold, mixed with the soot, was a terrible combination. Geist coughed as they rushed down the sidewalk, her lungs filled with the debris of House Solovyev.

Defiant and Battery stuck close to her. Dreamer kept watch from the back, Blick jogged in the middle, and Vergess took point. A few

Russians attempted to block their path, but Vergess shoved them into the street, practically breaking the arm of one man and busting open the eyebrow of another.

People broke into shops and looted the contents. Geist stepped over the shattered glass and kept Defiant close. Of everyone in her team, he hadn't been combat trained—and as long as she held into him, she could make him incorporeal as well, all thanks to Battery.

"How did you locate Victory?" she asked as they made their way around the corner of a government building. All the windows had been smashed and the stairs marked with paint.

Defiant leaned on her shoulder. "My uncle's research. When we developed the GH Gas, he made sure the weapon would seek out magic. We used… techniques… that…"

Geist didn't need him to finish. She had already experienced the gas firsthand. It *did* seek out magic. It had slithered toward her in the trenches and chased her out of the OHL. Somehow—some way —it sought blood. But how was it possible? The gas couldn't have a mind of its own. Could it?

"I used Blick's and Battery's blood to find Victory," Defiant continued, his voice low. "Their blood is similar. It calls to itself. That's how I know."

What kind of sinister magic did Defiant work on? Geist couldn't shake the terrible feeling that he wasn't telling her the whole story. Like there was some *other* aspect to the gas too cruel to mention—and that he would somehow reveal that secret if he explained himself.

But just like the Russian revolution, Geist had to put it aside. She had one objective: find Victory and escape with her team's lives intact. Once they were safe, she could examine all the other aspect of the operation.

Two Russians waving red flags stopped and pointed at Vergess. Thanks to Dreamer's illusions, Vergess looked like any other rioter in the street, but the two men asked something in Russian and Vergess was unable to answer. One withdrew a knife, and Geist was sure he would attack. Instead, the man flipped it around and tossed it over, hilt first. Vergess caught it with ease and then gave a sarcastic salute with the blade. The two men smiled as they continued down the road, the sidewalks and snow spotted with crimson.

A few more blocks and Geist realized they had entered an industrial district. Factories had been burned and bombed. Dozens of people were dead in the snow, most of which looked like police constables. No one had picked up their bodies.

"*Vedma!*" some Russians chanted. "*Vedma! Vedma!*"

Although Geist didn't really know the language, she recognized the word. *Witch.* She had heard it before, from the Russian immigrants to Austria. They muttered the words around sorcerers, their tone one of disgust.

Across the road, a group of Russians surrounded a teenage girl—herself Russian—and pointed rifles, knives, and pitchforks. The mob chanted and jabbed their weapons at her.

The young teen held a sash in her arms, clutching it tight to her chest. It bore medals from the Russian military and she guarded them from the rioters when they reached out to take it. She screamed at them, tears cascading down her face. Geist couldn't stand the sight any longer.

She let go of Defiant. "Watch him," she barked to Dreamer. Then she ran across the road, ghosting through carriages and never slowing.

They wanted to see a witch? Geist would show them a witch.

One man thrust his pitchfork out, his aim for the girl's arm. Geist appeared in the middle of the crowd, her invisibility flicking away for just a moment as she became corporeal long enough to grab the handle of the tool and push it aside. Everyone's eyes went wide at the sudden appearance of soldier. Even the girl leaned away, taken aback.

Geist went for the riflemen first. She gouged out flesh around their shoulders and arms. A gruesome affair—it left her hand hot and sticky with blood—but it would prevent them from using their weapons. Perhaps permanently.

"*Demoh,*" one of the rioters shouted.

Geist didn't need a translation. All she needed was their fear and panic. And when she attacked a man with a knife, while invisible, his leg rupturing as though split open, the crowd fled in every direction. Some men knocked others down in their haste. Then others ran over the ones on the ground, conducting themselves no better than a stampede of wild animals.

In the flight and desperation, Geist grabbed the arm of the girl and ran. The girl didn't struggle, even when Geist ghosted through a fence and into the safety of a factory that hadn't been ravaged. Even if the rioters came, the obstacles between them and the girl were enough for the teen to make a getaway.

When Geist let her go, the girl said something in Russian. Unable to reply, Geist nodded and turned back for her squad. The girl touched her shoulder and said something louder. What was she trying to communicate? Geist assumed it was a *thank you* and forced a second nod.

"I need to go," she said in English. "Stay safe."

"American?" the girl asked, her accent thick.

"Yes. American. You should hide."

She said nothing else.

Geist went invisible and ran back through the fence. Why did the Russians say that word with such confusion? *American.* There was always a hint of reverence, too. Geist understood, in a way. She had escaped her house and run to the United States, after all. She could have gone to a great many places—France, England, even Germany —but there was a specific reason she chose the United States.

It was a silly reason, and Geist dwelled on it as she rejoined the group. Defiant reached out and placed his hand on her shoulder, his grip shaky, betraying his anxiety. Her mind continued to wander as they broke free of the rioters.

Once, before Geist had joined the military, she had seen a parade through the streets of New York City. Soldiers marched and rode floats. They appeared to be like any other army, from any other nation, going through the motions. But what she saw changed her mind about the United States forever.

A group of chaplains marched by when a strong breeze stole the kippah from the head of a rabbi. The brimless cap flew through the air, and it was clear the man had become distraught. A Catholic chaplain removed his own cap and cut a circle from the olive green fabric and then handed it over as a makeshift kippah for his fellow chaplain to wear.

It was as if that Catholic wanted everyone to know that they weren't just chaplains, but that he was Christian, and the other man Jewish—and that they both wanted to shout the message, *While some countries kill each other for the difference in religion, America had people of all beliefs, working side-by-side, when the time came to help others.*

That tiny moment, almost insignificant in the grand scheme of things, had resonated with Geist. She wanted to add luster, not tarnish, to the reputation of the United States. She wanted to spread the ideals of tolerance and protection. Of cooperation.

And when she glanced between her teammates—two Germans, two Brits, an Arab, and herself, a woman, their leader—she couldn't help but realize that perhaps she had built exactly what she wanted.

It reinforced her desire to save Victory. She wouldn't allow her squad to be damaged or harmed. She would protect them.

Defiant squeezed her shoulder. "There."

The group stopped at a large gate. Beyond the fence stood a monastery, perhaps a century old. Its thick stone and dark windows weren't inviting, nor did it seem like anyone was inside. The building, two stories, complete with domestic quarters for nuns, waved the Russian and Eastern Orthodox flags.

"Our enemy is inside?" Dreamer asked.

Defiant shook his head. "I don't know about the enemy... but Victory is."

If Victory is in the monastery, so are the Eyes of the Kaiser, Geist thought. *We can't take any chances, and we can't waste the element of surprise. This might be the only time we'll get the drop on them.*

Dreamer made the sign of the cross. "It's a shame to see men who value nothing holy. This only adds to their many atrocities."

"Maybe they're men who lack faith," Battery muttered.

"That would explain how they manage to sleep at night."

"I'm going inside," Geist said. "Vergess, you'll come with me."

"I'd be honored," he said.

She didn't want to take any risks. If something happened—if

she were dominated—she wanted someone who could handle the situation. Hopefully it wouldn't come to that, but Geist knew it was a possibility.

"Battery," she said. "I want you to empower Vergess."

Battery snapped his attention to her. "Not you?"

"I want Vergess's *ruina* sorcery to be unparalleled. Once we have Victory, this place needs to be rubble."

Any hideout of the enemy, no matter how small, needed to be rooted from the Russian Empire. Defiant had already confirmed that the German Empire had been influencing the protestors for some time. It made sense that German operatives were hiding out in Petrograd, stirring up trouble, helping the people feel uneasy about their government.

They needed to go.

"Blick," Geist said. "You wait here by the gates. Shoot any enemies that exit the building. Careful, though. There might be civilians inside."

His eyes flashed a bright gold. "I'll be able to tell the difference."

"Good. Dreamer, I want you to protect Battery and Defiant. Your illusions are invaluable."

He stepped up to Defiant's side, his handgun at the ready. "By your command."

"Battery, we'll be back soon. With Victory."

He replied with his brow furrowed, but otherwise remained quiet.

She headed straight for the gate. It was locked. Geist ghosted to the other side, intent on using her sorcery to reach her hand into the lock and get the latch undone, but Vergess touched the heavy metal. In an instant, rust ripped apart the lock. It spread to the bars, then to the gate hinges, and straight to a pillar of brick. The devastating power—all thanks to Battery's sorcery—tore the fence apart in moments.

Vergess lifted both eyebrows. "I've... never wielded such destruction."

"It'll be fine," Geist muttered. "If you see the Eyes of the Kaiser, use it on them."

TWENTY-SIX

Blood Research

Geist and Vergess crossed the long lawn of the monastery. Chaos in the distance created a white noise over the property, drowning out their footsteps. The darkness of a moonless night hid them from sight.

Although it had been a long while since Geist had attended any sort of church, she knew the basic functions of a monastery. Most monasteries had people living on the grounds, but this monastery had overgrown grass, and the bushes were unclipped. Something wasn't right, but it wasn't like she could ask the locals about the status of the priests. No one in Petrograd cared about the happenings of a small monastery, not with a revolt taking place.

Geist walked to the wall. She tapped Vergess on the shoulder when he approached and tugged at his tunic, motioning toward the backside of the building. She continued around the building, and he followed, glancing around as they went.

Once they reached the back, Geist stopped Vergess and then knocked her knuckles against the stone. He grazed his fingertips over the monastery. Within seconds, the stone corroded, wasting away to sand. Metal pipes in the wall rusted and twisted, losing their sturdy nature right in front of Geist's eyes. She kept a good few feet from the destruction, well aware that *ruina* sorcery could spread to anything it came into contact with.

A rotted hole appeared in the wall—one large enough for a grown man to step through—and Vergess entered the monastery. The wonderful thing about his magic was that it damaged without sound, unlike explosives. *Makes for a convenient stealth tool*, Geist thought with a smile. She hadn't given much consideration to physical stealth in quite some time. She could walk through walls, after all.

Geist stepped into the monastery and took note of the dark hallway. Oil lamps hung on the walls with no sign the building had been fitted with electricity. Silence greeted her. It occurred to Geist then that people fleeing the riot should have been flocking to the church for safety, yet no one came.

No one.

"They're here," Geist whispered. "They've been here for a while."

Vergess nodded. "I had the same thought. The people of the Russian Empire must know this is a place for sorcerers."

"You know the enemy tactics better than I do. Where do you think they're hiding?"

"Below. Like at the OHL. They want privacy."

"Let's get going."

Geist, still invisible, remained close to Vergess as they traveled down the hall. They passed room after room, glancing in only to confirm they were empty. The moment they reached a staircase, Vergess nodded with his head.

"I think it'd be best if you took point," he whispered.

"I agree," she said—since Vergess couldn't see her nodding.

With careful steps, Geist made her way downstairs. The basement level, complete with rooms and a wine cellar, had an odd smell. It reminded Geist of leather and sweat. Had anyone cleaned the basement? She doubted it.

Geist entered a room and stopped dead in her tracks. The smell of blood—dried, old—hit her hard. She glanced around, curious to see empty glass vials stacked on countertops. She had seen them before—they were meant to collect blood from sorcerers.

Geist walked over to the far wall counter and stared down at the folders stacked near the wall. She flipped one open and read the German within.

SERGEI ANTONOV

Schools of sorcery: ignis, tempest

Subject possessed common magics. His vital liquid was collected and sent for further research. Subject became weak after first withdrawal. Died after second. The blood pressure became too low.

GEIST FLIPPED to the next page.

ALEXANDER KISLYAK

Schools of sorcery: communis, corpus

Subject possessed common magics. His arm was amputated and sent for further research. It appears physical flesh can also carry the traits for sorcery. Gas fusion an option. Subject remained alive through second amputation. During the amputation of the leg, subject choked himself on his own tongue. Ninth request for sedation has been sent.

GEIST WENT to another and then another. She stopped when she found a sorcerer with interesting sorceries.

MARIA GRININ

Schools of sorcery: obtinebris, animus, scorpius

Subject possessed exceptional magics. She was placed in confinement and drained. Died after eight days. Only extracted two vials worth. Willing participants are needed for sustained extraction.

. . .

SUCH INFORMATION DIDN'T STARTLE Geist. She had seen the research they conducted on the front lines. Now they were using Russian citizens—trapped in facilities underground—to carry out their next steps.

Geist slammed the folder shut. Despite her efforts and victories, the enemy continued to pursue their twisted goals. *And it won't end until the war is over.*

We have to win. We have to stop this.

"Who's there?" someone asked in German.

The question came from the hallway. Geist whipped around, her heart in her throat. She pulled her handgun as a metal clanging filled the basement. Her mind filled in the blanks with a picture of a grenade.

Geist dashed through the wall and entered the hall with her weapon raised. Pavel, the fleshcrafter of the enemy squad, stood down the corridor. A fragmentation grenade rolled across the floor, but before it exploded, Vergess waved his hand.

To Geist's shock, and horror, his *ruina* sorcery washed across the hall like a wave. He didn't need to touch the walls or floor or ceiling —his empowered sorcery spread through the air like a breeze, corrupting and rotting everything in the nearby area. And it wasted everything fast. Flakes from the ceiling fell to the floor, the walls twisted, and a hole melted in the floor in front of the fleshcrafter. Although devastating and thorough, the *ruina* sorcery dealt its damage without sound.

Pavel leapt away from the rot and pulled a pistol. If he fired, every enemy agent in the monetary would know their position.

Vergess lunged forward, faster than he had ever moved before. Battery's power not only gave him heightened destruction, but it also increased his *apex* sorcery as well. He was superhuman among normal men—a god of strength and agility. He grabbed Pavel by the arm, broke it with a brutal twist, and wrenched the gun from his limp fingers.

The second Pavel went to scream, Vergess crushed his throat with a vice grip. His fingers dug down into the skin, and his *ruina* sorcery took care of the rest. Flesh aged and melted, and then the bone became visible, crumbling into a fine sugar.

Pavel had tried to use his fleshcrafting sorcery—and perhaps a layer of skin came off Vergess's hand—but it wasn't enough.

The mess at Vergess's feet forced Geist to look away.

War has no pretty side.

"Stay where you are," someone commanded.

Geist knew the identity moment the words hit her ears.

An Eye of the Kaiser.

She snapped her attention to the end of the hall, but immediately glanced away when she saw the purple shine from his eyes. He had come along after Pavel, perhaps after hearing the clink of the grenade.

"Vergess," Geist shouted. "There! At the end of the hall!"

"Kill her," the Eye said.

Geist stopped breathing. Although she knew the situation, she denied it to herself. *Vergess would never get caught by their domination. He must've looked away in time.* But then he turned around and dropped the rest of Pavel's rotting body to floor. The expression on his face— almost neutral—confirmed the reality and dispelled the last of Geist's hopes.

"Vergess," she whispered.

He leapt down the hall with frightening speed, still empowered by Battery's sorcery. Geist took only one step back before he was on top of her. He couldn't see her—his eyes searched without focus— but his hearing and smell were far beyond human. *He'll know where I am!*

Vergess swiped his hand out in front of him. If Geist hadn't been incorporeal, he would've torn her arm straight from her body. The chill of magic sent shivers across her body. Should she attack him? Would they even have to fight? Could he harm her? What if she just stayed invisible?

As if moving to the next option on a laundry list of death, Vergess waved his hand and sent another round of *ruina* sorcery through the hallway. It caught the walls, ceiling, and floor. And then

Geist's boots. His overpowered magic would soon spread to the rest of her.

She scrambled to take off her military issued footwear, dropping her handgun in the process, but Vergess did it again, destroying more of the basement in the process. Her socks got caught by his sinister sorcery—the soles of her feet kept from slipping through the floor, but it also made them a contact point for the terrible sorcery.

Geist dove through the wall and landed in a wine cellar, desperate to put space between her and Vergess. She didn't want to attack. She couldn't. But she also couldn't let him kill her. Geist ripped off her socks, threw them aside, and then flinched when Vergess busted in through the door.

He would hunt her forever, with relentless speed and god-like power.

"That's right," the Eye called out, a laugh on the end of his words. "Bring me her corpse!"

When Geist went to dive through the wall a second time, Vergess cut her off with another burst of *ruina* sorcery. She jumped and went through the wall, her heart pounding, sweat running down her back. He was a trained killer. He would eventually formulate a plan to kill her. And if her focus ever wavered—if she dropped her sorcery for just a moment and became solid—he would tear her apart.

Geist ran across the hall to the opposite room and wheeled around on her heel, waiting the half second it would take for Vergess to catch up. She couldn't outrun him. She couldn't counter his *ruina* sorcery.

I'm so sorry!

Vergess destroyed the whole wall with a wave of his hand, his *ruina* sorcery destroying the basement enough that the building groaned in protest. When Vergess stepped into the room, Geist lunged. She reached into his leg, just above the knee, and took a chunk of muscle. Most men would have screamed and stumbled back, incapacitated. Vergess gritted his teeth and sent out another wave of *ruina*—his focus undisturbed.

Geist leapt up, hung onto his tunic, becoming corporeal after the rot passed, and hefted herself onto his body. Vergess grabbed her uniform in an instant. On instinct, and as fast as she could attack, Geist jabbed her hand into Vergess's gut. The look in his eyes —the shock—it must've been a long time since he ever feared for his life.

He swiped at her, his fingers like claws, no doubt hoping to catch a piece of her physical form. Geist went fully incorporeal just as his arm would've broken her bones and sent her flying. She ghosted through him, falling to the floor, taking her hand back from his torso —tearing bits of insides.

The moment she hit her back, Geist flipped up to her feet and dashed into the hall. She kept her eyes closed, her heart beating so hard she could barely hear anything else.

"Stop where you are," the Eye commanded.

But his magic didn't affect her. Geist ran straight for him.

"Get her!" the Eye of the Kaiser shouted. "Protect me!"

Geist pulled out her trench knife, thrust it into the Eye's body while still incorporeal, and willed it to become solid the moment she had it deep in his chest. When she ripped her hand away, soaked in his blood, she leapt backward, leaving the weapon in his body. Even if Vergess somehow defeated her now, the Eye of the Kaiser wouldn't last more than a few minutes.

The Eye wheezed and half gasped, his breath caught in his throat. He staggered, hit the wall, and tried to choke out something —say a few words—but he couldn't. Then his breaths came as wet hiccups and he collapsed to the floor, his suffocation so thorough Geist almost couldn't get enough air herself.

Rot in hell, she thought as she swiped her hand across his face, her fingers becoming solid as they went through his terrible eyes. He grimaced and rolled into the fetal position, unable to breathe or see. Geist took a few deep breaths and stepped back, certain of her victory.

Vergess hobbled into the hallway, his arm clutched tight over his stomach. He stumbled for a moment, shaking his head.

"Geist," he said. "I…"

She ran to him. "It's okay. I'm here." She dropped her invisibility, tucked herself under his arm, and helped him sit on the ruined floor.

Blood pumped from the gouge in his leg. Geist reached into the pouches of his belt, searching until she came to field medical supplies. They weren't enough, but they were better than nothing. She wrapped gauze around his knee and then sleeves from her uniform to use as more for his gut.

Although she had *corpus* sorcery in her veins—the type of skill to heal others—she had never trained it. In that moment, she regretted every decision that had brought her to the monastery. Why had she focused on *apex* sorcery when it wouldn't save the people she cared about? But regret was like quicksand for the mind. If she allowed it, the feeling would swallow her whole.

"You're going to be okay," she said, her voice unsteady.

"I'm sorry," he murmured.

"No. *I'm* sorry. Don't talk."

"This is the outcome I prefer."

Geist brushed the sweat-soaked hair from his forehead, her fingers trembling. Who were they going to get to heal his wounds? She had seen soldiers die of less. There was so much blood... It dripped onto the floor and pooled in the newly made cracks and shallow holes.

"I tried not to make it fatal," Geist said. "You'll be okay. Everything will be fine."

He nodded, his breaths shallow.

"Can... can you walk?"

"I will," he said.

An odd answer, but Geist didn't want to hear anything else. She held his tunic, her fingers twisted in the fabric, her chest so tight it felt as though it was collapsing inward. Hurting Victory, now Vergess? She couldn't stand it.

"You need to keep going," Vergess murmured. He stared at her, his blue eyes searching hers. "I can reach the others, but if there's any hope of getting Victory... we need to do it now."

"I can help. Let me stay with you."

Vergess half laughed. "Isn't that my line?" He shook his head.

"Listen… I'm sorry. I'm always worried about you, my intended. But one of the Eyes of the Kaiser has died. The enemy doesn't know what's going on. You have the upper hand in this situation."

"I… I know."

Geist couldn't deny any of his observations, and she knew she had to handle it. Although she wanted to protect him, like he wanted to protect her, the mission came first. She stood, helped Vergess to his good leg, and held him for a moment in a tight embrace.

"I'll be back," she said.

"You better."

Geist opened her mouth, but stopped herself before she spoke. Now wasn't the time for any more words. The basement corridor of the monastery crumbled bit by bit the longer she spoke with Vergess. Hesitation helped no one, but she did watch him hobble to the exit. His sorcery helped him—he could move despite his terrible injuries—and once she was satisfied he could make it, Geist turned to head deeper into the monastery.

I'll handle this. There're only two sorcerers I'm worried about, and one of them is a corpse in this hallway. I'll be fine.

TWENTY-SEVEN

Anti-Magic

A malgam felt it in his bones.

Geist had arrived.

His bait had worked perfectly, and now he would have her.

He pushed aside the wooden tables, clearing a space in the basement lab. Geist wasn't the type to give up without a fight. He liked that about her. She *never* just gave up. Amalgam smiled under his gas mask as he kicked a couple chairs into the wall. There would be nothing interfere with their confrontation.

"What're you doing to my lab?" a decrepit voice asked, floating out from the doorway to look the room over.

Amalgam stopped his rearranging. "What're you still doing here, Helmuth? I thought you left with Lieutenant Cavell and the others. Alexander Palace is soon to fall."

Helmuth, the newest magi-tech general, hobbled into the room. Years ago, he had resembled his nephew, Heinrich—thin, tall, and with thick black hair. But his features weren't right since his accident with the GH Gas.

Not right at all.

Helmuth walked with a limp, one foot twisted back around and elongated, like it had melted and then solidified into its grotesque, slug-like shape. His arms were longer than normal, his fingers reaching his knees. And he had four, an additional arm attached to his right shoulder, another attached to the left side of his ribs. Each limb was spindly—borderline skeletal.

His face, sunken in and wan, had the color of a dead fish. His asymmetrical appearance, combined with his beady eyes and intense gaze, gave him the feel of a monster from the horror stories of Germany's ancient fairy tales. It wasn't far from reality, either. Helmuth had consumed plenty of flesh since he embraced his transformation with the gas. Perhaps even from children.

"You're displeased to see me," Helmuth muttered.

"I asked what you were doing here," Amalgam said.

"The lieutenant didn't want my sorcery." He dragged both of his right hands across the wooden table as he shambled into the lab. "And I didn't want to leave our captives. What if they tried to escape?"

Amalgam didn't care about any of that. The longer Helmuth lingered in the room, the more he risked messing up Amalgam's plans. What if Helmuth tried to capture Geist for his experiments? His anti-magic sorcery could cripple sorcerers in the nearby area. Amalgam wasn't about to let it happen. He would have his fight. He would win. And then he would leave this place.

Helmuth lifted his hand and stared at it for a moment.

Although Amalgam's sight wasn't like those of normal men, the arm radiated a twisted aura. Each finger, each bone—even the muscles—weren't Helmuth's. They were stitched together and fused to Helmuth with GH Gas, replacing the limb Helmuth lost when he melted his own arm away.

Helmuth was a Frankenstein's monster of body parts, not just his four arms... For some reason, Helmuth didn't just want blood, he wanted organs—*pieces*—to use for his ever-growing collection of sorcery.

Fucking gas, Amalgam thought.

He didn't know how it was made or how it worked, but it somehow *did things* to flesh that should never happen. Although Helmuth had stolen fingers, he tapped his fingernails on the wood, testing out the control of his twisted hand. Although his anti-magic sorcery could shield him from the effects of the GH Gas, he allowed it to twist him for a small moment, long enough to attach a new limb or flesh. Before the gas could degrade his body into a puddle of fleshy ooze, Helmuth activated his sorcery and halted the change, resulting in a clean attachment of limbs and organs.

"What *are* you doing?" Helmuth asked, his German formal and harsh. "I thought you left with Otto and Pavel."

"The Ethereal Squadron has arrived. I'm preparing."

"They found us?"

"You should leave," Amalgam said. "I'll handle the situation."

"By yourself?"

While the words were innocuous, his tone was thick with condescension. Amalgam rotated his shoulders, his attention glued to Geist's ever-nearing location.

Helmuth continued, "The Ethereal Squadron has so many useful sorceries. We shouldn't squander our opportunity to catch them. And your long history of failures doesn't instill confidence."

"I said I would handle it," Amalgam growled, his hot breath trapped in his gas mask.

Even Helmuth—a monster himself—clearly thought him nothing more than a dog. It stung, but Amalgam pushed the thoughts from his mind. Geist's presence, her aura of magic, soothed him. He enjoyed her proximity and wouldn't allow Helmuth's snide remarks to agitate his mood.

Besides, if Helmuth pushed his luck, Amalgam would just tear him apart, starting with his stolen liver. Although the man had acquired several schools of sorcery, he had yet to master any of them. Now would be the time to put him down, if it were ever going to happen.

Geist started her descent down the long staircase. Closer and closer she crept, at a steady pace, but cautious.

"Leave," Amalgam said. "Or you'll be a part of this."

"Don't fail us."

Helmuth shuffled back toward the door, dragging his stump of a foot, the flesh dragging across the stone floor, creating a slithering sound. Not all the parts of his new body functioned like they should. Perhaps next time he would find a sorcerer with limbs the same length; then he wouldn't have such an awkward gait.

Alone, and ready to face Geist, Amalgam's blood raced through his veins. Each second that passed reinforced his desire for their reunion. Although they had fought throughout the Russian Empire, they hadn't been alone. Hans, Otto, even Pavel—they had been in the way, threatening to destroy Amalgam's plans.

Not now.

Geist came to the basement door and stopped. Her magic aura, different than most, had a song about it. Like giving melody to the sparkles of early morning light or the tranquil peace of a starry night. Abstract, yet comforting. And the closer she got, the clearer the song became.

Come on, Amalgam thought. *What're you waiting for? You know this is the only place you'll find Victory.*

She slipped into the room, ghosting through the door, silent as a corpse. Then she stopped, her whole body tense. For some reason, she had no boots.

"I've been waiting," Amalgam said, wanting her to know he knew of her presence.

Geist didn't move for a moment. Then she ended her sorcery and stood straight, her presence filling the room—and Amalgam's mind. It consumed his thoughts, like a drug, and he waited for her to speak.

"Where is he?" Geist asked.

Who? was his first thought, but Amalgam shook his head, dispelling the confusion. She had come for Victory.

"He's locked away," Amalgam said.

"Alive?"

"Unharmed, as far as I know."

"You…" She took a shaky breath. "Didn't take his blood?"

Amalgam gritted his teeth. He didn't care about Victory, and it wouldn't matter soon regardless. On the other hand, he knew Victory's safety meant the world to Geist. He couldn't disregard it, or else she would panic.

"I didn't want to risk his death," he said. "He had to be alive or else you wouldn't have come, would you? So don't fret. He lives."

Geist took a hesitant step farther into the room, still tense. She reached for her sidearm, but her hand landed on an empty holster.

"Why?" she asked. "Why do you care so much about *me*? Is it because you want revenge for me throwing you in the GH Gas? You want me to suffer the same fate?"

Amalgam didn't answer. Revenge would be logical. She had been the one to push him into the gas-filled trench. But it wasn't that. He just wanted her company. Her calming aura. Her.

"I should've killed you on the operating table," Geist said, her tone icy. "When you were helpless. But I didn't. I thought we were alike. You had lost your brothers-in-arms, and so had I. And now you're targeting Victory, my teammate, just to get to me? I thought you would know better than anybody. I won't allow you to do this ever again."

"You're going to kill me?" Amalgam asked with a smile.

"Monsters deserve no better."

Her thoughts, tangled and confused, flitted into his mind.

… he's left me no other options … it must end tonight …

Amalgam gritted his teeth and flexed his fingers. "Come at me then."

This was it. He would subdue her and create another monster— one with her aura—and they would be intertwined by circumstance.

Geist wrapped herself in *specter* sorcery and lunged forward. When she neared, Amalgam lifted his arm and flooded the basement room with sickly green fire. Instead of just aiming for her, he cast it in all directions, catching some of the tables. The magical fire wouldn't pierce his magi-tech armor, but it would catch Geist, even if she was incorporeal. She wasn't immune to temperature, after all. Better to surround himself with it and drain her of stamina.

She darted around him. Quiet—*fast*—with the grace of a cat. Her *apex* sorcery had developed in leaps and bounds. When she went to attack him from behind, Amalgam teleported. He shifted his location to a button he had tossed in the corner. Hundreds of buttons littered the monastery, just in case.

Geist wouldn't escape.

He used his stolen *ignis* sorcery again, throwing another wave of flame into the room. Geist leapt to the wall, kicked off, and landed beside him, her acrobatics beyond impressive.

She snatched his Luger pistol from its holster and fired, all within a blinding second. The bullet clipped Amalgam's gas mask, cracking the mirror-like glass over his left "eye." His sorcery might not save him if she fired straight into his skill.

Amalgam staggered back and unleashed a furious eruption of fire.

Geist jumped away, and she hit the wall, not ghosting through. Flames washed over her. She cried out as she dashed away.

The sound she made—one of agony—it hurt him more than the sting of bullets or the cutting of barbed wire. Amalgam didn't want to kill her. Far from it. But he had to win. *I need to be careful. I can't lose control.*

Geist fired again. And then again. Amalgam turned away, the bullets hitting his arm and chest. His *corpus* sorcery knit flesh back into place and pushed out any lead lodged in his body. It couldn't last forever, though. Blood that spilled out wouldn't make it back in.

Amalgam teleported to another button, in the opposite corner as Geist. She caught her breath, and that was his opening. He rushed forward and slammed his fist into the side of her head. His magi-tech gauntlet prevented her from ghosting through his attack.

Geist spit blood, but she rolled with the hit and then ghosted through the nearby wall. Amalgam took a step back, tense. He could follow her movement, even if she was two stories above him. But she didn't move. She waited in the other room.

Why?

The answer hit him quick—she wanted time to recover. He had wanted to knock her out, and perhaps he got close, but now she could take all the time she wanted in catching her breath. If Amalgam tried to enter the hall and walk around to the other room, it would take too long. Fortunately, he knew she wasn't leaving. She had made it clear—she wanted him dead and that his continued attacks on her squad couldn't be tolerated any longer.

After a few seconds, Geist dove back into the basement lab, her movements just as fast as before, perhaps more so. Amalgam was ready. When she fired, he teleported again. Soon she wouldn't have any bullets.

But then a terrible feeling blanketed the room. It clung to Amalgam like tar across his body, slicking in his throat and choking him. His breaths came strained and his chest twisted in agony.

Anti-magic. Powerful and deadly. It silenced the thoughts of others and nearly blinded Amalgam. He grabbed at his head.

"Surrender," Helmuth said from the far door. He punctuated his command with the loading of a handgun. "Or I kill this one."

It took all of Amalgam's concentration to "see" Victory was also in the room.

Damn him.

Helmuth wanted to interfere with his plan? Even when he told him not to? *I'll kill him,* Amalgam thought. *I was supposed to fight without this interference.*

Geist moved a few inches closer, but Helmuth pressed the barrel of the weapon against Victory's skull.

"I'll shoot," Helmuth said. "And then our monster, Amalgam, will rip you apart. But if you surrender, there's a chance at least one of you will live to bring a message to the Ethereal Squadron in Verdun."

Helmuth was no doubt making up nonsense, but the proposition seemed to give Geist pause. Was she considering it?

Amalgam hit the floor on one knee, his mind a blur of thoughts and darkness. The anti-magic took everything from him. He wasn't a monster, just a corpse that didn't know it was dead.

Geist is right here… She's the only person who matters. I can't let anyone of these bastards touch her—especially not Helmuth.

TWENTY-EIGHT

Coward

Geist struggled to breathe.

Defiant warned me his uncle was here! she scolded herself. *I should've taken it into consideration. Without my sorcery, what can I even do?*

Victory had seen better days. His uniform was torn, his identification tag was missing, his hair matted with blood—and although he could stand, he shook, as if cold or weak from hunger. Had they fed him? Were they planning to torture him to death through starvation?

Defiant's uncle, a man well into his fifties, didn't look right. He had two different-colored eyes, and his skin looked patchwork at best. He wore long sleeves over his four awkward arms, and his collar high, so Geist couldn't make out more detail about his flesh. His one foot, melted and long, trailing behind him, reminded her of a slug. Despite all that, he resembled Defiant enough to mark them as relatives, even if the sorcery wasn't a dead giveaway.

Looking at him for longer than a few seconds got Geist's stomach churning. He was a walking charnel house.

The anti-magic researcher slid his finger over the trigger of the handgun.

"Wait," Geist choked out.

Victory met her gaze. He had the hard look of someone unafraid to die.

She knew what he would say—not to give into the enemy demands—but Geist still felt the sting of her earlier failures. She had let him down on multiple occasions. He had been injured and thrown into danger. *She had attacked him.* And Cross would be devastated if Victory died. As a soldier and a leader, Geist understood that sometimes not everyone could escape a fight, but that didn't mean she could use it as an excuse to save her own life.

Geist steeled herself to her ultimate desires. If she *could* save her teammates, there would be no price she wasn't willing to pay. No matter what, she would make sure Victory made it free.

"I surrender," Geist said. She threw down the Luger.

"*Geist*," Victory snapped. "What're you doing? They'll kill us both!"

Defiant's uncle chortled. "Well?" he barked at Amalgam. Then he pointed at Geist. "Restrain him. Put him with the others."

Amalgam pushed himself up to his feet, picked up his stolen Luger, and then placed a heavy hand on Geist's shoulder. She didn't resist when he torqued her arms behind her back. Without her *apex* or *specter* sorcery, without her rifle or handgun, what did she have? And the enemy still had a gun to Victory's head.

The anti-magic sorcerer pushed Victory down the hall, his bizarre hands gripping Victory's torn clothes.

"Don't struggle," he muttered. "You'll follow me."

Geist closed her eyes and allowed Amalgam to manhandle her deeper into the basement. The lights remained dim, but the smell of blood hung thick in the stagnant air. Her imagination filled in all the blanks. It reminded her of the OHL. The monastery was where the enemy was experimenting—they used underground facilities to prevent things like the GH Gas getting out too quickly, or from being discovered by spies and biplanes.

Geist knew it all too well.

When Victory and Defiant's uncle went in another direction, she almost struggled to go with them, but she bit back the urge and continued forward. Now wasn't the time to fight.

They entered a back room with lights. It didn't bother Amalgam —he continued in and rummaged through the items in the room without hesitation. He tied her hands with coarse rope, and Geist half smiled to herself. The instant the anti-magic effects faded, she would slip the restraints. Even if she had surrendered to save Victory's life, that didn't mean she wouldn't look for an opportunity to escape.

"This isn't how I imagined it going," he whispered, his voice made sinister through the gas mask.

Although Geist wanted to avoid confrontation, she couldn't help but dwell on a myriad of questions. Amalgam didn't make sense to her. Why? All of his actions, all of his dealings—since he became twisted by the gas, it was like he lost his motives as a soldier and adopted something perverse in their stead.

"What do you want with me?" she asked.

"I want you close."

He offered nothing else.

"You're going to use the gas, right?" Geist asked. "As revenge for what I did to you?"

"I'll use the gas. But not as revenge."

"Then why?"

Geist didn't understand. What other reason was there than revenge? What possible motive could there be to track her down through one of the largest nations in the world? To stalk and kidnap a special forces member of the Ethereal Squadron? Why so much effort?

Amalgam pulled her close. "Once you're like me, there'll be no reason to return to Verdun. The Ethereal Squadron won't take monsters. And then your calming aura... I won't have to lose it."

Aura? Like a magic aura? He didn't want to lose *that*? That was the motive for his insane dedication to finding her?

"What's so special about my sorcery?" she asked. "It can't possibly be anything—"

"It reminds me of what I used to be," Amalgam growled. "You won't understand until you feel the claws of the gas rearrange your flesh. Then you'll know. Nothing feels right anymore. But you...

Your presence removes that sick feeling of worthlessness. If I can keep you close, through circumstance or restraint, I will. I can't live without it. Not anymore."

Geist didn't understand. Her sorcery never did anything but help her kill people. Now Amalgam wanted her presence to feel himself? *What a twisted life he's led.* But she couldn't feel pity for him. He fought for the enemy.

"I won't stay with you," she said. "And if you try to keep me, one of us will end up killing the other."

"What?" he asked, genuine disgust in his tone.

"It doesn't matter what you do to me. I'll always return to Verdun."

Amalgam tightened his grip on her arm, his fingers leaving bruises. "I told you. They'll never accept a monster. One I use the gas—"

"I'm a member of the Ethereal Squadron," Geist stated. "Even if I'm warped by fell gas, it'll never change that. A soldier is a soldier, even if they lose their leg to the mines, or their fingers to the barbed wire, or their life to the enemy rifles—*you* might've lost your way, but don't think we're the same."

Geist had once doubted. She had thought that if her teammates discovered her identity as a woman, they would reject her. But they hadn't. And each day that passed, each battle she fought alongside them, reinforced her loyalty to the cause. If she ever gave up, for any reason, she would be letting her squad down. Geist wouldn't let that happen.

"You're a fool," Amalgam said. "If you hobbled back to them, broken and bleeding, they'd treat you like the dog you are. They'd use you till there was nothing left. And somehow you feel pride for that?"

Geist shook her head. "You're wrong. I've seen them. They honor those who give themselves for the cause. That's what all men of war do."

"That's not what happened to me," he shouted. He shook her by the collar of her tunic, his grip so tight Geist thought he would rip it straight off her uniform. "I returned to my commanders and they tied me down, performed experiments, and brought me back from the brink of death only to serve them as a monster! They don't care if I die—they may even prefer it. Then they could have my blood. That's the last thing that makes me valuable to them."

Geist stared up at the mirror-like glass of his mask, her reflection staring back, her eyebrows knit and her face bruised from her earlier fights. She remained silent, absorbing Amalgam's anger-laced words.

Amalgam growled, his teeth grinding in the process. "I'm *nothing* to them, and they've made it clear, time and time again. That's what would happen to you, too. Your allies will see you as a broken tool, and they'll treat you like one. At least—together—we could be monsters set apart."

His yearning to connect with someone struck a chord. Geist had always felt separated from her teammates when she clung to her secrets and kept her identity hidden. Only Cross—another woman —had been a true friend. She suspected the others would have discarded her if they knew, like she didn't matter. Again, Geist sensed a kinship with Amalgam that was difficult to articulate. Even conveying it to him seemed impossible.

Geist took in a shaky breath. "Amalgam," she whispered. "Being altered by the GH Gas doesn't make you a monster. Your commanders—the men who use you like a tool—*they're* monsters."

He didn't respond.

Grasping at straws, and thinking about what Victory would say, she continued, "Your commanders never should've abandoned you. A real leader will make you a better person." She grimaced and shook her head. "No. I take that back. They don't *make* you a better person—you do that yourself. Because a leader inspires you to be the best you can. If your generals and lieutenants tore you down to take your power for themselves, they're the antithesis of what they stand for."

He took in a sharp breath, perhaps to speak, but Geist didn't want to hear it.

"Stop making excuses," she said, her own anger coming back in full force. "Their actions can only explain away so much. A man isn't defined by how others treat him. A man is defined by his own actions."

"It's not that simple. They determined I would serve as a cog in their plans. I have no other options."

"*You* determine who you'll be in this life. A soldier, a dog, *a monster*—don't you dare say you can't change course now, or else you're less than a monster. You're a coward."

For a long moment, they stood in the dark room, his breathing in the gas mask the only sound between them. Was he giving her words thought? Would he be enraged and lash out at her? Would it even matter? Maybe he was too far gone. Maybe they had messed with his brain and his insides. Maybe he couldn't feel things like a normal soldier.

Or maybe I'm wasting my breath, but if he doubts his loyalty to his cause, perhaps he'll give up this wretched fight and leave the Russian Empire. After that...

Amalgam loosened his grip. Geist widened her eyes, a faint sense of hope stilling her thoughts. Without speaking, he led her out of the dark room and down the hall, following the path of Victory and his captor. What was he doing? They went deeper into the monastery, far from the exit.

"What's going to happen?" she asked, struggling with her restraints. The suffocating presence of the anti-magic messed with her thoughts. "Where are you taking me?"

Amalgam never acknowledged her. The next room they entered had lights strung along the walls and ceiling. The harshness of the bright bulbs stung Geist's eyes, so she kept her gaze down. She still caught the contents of the room, however.

GH Gas grenades. An operating table stained with blood. Individual air-lock chambers meant to keep people in with gases or deprive them of air. Devices of mutilation and torture.

Goddammit! He's too far gone!

Victory stood with his back against the wall while the anti-magic sorcerer placed vials down on an operating table. The researcher held his gun in one hand, vaguely pointed in Victory's direction, while the other three hands went to work organizing. With the bright light streaming down, Geist couldn't help but notice the many shades of skin his hand had. Each finger seemed different—darker, lighter, crooked, soft—she had a guess, but she didn't want to voice it, not even in her thoughts.

Heinous.

"There you are," the researcher said. "Took you long enough. Tie that sorcerer to one of the tables. We can make ourselves useful while the others deal with the tsar."

"This one is mine, Helmuth," Amalgam said. He walked over, grabbed a bandolier of GH Gas, and slung it over his shoulder. "I'm leaving."

"No, you're not." The anti-magic researcher—*Helmuth*—gave Amalgam a puzzled glance, his mismatched eyes intense. "You'll stay here and help me deal with these two. We need their blood."

Geist focused on the containers of gas, and she kept herself still to avoid drawing attention to herself. The tension in their conversation had escalated with each word. Did Helmuth intend to kill Victory? Right here, right now?

Sorcery or no sorcery, she thought. *I can't allow that.*

Amalgam picked up a bottle of pink liquid and a syringe. "Don't push me, old man."

"I've tolerated your insubordination for far too long. When I speak to the lieutenant, I'll have him carve subservience into your hide."

"Is that right? I doubt it'll work. Haven't you heard?" Amalgam chuckled. "I'm unstable."

He spoke with perfect articulation, which added an air of psychopath to the *I'm unstable* statement. Geist didn't know if he was joking or serious. And it didn't look like Helmuth knew, either.

"You're a dog," Helmuth muttered. Then he turned back his work. "A simpleton like you couldn't help me anyway. Leave us."

Despite the insult, Amalgam headed for the door, not a word offered to anyone. Geist fought against his grip, her breathing shallow and panicked. Leaving Victory was as good as killing him. There would be no escape from the monastery if he was left in the basement.

"You said you'd let one of us go," Geist said, digging her bare heels into the cement. "Release Victory. He has family waiting for him. He doesn't deserve this."

Amalgam didn't reply. Neither did Helmuth.

"A man would never go back on his word," she growled.

Although Geist couldn't see his face or know his expression, his slow step into a stop told her she hit a nerve. He waited for a moment—and she thought he might attack her with the syringe he held in his other hand, but he didn't move.

Helmuth glared. "What is this? You're goaded into action by enemy sorcerers? You're a disgrace."

"Mind your own business," Amalgam growled.

"Lieutenant Cavell will be informed of your behavior."

Lieutenant Cavell? Geist closed her eyes, her father's face as clear as day in her mind's eye. *He's here? Of all the people—why does my past continue to haunt me?* She opened her eyes again, determined to escape the monastery before her father reached them.

For a moment, no one said a word. Then Amalgam faced Helmuth. The two stared, the researcher becoming increasingly unsettled—fidgeting with the handgun and taking a step back, his stumpy leg almost catching underneath him.

"Amalgam?" he said. "Stand down, you cretin."

In a showy display of insubordination, Amalgam let go of Geist, drew his Luger, and shot Helmuth. The bullet hit the creepy old man right in the chest, and the bang echoed in the room with enough thunder to batter Geist's ears. She grimaced and stumbled back into the wall, wracked by a state of disbelief.

Helmuth hit the floor with a cry, his own weapon tumbling from his weak grip.

Amalgam tucked his handgun away. "Now I've held up our end of the bargain," he said. "Victory is free to go."

When Victory met her gaze, Geist replied with a curt shake. Victory couldn't handle Amalgam, especially as the anti-magic aura over the basement began to lift. It was best for Victory to leave while he still could. Once he was safe, she could attempt an escape without fear for his life.

TWENTY-NINE

Lieutenant Cavell

Amalgam jabbed the needle of the syringe into the bottle of sedative. The pink liquid had been created by Helmuth himself. Perfect for subduing sorcerers. The moment he had enough, Amalgam turned to Geist. She had her attention on Victory—the two speaking in glances—and he used her moment of distraction to grab her arm.

She turned to him just as he stabbed the syringe into her bicep.

"What's that?" she asked with a slight gasp.

"A sedative," he replied.

He couldn't risk her getting away. Not now. Not after everything he had done. Shooting Helmuth was the final act of treason. He wasn't on anybody's side.

Amalgam tossed the used syringe to the floor and tucked the liquid away. Geist ghosted through the ropes holding her wrists, but she couldn't ghost through his anti-magic gauntlets. He maintained his grip on her arm, refusing to let go under any circumstance.

"Don't run now," he said through gritted teeth. "Or I will resort to drastic measures." He motioned to Victory, still standing by the far wall.

"What does this sedative do?" she asked, a slight panic in her words.

"It'll take a hold in less than two minutes. You'll lose feeling in your body and eventually fall unconscious."

Then he would be able to teleport with her to any of his many button locations. That was all he really needed. He could escape everyone, including the Russian Empire, so long as he could take Geist along his short-distance teleportation route.

After that, he could give her words more thought. What did it really mean to be a man? Or a coward? The words rattled in his skull until they had lost meaning. He didn't care to dwell on it, not when he was so close to his goal. Her words wouldn't shake him. He refused.

A terrible realization hit him a second later.

While Helmuth had his anti-magic active, Amalgam hadn't sensed anyone beyond the walls of the room he had been in. Now that he had his "sight" back, one of his worst fears had come to fruition. His heart pounded against his ribs, and his gas mask felt constraining.

Lieutenant Cavell had returned to the monastery.

No doubt he had found the bodies of Otto and Pavel. He would demand to know what happened, and the moment he found out his daughter had murdered them, it would be all over. Lieutenant Cavell wanted to kill her, after all, so he could offer her blood to the prince. He would take her from him.

"Geist," Victory said as he crossed the room with a slight hobble. "Something terrible has happened."

"What is it?" she asked.

"Your father. He's here and… has taken the blood of from one of the Eyes of the Kaiser."

There were no words after that statement. Amalgam had been right. *He must've stumbled on the body in the basement. Then he stopped to get himself enough to fuse into his body. What a bastard.*

"We need to leave," Geist said, her voice shaky.

Victory pointed to a far door. "There are other sorcerers here. We should release them."

"They're sedated," Amalgam said. "No use bothering with them."

"We could remove the restraints. The sedatives will wear off, and then they can flee."

Amalgam didn't care. The POWs and science experiments couldn't help him fight Lieutenant Cavell, and he was the only thing preventing Amalgam from rushing out the front door.

Not waiting for further discussion, Victory went straight to help the others. Amalgam didn't stop him. Instead, he tensed in preparation. If he didn't fight Lieutenant Cavell—if he didn't *kill* Lieutenant Cavell—he would take Geist. It was unacceptable and he had to have a plan of attack.

Surprise, he thought.

Geist slumped a bit, her legs trembling. *The sedative must've taken hold. That's fine, I can use her.*

Amalgam nodded to himself. If he "presented" Lieutenant Cavell with a disabled Geist, there would be no question of his loyalty. And when the lieutenant went to take his daughter, Amalgam could strike. If he could kill Cavell in one blow, he wouldn't have to deal with a master of *specter* and *apex* sorcery. Then he could escape with Geist with no one chasing him.

I just have to make sure my one strike counts.

Helmuth writhed on the floor, his whole body mimicking the motions of a slug with salt on its skin. He hadn't died. No. That would be too simple. His freakish body, filled with parts of others, would need a little more repair, but the man would be back up on his feet within a matter of days. Amalgam could shoot him a few more times and finish it, but he didn't want the gunshots echoing throughout the basement.

"We're going to meet your father," Amalgam said. He yanked Geist through the door and into the long corridor. "But I won't let him hurt you."

"Why?" she asked.

"I thought I made myself clear. I don't care about my nation, my comrades, or my old duties—my only goal is to keep you by my side."

239

Geist forced half a smirk. "Not that. Why would my father hurt me?"

"Ah. To take your blood and give it to Prince Leopold. As an apology for you running away from your marriage proposal and attacking him during the attack on Paris." He pulled her close. "Come."

Geist radiated warmth, the exact opposite of the GH Gas. The gas sucked life away and destroyed it, and her aura reminded him of a pleasant spring morning. Amalgam tried not to dwell on the sensation. He could get lost in the euphoric feeling, which would give Lieutenant Cavell the upper hand.

Together they hustled down the basement hall. The destruction continued throughout the building; each brick and cement slab was infected with powerful *ruina* sorcery. Soon it would all collapse. Yet another pressing reason to escape before it was too late.

Lieutenant Cavell headed in Amalgam's direction. There was only one route up and down, after all. They would cross paths no matter what happened.

"Is my brother here?" Geist muttered.

"He's at Alexander Palace."

"R-right now? During the riots?"

"He's helping to incite the riots."

It wasn't hard. The Russian Empire had been in a state of disarray for decades. The ruling class, separated from the life of the common man, had stagnated. While the rest of the world twisted and changed, the Russian Empire clung to old ideas and practices. Their tsar took to the battlefield, not because he had a talent for war, but because *he was the tsar*. Once the Russian military crumbled to the enemy, morale across the country broke.

That was when the Bolsheviks really got a foothold. They promised change, and all they needed was violence—something the starving people of the empire were ready to engage in.

Amalgam headed for the lieutenant. Once he reached the top of the stairs, he stopped. The entrance room would give him enough space to attack the lieutenant, and it made sense to prepare ahead of time if he wanted to have the upper hand.

Geist leaned heavy on his arm, her breathing ragged. The rough breaths weren't supposed to be a side effect of the sedative, and Amalgam wondered if she somehow had taken to it poorly. But he didn't have time to investigate. Lieutenant Cavell stopped on the other side of door, his sorcery up and his footsteps silent. His magic aura betrayed his presence, however.

"I thought you went to the palace with the others," Amalgam said.

Lieutenant Cavell stepped through the door and allowed his sorcery to fade from his body. He teemed with twisted magic, no doubt due to the blood he stole from the Eye of the Kaiser. After he rotated an arm, Lieutenant Cavell smiled.

"I came back when Otto and Pavel failed to rendezvous at our gathering point. I came back to find their corpses in the hallway."

Not even a hint of remorse or sadness for teammates who gave their lives for the cause. That was the new reality the GH Gas brought. Everyone wanted *blood*, especially from the powerful. How much longer could Europe handle such a sad truth? Amalgam smiled under his gas mask. How long would the royal families last?

Lieutenant Cavell glanced over at the limp body of Geist. "Florence?" He returned his attention to Amalgam. "Your plan worked? She came here for the other member of the Ethereal Squadron?"

Amalgam listened for his inner most thoughts.

... I can't believe it ... this solves my problems ... maybe this dog is useful after all ...

It was working perfectly. Lieutenant Cavell had no idea. He thought Amalgam a loyal soldier, and soon he would come to take his daughter. That was when Amalgam would strike with everything he had. He tensed as he took a few steps closer to the lieutenant.

"I told you she would come," Amalgam said. "And I've already injected her with sedative. There will be no escape."

Apex sorcery had many strange side effects. Lieutenant Cavell could sometimes smell people lying. They sweated more than usual and gave away their nervousness through their traitorous pores. But Amalgam wore a suit of leather and anti-magic, complete with a gas mask, all sealed to hide his skin. Lieutenant Cavell never guessed what was coming.

"Good," the lieutenant said. "You've done well."

Amalgam dropped Geist to the floor, through it hurt his soul. She crumpled to the cracked cement with a groan, her whole body trembling. Lieutenant Cavell stepped forward and reached for the collar of her uniform. Amalgam lifted his arm and focused his sorcery, his putrid green flame gushing forward in a powerful stream of fire. The heat flooded the tiny room. Amalgam didn't care if it hit the wall or the door, so long as he got most of Cavell's body.

With a shout and a grunt, Lieutenant Cavell leapt backward, a good five feet from his original position, his speed and strength far beyond anything Amalgam could bring to the table. But the lieutenant didn't strike—he grabbed at his singed face, and Amalgam knew he had a small window to finish the man.

He rushed forward, lifted his arm a second time, and lit up the basement. When he concentrated hard enough, the heat of his twisted fires grew in intensity. He knew Cavell's *specter* sorcery wouldn't save him from flame, and if he failed to get out of the way, he would lose his concentration to the burns and succumb.

At least, that *had* been Amalgam's plan—up until Lieutenant Cavell dashed forward, through the fires, and backhanded Amalgam hard enough to shatter the glass of his mask.

Amalgam hit the floor, barely aware of what had happened.

The moment he had an ounce of concentration, he teleported to a button, slipping from one floor to another. He couldn't picture his destination, and when he forced himself to his feet, confusion gripped his thoughts. Where had he gone?

A ringing persisted in his ears, and Amalgam knew pieces of gas mask had embedded themselves in his skin. *Damn.*

It didn't take long for Lieutenant Cavell to track him down—Amalgam had only teleported to the corridor over. Before Amalgam got another strike to the face, he teleported again, this time back to the top of the staircase. His thoughts escaped him, like water between fingers, but there wasn't much else he could do. He was on the run, and if he couldn't find an opening, he would die.

Technically, he still had a couple of GH Gas grenades. His suit would protect *him* and not Cavell, but it would also kill Geist. She was on the floor, her arms posted beneath her. She wasn't yet unconscious. An unfortunate fact that could cost them.

He couldn't use the grenades.

Lieutenant Cavell stepped back into the room and opened fire with his Luger. Amalgam's armor absorbed most of it, but a couple bullets slammed straight into the soft flesh of his side. Amalgam dropped back to the floor, pain searing his insides. Agony sometimes angered him—reminded that he was weak and he existed on the edge—but now it weighed heavy on his mind. This could be the last time he felt anything.

After wrapping himself in invisibility, Lieutenant Cavell rushed forward. He still hadn't figured out that Amalgam could sense his every move. The second he drew close, Amalgam used the full strength of his fire. Lieutenant Cavell put an end to Amalgam's sorcery with a powerful kick to the side, right in the bullet wounds. Amalgam half screamed as he tumbled to the floor. His lower ribs were broken. Amalgam knew the feeling well. Each breath was like a stab to the lung.

He could heal it, if he had enough time and focus, but…

"You're unstable," Lieutenant Cavell growled as he became visible. "A dog that needs to be put down."

His thoughts echoed the same sentiment.

… the gas has messed with his head … he's not right … better off dead …

Amalgam couldn't find the concentration to teleport. The flares of pain from his chest hurt too much.

Cavell approached him, his Luger at the ready. Amalgam smiled to himself. At least Geist was nearby. Her warmth… it chased some of the darkness away. And it grew warmer and warmer… enrolling him with a relaxation he no longer found in life. Perhaps dying wouldn't be so bad. He deserved it, after all…

That was what monsters got.

THIRTY

Father Dearest

G eist knew she wouldn't have the element of surprise long. It was now or never.

She leapt up from the floor, her bare feet silent as she lunged for her father. He glanced around right as she reached out her hand. Geist would've gotten his chest, but he twisted, and instead she clawed through his side, right along the contents of his guts. She became corporeal, ripping out flesh, but not a killing blow.

Fuck! Her eyes widened, knowing full well that had been her moment to win the fight.

Her father didn't flinch. He brought his handgun around and fired. The bullet sailed through her and ricocheted off the cracked cement.

"You ungrateful wretch," her father growled, the intensity in his eyes betraying his overwhelming hatred. He stepped away until his back hit the opposite wall, blood seeping into his Austro-Hungarian uniform. "I thought you were sedated!"

She *should* have been sedated. But when Amalgam had gone to stick her with a syringe, Geist had allowed the liquid to ghost through her body. A normal man might have seen the medication drip onto the floor, but Amalgam didn't have eyes... Geist didn't

244

know how he saw, but he didn't pick up on that, so she acted as though she had been affected, biding her time until she could act.

And then her father had shown up, ready to kill them both. Even though his uniform was charred, his flesh raw, and his stomach bleeding, he still had the power and strength to remain standing. He didn't tremble or hesitate—or even slow.

Geist wrapped herself in invisibly, and her father did the same.

"Florence," he said. "I'll bring you back to Austria in pieces."

Her heart leapt into her throat. Her father had twenty years more practice with his sorcery than she did—he was a master of *apex* and *specter*—and had been a lieutenant since the beginning of the Great War. Why did it have to be him? Why was he in the Russian Empire?

She calmed herself when nothing happened. Seconds ticked by, and the walls crumbled a little further, the whole monastery trembling. If they remained incorporeal, they couldn't fight, even if her father was far better than she was. But Geist knew that wasn't an option. Victory was still down the stairs. She couldn't leave him, and if her father discovered him, there would be bloodshed.

And Amalgam…

He lay broken and bleeding against the far wall. Should she leave him? He was unstable, but he had tried to defend her against her father. *That's not enough to justify helping him at this point. He almost murdered Victory just to get to me.*

Geist dropped her invisibility but remained ghost-like. She wanted to speak, but her father appeared in an instant, inches from her, and swung for her throat. His hand passed right through, but Geist could sense the force behind the attack. He meant to kill her in that single strike.

"Is that all you've got?" she asked.

It was a terrible taunt, and she knew if they went fist-to-fist that she would lose, but if she didn't fight, there was no way to win. She had to take the risk—had to catch him corporeal—and getting him reckless might give her an opening.

He smiled. "Why don't I show you some of the new sorceries I've gotten a hold of?"

The statement caught her off guard. Her father held up a hand, and a strike of electricity arched from his palm. It hit Geist, sent her into the wall, but the power wasn't there. He hadn't mastered *tempest* sorcery; he had just started learning. Still, sorceries like that could pierce through her incorporeal state.

Geist vanished and rolled to the side. Her father disappeared as well, and another round of panic set in. Like submarines, they could circle forever until they bumped into each other. How was she going to outsmart him?

He has to make himself corporeal to attack, and he attacked me immediately when I appeared…

She ripped off her tunic, thankful she had an undershirt. After two seconds of silent counting, she steeled herself to an attack and threw her uniform forward. The instant it left her hand, the garment became visible. In the next instant, her father struck—ripping the tunic clean in half with his strike.

Geist was already on her feet. She reached out and caught him as he tore through the fabric. She made her hand physical as she caught him under the ribs, right on the spleen, and clawed at the soft organ.

Her father barked out a shout of pain and surprise. He backhanded the area, but Geist had been fast enough with her *specter* sorcery to avoid the hit. It was only a matter of time, however. Her attacks were small. It would take hundreds to bleed out her father. All it would take was one strike from him and she'd be dead.

Blood poured from Lieutenant Cavell's side, soaking his tunic down to his belt. He placed a hand over the injury, his intense gaze locked on Geist. She stumbled back, unable to concentrate enough to become invisible.

Her father had always hated her. She had never been enough. His words rang out in her memories, always about her failings. He wanted more than her—more than anyone could give—he wanted control and power and obedience. When Geist hadn't provided it, he got angry. She remembered what it felt like to be struck by him. The memory haunted the skin of her cheek.

"You were always a disappointment," he growled. "And now you have the audacity to attack me?"

Perhaps it was the drugs in her system or the fact she had broken away from his control years prior, but in that moment, she didn't take his words seriously. "And here I thought you'd be proud of me," she quipped.

"Proud of some crossdressing snake who betrayed me?" Her father laughed. Blood coated his bottom row of teeth. "If you'd have *just listened*, none of this would've happened!"

Green flames erupted from the corner of the room, soaking everything in heat. Geist leaned away, but her father hadn't been so lucky. He arched his back and whipped around, hatred written across his face. He dashed across the room, and Geist followed.

Amalgam had helped her again. She decided in that moment—if she could save him as well, she would.

The second her father appeared, Geist realized he couldn't ghost into Amalgam due to anti-magic armor. *The anti-magic.* It would harm him. It was the only substance capable.

She lashed out, but her hand went right though her father's chest. "Fight me," she shouted. "I thought you were going to take me back to Austria in pieces!" Then, in French, she said, "Use your armor, Fechner!"

Geist didn't know if he knew French—all she knew was that her father didn't. And if she used Amalgam's "real" name, he would know he was being addressed, even if he couldn't figure out the rest of the sentence. They had to fight together. It was the only way.

Her father wheeled on her, practically smiling.

"You'll regret this."

Amalgam got to his feet and swung with his anti-magic gauntlet. Sure enough, it connected with the wound on her father's side. Blood splattered to the charred cement, and this time he called out. In that moment of lapsed concentration, Geist lunged forward. She dug her hand in around his collar bone and twisted, trying to desperately to get an artery. Her father, his gaze locked to her, had the most sadistic and twisted expression she had ever seen on another human being.

And in that second—where she was physical enough to hurt him —he backhanded her. The blow sent her into the crumbling wall. She hit with enough force that she woke on the floor, unable to remember how she got there.

It took several seconds for the world to stop spinning. She witnessed her father disappear and heard his bootsteps echo in the hallway. He had fled. But why? Had they injured him that badly? Geist wanted to smile, but she couldn't bring herself to muster the energy. If he was running, they must've been close to gutting him once and for all.

"Commander Geist!"

The feminine voice straight in her thoughts didn't help. What was going on?

"Alexander Palace is under attack! The grand duchess has asked that you return at once to evacuate the royal family. Our soldiers are being overwhelmed by fell sorcery!"

The new information shook Geist. One problem led to another and then another. The added situation piled on top of her weakened body, and it felt as though she were drowning. How many more things could possibly go wrong? But she didn't have time to doubt or complain. She was a soldier, dammit. She had to get up. If there was still life in her body, *she had to get to her feet.*

Geist rolled to her side and screamed. Her arm—it was shattered to the bone. She rolled to her other side, half sobbing. Never before had her bones been so destroyed. The agony helped wake her up, however.

"Geist!"

Victory stood over her. He leaned down and offered his shoulder. "We need to leave. I've helped the sorcerers in the basement, and I think there's enough time for them to flee, but I know if *we* don't exit immediately, dire consequences will result."

"The palace," she muttered, her chest so tight it made it difficult to breathe. "We have to return."

"It's under attack by the Russian military itself."

"We need… to go back."

Geist got to her feet thanks to Victory. Still shaken by her encounter, she half expected to see an enemy nearby. A soldier, a researcher, another Eye of the Kaiser—someone—but to her delight, they had all gone. All that remained was the blackened basement room. What had happened? Then she spotted Amalgam slumped in the corner. He sat leaning against the wall, the glass of his mask completely shattered. He didn't move, but his heavy breathing echoed in the room

"What're we going to do about him?" Victory asked.

We should kill him. That was what she wanted to say, but she stilled her order. There was no duty owed to him, nor had they ever been allies. Still, he *had* helped her and even betrayed his own team to make sure Victory could go free. There had been no incentive for him to do that, other than to keep his word to her.

It was as if he didn't fight for a nation—just her.

"Amalgam," she said. "Get up."

He stirred for a moment, but when he tried to get to his feet, he slumped back down to the floor. Blood, darker than a normal, spilled onto the floor. It leaked from his armor, down to his trousers. He shook his head and placed a hand on his mask.

"Get up," she commanded.

Victory turned to her, a look of concern written on his wary face.

Could Amalgam get himself out of the monastery? Geist didn't know, but she wanted to see him escape before it was too late.

With a show of effort, Amalgam leaned on the wall and dragged himself to his feet. His body shook, and his legs almost buckled, but he remained standing. After a long moment, he pushed away from the corner and stumbled toward the door.

"Your comrades are attacking the palace," Geist said. "What's their goal? Where will they be?"

He turned his broken gas mask face toward her, his breathing just as heavy as before. He said nothing. Was he withholding the information?

"I'm going to the palace," she muttered. "If I'm going to have any hope of escaping alive, I need to know what they're doing."

Amalgam shuffled out the door. "They're going to collect blood under the cover of the riots. They knew the royal family stays in the inner sanctum… That's where they're heading."

She knew he was telling the truth—he didn't want her to die, after all. And she felt better knowing he had the strength to respond and move around on his own. He would be fine, even if they left him.

"Let's go, Victory," she said.

"Don't leave me," Amalgam said, his voice wet and half muffled by his mask. "Please. Not yet. Just… a little longer."

Victory held Geist close. "It'll be easier if we walk with him to the entrance hall. Then we can separate."

She nodded. *Whatever works.* And if Amalgam wanted a few more minutes with her, to help him cope with the reality of their separation, so be it.

Victory helped Geist to the corridor. The longer they walked, the more Geist regained control of her body. Pain pulsed from her shoulder to her wrist, threatening to steal her concentration, but an icy numbness quickly set over her entire body. It felt a second wind, but she knew better. *I'm so injured I might even go into shock. I have to ride this adrenaline high, though. I can't stop now.*

"Thank you," she muttered.

Victory held her close, his wan skin coated in sweat. "I should be kissing the ground you walk on. I was certain I wouldn't make it."

"Cross would never forgive me if you die."

"This is twice I owe my life to you."

"You've saved me countless times with your future sight," she replied, half chuckling. "Just… try not to get yourself captured by the enemy anymore, got it?"

Victory offered a genuine smile. "Deal."

Slower than Geist wanted, they made their way out of the crumbling building. Rocks fell from the ceiling, some doorways had collapsed, but they still had a way out. When they made the front entrance room, Blick stepped out from around a wall, his rifle up and his gold eyes shining.

"Victory!" he shouted. "Geist!" He dashed over, his eyebrows knitting together. "What happened? You both look like you've seen Hell and lived to tell the tale."

"How is Vergess?" Geist asked.

"He… isn't in good shape. Defiant knows medicine, apparently, and wrapped him up good, but the guy keeps bleeding. I don't think we can wait here any longer."

Blick lifted his rifle, his eyes locked on the weakened Amalgam, who stumbled into the room. Geist placed her hand on Blick's rifle and pushed it down.

"It's okay. He won't hurt you."

"We're going to let him live?" Blick asked. "He's an enemy agent."

"He betrayed his nation, and I owe him my life. We're going to let him go for now." She grabbed his tunic and gripped the shoulder of the sleeve tight. "I have to get back to Alexander Palace."

"Why?" Blick shook his head. "We'll never make it. Half our squadron is in bandages. We might not make it through the rioters."

Geist knew he wasn't exaggerating. Vergess needed medical attention. Victory needed nutrition and rest. Geist needed a cast for her shattered arm. Defiant had lost his glasses to the Eyes of the Kaiser. Who did that leave? Blick, Dreamer, and Battery. But the three of them had no hope of making it into the palace and escaping with the royal family.

It has to be me. With Battery's help, I can ignore more of this pain and help ghost people from the palace grounds. She closed her eyes. *And maybe Dreamer. He keeps calm no matter the situation. We can work as a group.*

"Blick," she said. "Help me."

He offered his shoulder and Geist leaned on him. Unlike the rest of her squad, he was notably muscular, and her weight didn't seem to hinder him in the slightest.

"Me, Battery, and Dreamer are going back to the palace," she said. "You will lead the others to safety beyond the city lines. Victory is here now. He can set you on the right path to avoid confrontation. And if sorcerers show up, Defiant can neutralize them."

"I understand," he said.

"Wait," Amalgam called out through a wet cough.

Blick stopped.

Amalgam held out a bandolier of three GH Gas grenades. For a moment, Geist considered taking them, but she ultimately shook her head. The gas had too much potential to harm the citizens of the Russian Empire. There were riots happening everywhere, and if a grenade went off, it would no doubt kill hundreds.

Confident in her decisions, Blick continued to help her outside.

The cold Petrograd air greeted them with a waft of embers. While the whole city seemingly burned, Geist's goal became clear in the distance. Grand Duchess Anastasia and her family needed help. Once she did this... the one last thing... then she could finally go.

At least I hope it's the last, she thought with a wary smile.

THIRTY-ONE

The Last Grand Duchess of Russia

U sing only one arm to hold onto Dreamer, Geist kept herself as still as possible. The power her father displayed with his strike rocked her. *Apex* sorcery was powerful. Even her ribs, collar bones, and spine felt sore, as though the blow had shaken her entire body. *If it hadn't been for Amalgam's anti-magic, I don't think I would've gotten away.*

"Blick saw your father fleeing the monastery," Battery said as they ran through the back alleys of the city. Dreamer had given them the rags and appearance of street urchins. For some reason, it looked the most compelling on Battery.

"In what direction did my father go?" Geist asked.

Battery hesitated before replying, "Toward the palace."

No. She shook her head. *Everything will be fine. He ran because he was injured. He wouldn't risk attacking me again until he knows he's safe. We'll still be able to get the royal family to safety.*

"Your father can't see through illusions, can he?" Dreamer asked between controlled breaths.

"I... don't think so."

But she didn't know anymore. He never had *tempest* sorcery, but he had used a bit of it in the basement. *And Victory said he had taken the domination power from the dead Eye of the Kaiser. Why is he amassing so many sorceries? Just to have them? Just to be the most powerful? He can never master all of them. It's too much.*

They reached the edge of the city and stood between buildings, examining the long road to the palace. Russian soldiers fought with protestors, so chaotic it was difficult to discern who was fighting who. Geist quickly noticed the distinction—some men wore red, and others wore white. They were two armies, each made of civilians and military personnel. One the Bolsheviks, and one opposed to them.

Through the fighting and carnage, Geist spotted a man atop a horse. She recognized him. General Volkov, the sorcerer general who had questioned her intent with the tsar. Although he had said his ability was to detect lies, he waved his sword and sent a wave of rot into the enemies—much like Vergess's empowered *ruina*. He cleared through waves of people, fighting under the white banner. His men rallied when he shouted, each fighting harder than before.

Sorcerer General Volkov rode his horse into a grouping of the enemy, clearing away as much as he personally could. His shouts were in Russian, but Geist could sense the charisma.

"We fight with his army," Geist said. "And we make it close to the palace."

With a wave of his hand, Dreamer gave the group white handkerchiefs. Together they made their way through the battle. Battery used his personal handgun to down enemies. Dreamer used daggers and his rifle. Geist held out her hand, took the empowerment from Battery, and then rushed forward as an invisible force of death for the White Army.

When they reached the fence, she waited until Dreamer and Battery were close. With her empowered sorcery, she ghosted them through the bars. Then they ran as a squad to the walls. Bullets rained down from the windows, but Geist protected them both. Her "bubble" of incorporeal made it so the fast-moving bullets slid right through her teammates.

Once inside, Geist cursed under her breath.

Both the White and the Red Army were looting the luxuries.

Fires had been set to the rugs and tapestries that were too large to move, and the servants had all been slaughtered. The once regal home had become a nightmare prison for the inhabitants.

"Wait here," she told Battery and Dreamer. "Secure this hallway. I'm going to bring the royal family here, and then we'll escape together."

They responded with curt nods.

Satisfied they would follow her orders, Geist rushed into the palace. She ghosted through walls, dashed across rooms, and ignored the furniture standing in her way. The inner sanctum was the area with Anastasia and her brother, Alexei. Geist had seen it before, when she went snooping around. Now the corridors were filled with the bodies of the Imperial Guard, as well as civilians with red scarfs.

"Commander Geist."

She stopped in her tracks, her breath a fire that scorched her lungs and spread to her shattered arm.

"One of the governesses was a secret Bolshevik all along. She's using her potentia *sorcery to empower an Eye of the Kaiser. Warn your team—if you even hear his voice, you'll be dominated."*

One fucking problem right after another, Geist thought. Each problem added to the next, and the situation almost became so dire it was hilarious. It was just *her* versus the enemy. She had to save the tsar and family. How could she do it?

When Geist made it past the stairs and elevator, she came to an abrupt stop.

The landing for the highest floor looked as though rabid dogs had been let loose. Men and soldiers had been mauled by some beast, their throats ripped out and their ribs broken open, exposing their organs. Blood soaked the carpet, changing it to a dark black with a sheen of crimson.

Among the bodies, Geist recognized Tsar Nicholas II. Unlike the others, he had no blood draining from wounds on his body. He was a husk—a dead carcass—his skin hanging and his eyes shriveled. Geist stared for a long moment, her heart slamming against her ribs.

Next to him sat the corpse of a woman with a beautiful silver gown. She may have once been exceptionally beautiful, but after having her blood drained away, there was not much left. Had she been the tsarina?

Geist had been too late.

Screaming from down the hall broke the spell the corpses had cast.

She ran for the commotion, determined to save *someone* from the hellish nightmare of the palace. But she stopped when she recognized the door to Alexei's room. Bolsheviks stood in the hallway, some kicking and spitting on the Imperial Guard corpses. Inside the room, Geist could hear the faint sound of Russian—and then she detected a conversation in German.

"How long?"

"The boy is almost drained."

More screaming. Then sobbing.

Of the two people talking, Geist knew one of them had to be the Eye of the Kaiser. Which meant, if she rushed in and attacked, he would issue a command. Even without looking him in the eye, she would be dominated thanks to the empowerment. Fighting couldn't be an option. However, she could still slip in invisible. But then what? *And what if he said a command to the group and just happens to catch me?*

There was no time to debate and weigh the options.

Geist went through the wall and entered Alexei's bedroom. To her horror, two men held Alexei—a child no older than thirteen— while they allowed blood to gush from his slashed jugular. Anastasie struggled against the hold of her captors, her face wet with tears and her hair matted with dried blood. The Bolshevik soldiers growled something in Russian and twisted her arms. She yelled, but she never stopped fighting.

An Eye of the Kaiser and an Austro-Hungarian soldier also stood in the room—the soldier wearing a gas mask similar to Amalgam's. Who was he? Was it her brother? Geist couldn't waste precious moments debating. Instead, she took the gas mask as a warning.

They had gas on them, and they were prepared to use it.

Geist ran to Alexei. She touched his shoulder and wrapped her *specter* sorcery over his whole body. He fell through the bed and then the floor. She let go of him after that, returning him to a solid state. While everyone in the room gasped and stared—shock written across their faces—she ran for Anastasie.

With one swift touch, Geist and the grand duchess also fell through the floor. A second later, Geist made them physical. The landing sent pain flaring up from ankles to her knees, but Geist pushed through it. And it wouldn't take long for the Eye of the Kaiser to figure out what happened.

Muffled yells from above rang through the ceiling.

"Find her!"

The magic behind the words clawed at Geist. For a moment she thought she had been dominated, but then the feeling faded. She had found Anastasie and completed her command, apparently.

We need to leave right now!

Anastasie must have thought the same thing. She pushed herself to her feet and rushed to her little brother's side. The boy didn't move or respond when she shook him. Instead of trying a second time, Anastasie hefted him into her arms, her whole body shaking.

"Let me help you," Geist said.

Not just because the grand duchess was struggling—but because she could use her sorcery to ghost through them through the whole building.

Geist offered her good shoulder and took one half of Alexei. Anastasie continued to cry, fresh tears streaming down her face by the minute, but she never took her eyes off her brother. Then Geist pushed her toward the wall. Compliant, they hustled forward as fast as they could. Anastasie closed her eyes hard right before they "collided" with the building.

Running knocked Geist's broken arm around, especially with Alexei in her grasp. Geist bit her tongue to distract her from the terrible sensations of her side, determined to escape the building no matter what.

Unlike Amalgam, who could sense where she was at all times,

Geist knew the Eye of the Kaiser would never find her if she just ran through the palace fast enough. He would be left behind.

Geist and Anastasie burst into the secure hallway with Dreamer and Battery. Both men jumped to her side the moment she dropped her invisibility. When they reached for Alexei, however, Anastasie took him for herself. She wrapped her arms around his chest and clung tight. Blood had soaked his officer's uniform, and he didn't move.

Not once.

"We have to go," Dreamer said. "How do you want to go about this?"

"The way we came," Geist said. "We don't have any time to lose. The Eye will know it was me, and he'll search this entire palace. If we don't leave right now—"

She stopped herself short. If the Eye of the Kaiser knew it was Ethereal Squadron that had taken the Grand Duchess, there was a chance they would be stalked all the way to the ports. But what else could they do?

Geist turned to Dreamer.

"Corpses," she whispered. "Dreamer, illusion some of these corpses. Make one look like the grand duchess and another to look like her brother. We'll leave them in the hall. It'll look like they got shot—when the enemy stops to take their blood, they'll get nothing but a random soldier."

"There are no corpses the size of the boy," Dreamer said as he glanced around.

Even finding one the size of Anastasie would be difficult, though it wasn't impossible. However, Dreamer was correct. They had no child corpse to use as bait.

Battery touched the neck of Alexei and waited, his brow furrowed. When he pulled his fingers away, he grimaced. "He's dead," he intoned. "We can just leave his body."

"No!"

Geist, Dreamer, and Battery snapped their attention to the distraught grand duchess. She held her brother tighter than ever, her fingers digging into his back. Then she crumpled to the floor on her knees, her whole body shaking.

"I won't leave him. P-Papa gave me o-one duty. I have to p-protect him."

She spoke her words through strangled sobs.

Battery shook his head. "If we carry him... it'll slow us down."

"You must leave him," Geist said.

Anastasie tightened her grip. "Never. I'll never leave him. I'll die here in this p-palace with the rest of my family. I'll... I have to... be with them..."

Leaving her would be the same as giving the enemy her blood. While Geist wanted to honor the grand duchess's wishes, she knew that wasn't an option.

We don't have time to convince her of her foolishness! Geist snapped her finger and pointed from Dreamer to Anastasie. There was no other way. It had to be done.

Dreamer, without a question or word, lifted his rifle and walked over to the grand duchess. Before she could protest, he struck her across the face, rendering her unconscious. She fell to the floor, her strawberry blonde hair spilling across the charred rug. Dreamer then picked her up off the floor and held her close—the body of her brother left in the middle of the hallway.

Battery took the grand duchess as Dreamer grabbed a corpse and tore through the clothing. Then he waved his hand, and illusions spread over the fabric and flesh. The body was already burnt, but now the skin looked as though it had once been soft and smooth. The torn uniform resembled a tattered dress that had wasted to ash in the flames. In all ways, it looked like the corpse of a young girl caught in a terrible fire and unable to escape.

"This is the best I can do," Dreamer said. "And I can hold it indefinitely."

"Good enough," Geist said. She motioned to the wall. "Come. We have to escape. Touch my uniform." She would use her empowered *specter* sorcery to take them through the war.

Just a little longer, she told herself. *Then I can rest.*

Battery helped her stay on her feet. Together, they dashed

through the wall of the palace, made their way through the gate, and then traveled the long road through the riots.

Alexander Palace burned behind them, the blaze intense enough to imitate the morning sunrise. Embers and ash rained over Petrograd, like the snow on a fresh winter day.

THIRTY-TWO

The Last Russian Empire

G eist rested on the bench of their stolen carriage. Her vision faded in and out as they hit bumps and cracks along the road. Her arm, a throbbing mass of useless flesh, bothered her the most. The rest of her thoughts were dedicated to Vergess. Would he make it? The others couldn't seem to tell her.

Defiant stayed close to her the entire time, speaking in German about the usefulness of modern medicine. Geist didn't catch what he was talking about, but she was glad he was close. For some reason, in her addled state, she still thought she needed to be nearby in order to protect him, even though that was foolish, given her current condition.

Despite the fog of her mind, Geist knew Blick drove the carriage, Dreamer tended to Vergess, and Battery held Anastasie close. Victory slept on the corner of the bench, his haggard appearance far from what he usually displayed.

She closed her eyes. They were making their way out of the nation. Soon they would be free of the chaos. Soon they would return to Verdun.

THE BOAT RIDE only made things worse.

Geist kept to herself the entire trek, her arm finally wrapped, but not healed. They would have to wait until they reached Cross to get a full recovery. The sway of the boat messed with her insides, and more than once she had to hold back the urge to vomit.

The door to her tiny room opened and closed with a metallic slam, the bulkheads of the ship practically shaking from the force.

"Sorry," Blick whispered. "It was an accident."

She didn't respond. She stayed on her cot, unmoving, and stared at the steel in front of her. The last 72 hours rushed through her mind in a blur.

"I think Vergess will be okay."

Again, she couldn't manage to speak.

"Defiant said he would've turned a certain color if things were infected, and he said since Vergess can still talk and hasn't lost cognitive ability, he'll be fine." Blick took a seat on the metal frame of the cot, careful not to disturb Geist. "He's smart, right? He knows things like this. He almost sounds like a doctor."

With all the research he's done on the human body, I think it is close.

"Look," Blick said. "Victory said he likely lives, so that's good enough for me. You can stop worrying about him. What you should focus on is the grand duchess. She's... uh... not right. With what happened." He rubbed at the back of his neck. "Normally I'm good with women, but she's deep in regret. Dreamer said we should watch her. Make sure she doesn't throw herself off the side of the boat. Then Victory said we need to keep an eye on our handguns..."

Geist closed her eyes. Anastasie cared about two things: her family and her nation. Now her family was dead, and her nation was burning. To make things worse, Anastasie had been unable to do anything about it. She couldn't stop the Bolsheviks—she didn't even know what they wanted—her father kept her away from her countrymen. Everything had been taken from her, and all in a single night. Such a helpless feeling would drive the toughest of soldiers to the brink of their sanity.

"Do you want me to leave?" Blick asked.

Geist opened her eyes and forced herself to answer with a shake of her head. She wanted company.

"Good, because I wanted to tell you something else. Thank you for getting Victory back to us. I swear, you're the one person who gets us out of every scrape. You and your damn *specter* sorcery." Blick flashed her smirk. "Would you teach me that someday?"

She gave him a questioning glance.

"I don't have the sorcery in my blood. No one in the Hamilton family has it. But at the rate things are going... maybe one day I will have it."

The thought chilled her. Was Blick implying they would steal *specter* sorcery from the enemy? Her father certainly had it, and he needed to be eliminated, but did they want to merge blood from others into their body? Geist hated the sinister gas.

"I'm joking," Blick said as he patted her shoulder. "I'm not going to get that gas anywhere near me. After everything we've been through, I feel like I need to stay away from any freaky shit. Victory told me about Defiant's uncle. Now *that's* a monster."

The ship rocked with the waves of the Baltic Sea. How much longer until they were home? Geist didn't want to wait any longer.

Blick leaned his back against the bulkhead. "If you need anything, just let me know." He crossed his arms. "You don't look so good."

With a strong exhale, Geist relaxed a bit and tried to fall asleep.

Her team would handle everything. *I just need to reach Verdun to make my reports. Then everything will go back to normal.*

GEIST SAT in Major Reese's conference room, her breathing shallow and her skin coated in sweat. Cross stood next to her—an angel wearing a nurse's uniform with a crucifix hanging around her neck. Each slight touch of Cross's fingers sent a pulse of healing through Geist's body. It was far better than anything she had experienced before.

"You're getting better at this," Geist muttered.

"I've had to use it a lot," Cross said, her words more morbid than her tone implied.

Major Reese paced behind his desk. He had lost weight, and the dark bags under his eyes marred his face. "Geist, my boy. I've read through your reports."

"Yes, sir," she muttered.

"You recovered one sorcerer from House Kott."

"That's correct."

"House Menshov made it out of Petrograd, but they fled the nation without their wealth. The family has requested assistance from the sorcerers of the Ethereal Squadron."

Geist allowed the information to soak while Cross continued to mend bone and stitch flesh. The warmth of her healing touch offset the normal chill of magic use.

"House Solovyev was destroyed," Major Reese said with a huff. "The people you managed to rescue from the fires were nothing but servants or the family of servants. Not a single sorcerer escaped."

The knowledge hurt. "I understand, sir."

"And that brings us to House Lungin. For whatever reason, we have no information on them. They probably escaped during the riots, but they haven't contacted the Ethereal Squadron since their departure."

"I don't think the enemy got to them," Geist said. "Their home didn't look invaded, just wrecked from the Bolsheviks."

"My intelligence confirms this. We'll count them among the living for now."

The mood in the room shifted the moment Major Reese stopped pacing. Geist knew what he wanted to say. The tsar and his family were dead—all except for Anastasie. And no one knew about her. All the newspapers were reporting her death at Alexander Palace, her corpse recovered from the wreckage. Dreamer's illusions had been flawless, and none of the golden eyed sorcerers would think to check a dead girl for deception.

"We don't know what'll happen to the Russian Empire," Major Reese said, his intense gaze locked on the floor. "General Volkov has been lifted up as a potential leader of the nation. He openly claims he's a sorcerer and capable of ushering the Russian Empire into a new era of prosperity. He says he leads the *White Army*."

"What about the Bolsheviks?"

"They're led by a man named Lenin, and he claims he's forming the *Workers' and Peasants' Red Army*. He wants to wrest control from the military by declaring General Volkov a traitor. It seems the nation will dissolve into civil war."

"Aren't we an ally to the Russian Empire?" Geist asked. Her strength came back in pieces the longer Cross healed her. "Shouldn't we send soldiers in and help General Volkov?"

"We don't have the manpower to spare. The Russian Empire has officially withdrawn from the war."

"What?"

"That's right," Major Reese stated, his voice becoming louder with each word. "The Germans and Austro-Hungarians no longer have to fight a two-front war. They can focus their efforts on France, which means we shouldn't divide ourselves. The Russian Empire will have to handle the revolution themselves."

"Without a tsar?"

"There's nothing we can do about that."

"We could reveal the grand duchess and she could return to claim her nation."

Major Reese shook his head. "That would be sending her to the slaughter. You know as well as I do that the enemy wants her. It would be best to allow Lenin and General Volkov to fight it out. Whoever wins will have the power to protect Anastasia when she reveals she's alive."

The Bolsheviks won't care about her, though. They tried to kill the tsar themselves.

"Are the rest of the royal houses safe?" Cross asked.

"No," Major Reese replied. "We'll be sending warnings to our allies, but for now, we need to focus on gathering our strength."

"What's going to happen to Grand Duchess Anastasia?" Geist asked.

"She will rest here in Verdun. After that, I will ask she fight for the Ethereal Squadron."

Both Cross and Geist stared, their eyes wide. It wasn't that Geist thought that was a bad idea—she loved the idea, actually—she just couldn't believe Major Reese was the one to suggest it.

"I thought you said women shouldn't suffer at the hands of war?" Geist asked.

"I don't think they should. Anastasia's sorcery is used behind enemy lines and can work to France's benefit. If she stays as an operative of the Ethereal Squadron, we could have a valuable team member."

"So… as long as she's not fighting on the front line, you're okay?"

He nodded. "I understand women play an important role in the war. I just don't want to see them harmed. Men started this war; men should finish it. And Anastasia has made it clear she wants to support our efforts against Germany and Austria-Hungary."

The news brought relief to Geist. *This is perfect.* The grand duchess wanted to help, and now she could. Even if her family and home had been burned to the ground, she could still fight in their stead.

"What's our next move?" Geist asked.

Major Reese turned and smiled. "I've spoken to several generals. There's been an agreement. We should bring the fight to the enemy. The Ethereal Squadron will infiltrate the royal houses of the Kaiser and the Austro-Hungarian Emperor."

THIRTY-THREE

Brothers

Hans Lorenz stood in the court of the Kaiser, his hands unsteady. The words on the report didn't make sense. They said his brother, Otto, had died by the hands of the enemy in Petrograd. His insides had been torn apart and his eyes gouged. But that would never happen to Otto. Never. He was the Left Eye of the Kaiser. An untouchable sorcerer with powers unrivaled.

A hollow feeling lingered in Hans's chest. He had known for quite a while his brother had died. He felt it the moment it happened. Even while Alexander Palace burned, he mourned the loss of his only companionship in life—the one person who knew him—his first and only lover.

Lieutenant Cavell had penned the report. He made it clear that *specter* sorcery had been used to kill Otto, and while Hans wanted to accuse the man, just to purge him from the world, he knew that Geist, the woman from the Ethereal Squadron, was the one to blame.

A woman. Lowly scum not fit to breathe the same air as Otto.

Hans crumpled the report and squeezed it in his hand until his nails pierced the paper and dug into his skin. Crimson soaked the report.

I'll make sure everything she loves is burned to the ground. Then I'll gut her and bring back her organs. Anything to avenge Otto. Anything to make sure he rests in peace.

"Hans?" the Kaiser asked, his voice strong yet distant.

"My Kaiser," Hans said, never looking away from the paper. "Allow me the use of the Kaiser's Guard. I want to eliminate a branch of the Ethereal Squadron. I want to bring our enemies to their knees and collect their sorceries myself."

Otto.

His brother.

Hans couldn't stop thinking about him. Had he suffered in the end? Had that witch tortured him by ripping out his eyes? *She'll never escape me. I'll make sure her torment lasts an entirety. She'll beg for death by the end of it. They all will.*

The Kaiser chuckled. "Now that the Russian Empire has fallen, that was the exact assignment I was going to give you. Bring me the blood of the Ethereal Squadron."

Thank you for reading!

Please consider leaving a review—any and all feedback is
much appreciated!

ABOUT SHAMI STOVALL

Shami Stovall grew up in California's central valley with a single mother and little brother. Despite no one in her family having a degree higher than a GED, she put herself through college (earning a BA in History), and then continued on to law school where she obtained her Juris Doctorate.

As a child, Stovall enjoyed every portal fantasy, space opera, and magic series she could get her hands on, but the first novel to spark her imagination was Island of the Blue Dolphins by Scott O'Dell. The adventure on a deserted island opened her mind to ideas and realities she had never given thought before—and it was the moment Stovall realized that story telling (specifically fiction) became her passion. Anything that told a story, especially fantasy series and military science fiction, be it a movie, book, video game or comic, she had to experience.

Now, as a professor and author, Stovall wants to add her voice to the myriad of stories in the world. Everything from sorcerers, to robots, to fantasy wars—she just hopes you enjoy.

See all future releases with:
https://sastovallauthor.com/newsletter/
Or contact her directly at:
s.adelle.s@gmail.com

Other Titles by Shami Stovall:

The Ethereal Squadron

Star Marque Rising

FRITH CHRONICLES:

1: Knightmare Arcanist

2: Dread Pirate Arcanist